Lifehack

2nd Edition

Joseph Picard

hey Pat!
I hope ya like it...!
email me feedback!

ISBN 978-1-4357-3633-7

Foreword

I've heard it said that no creative work can ever be truly complete, but when I was asked to have a hardcover version made, I saw it as an excuse to correct (and improve) the many oversights in the original. Even now I'm aware of a handful of things I would have done differently if I were starting the book from scratch today, but Lifehack is its own creature, created as much by the characters as by me. Some lessons are better kept for future books in Ayguola. "Watching Yute" is well underway...

Thanks to all the support involved, both in this second edition, and in the first, "AZU-1:Lifehack". Helpful folks on message boards, reviewers, friends and family, all helped to establish the first edition- as flawed as it was. As it was my first book, I was in a hurry for no other reason than impatience. With the deed done and in my hands, this impatience was satiated. I could then relax, and see the errors that evaded me before.

Special thanks go to my volunteer editing force: Dolores (my mum) Adam Zilliax, Meggin Dueckman, and Carrie Shannon who has also been a great supporter in the launch of the first edition.

Chapter 0: Nanites

Want a programmable molecule? Build a machine. Build the smallest machine you can, then make it build things so small that you yourself could not have made it. Make this tiny new machine build something even smaller.

If you continue along this path until you can't even see your machines without a microscope, even smaller than one millionth of a meter, you've entered the realm of nanotechnology.

In 2008, these machines are already being used to create new materials for every day use, such as clothing, packaging, various chemicals, and incredibly small circuitry, but research is striving towards much more ambitious ends.

In effect the science is about manipulating microscopic particles, perhaps down to atoms, using these microscopic robots, called nanites. Essentially these would be programmable molecules. And, to make things easier, a few could build more, making construction of nanite fleets nearly self-automated.

Construction could one day be as easy as leaving raw materials out for well programmed and directed nanites and watching what you want built, molecule by molecule. It would seemingly grow, and the speed of this would be related closely to the size of your nanite fleet. But of course you build many nanites, because it would be easy to once you taught nanites to do it for you.

Curing a disease would only be a matter of teaching a fleet of nanites what to destroy, injecting them into a patient, and having the nanites work faster than the cells of the disease could grow. They could be programmed to hunt any number of harmful elements in a body; a virus, bacteria, and cancers. Theoretically they would all fall with similar ease, regardless of their resistance to medications as we know them. A new immunization could be as easy as downloading the latest patch and updating your nanites. Poof. Suddenly they also attack the dreaded bird flu, mad cow, or any other new scary thing they discover.

Food could be created on a molecular level as well. Who needs an actual plant when an armada of microscopic robots could be given dirt, water, and sunlight, and continuously produce endless identical, perfect fruit, until one of the base ingredients were used up?

The potential applications seem limitless. Nanite clothing might change to whim and continuously clean themselves, or clean the wearer. Buildings or furniture laden with nanites might change to suit purpose or just melt away temporarily when unwanted. Airborne nanites that avoid being inhaled, and spend their time cleaning the air, or waiting for other commands.

And you could do it all without anyone even noticing the nanites themselves.

Of course, any technology goes through difficult spots in its infancy. What would you do with a programmable molecule?

Chapter 1: Little Spats

Regan threw a second high heel shoe at her newly *ex*-girlfriend Kris with every ounce of strength she could. The shoe missed its target and struck the bedroom doorframe. "It's fucking over, you slut! Strike goddam three! That I *know* about!" Regan's wavy black hair tossed across her face, but her enraged brown eyes glared clearly though at Kris.

Kris calmly took another cautious step forward with a gentle smile and a sympathetic look from behind her thin rimmed glasses. "Honey, I said I was sorry! You're not going to throw it all away just-"

Regan launched a blouse at Kris that she had borrowed. It didn't fly as well as the shoe. Why couldn't it have been another shoe, or a harpoon? "Throw *what* away? Eight months of trying to make this work while you screw anything that catches your eye? I'm really gonna miss that!" She mashed down on the lid of her suitcase. Its contents, that of her duffle bag, and the outfit she had on, were the sum of her worldly possessions. That and the bus ticket waiting for her at the terminal that cost her the remainder of her liquid assets.

"Honey, I-" Kris was cut short, and had to make a hasty side-step to evade the suitcase as Regan barged out of the bedroom. "Regan, do you know how silly you look, running away from home like this?"

Regan growled as she stomped on. She stopped and spun on her heel to glare back at Kris. Past Kris lay the bed in which Kris had once again betrayed Regan. The first time was painfully forgiven. The second time was forgiven with disgust at herself for allowing Kris to get away with it. This third time had driven Regan into boiling rage. There was likely more which she had never learned about.

"Running away from home? Home is where the heart is, Kris." Regan stormed to the front door, duffle bag swinging from her shoulder, suitcase hitting walls heedlessly as she dragged it. She grabbed the black leather jacket hanging by the door and threw it on over her tank top and the strap of the duffle.

She pushed herself and her luggage through the door, and turned to close it. Pity the door swung into the apartment instead of out. It would have been very satisfying to kick it shut with her punk-ish boots. Nah, fuck it. If she couldn't close it her way, let Kris close it. No, to hell with that, she needed the satisfaction of the slam. She reached in for the doorknob with one final glower at Kris, and yanked it shut. The impact resonated through the walls.

Regan stood in the hall and took a deep cleansing breath. Was she crying? No? Good. Kris was only allowed to see the hate. Save the tears for the day when the pain is far behind.

"Inky or Pinky?" Jonathan Coll leaned over the table-top arena walled by clear plastic, and stared down at the two quivering, blood matted rats.

"Doctor Coll, you know I'm not really into that." Across the lab, Jonathan's pet intern tended to the most recently assigned task of tedium.

Jonathan chortled, and brushed a raven bang out of his eyes. "Oh come on Scott. Scotty, Scotterino. Inky or Pinky?"

Without pulling his attention away from his work, Scott sighed in mild exasperation. "Oh, I don't know. Which has the series fourteen nanites, and which has the fifteen series?"

"Ha ha!" Jonathan gleamed, proud of his work. Both rats were teeming with microscopic machines which could one day allow a person to continue to go on despite considerable injury and get medical attention later. Eventually the nanites would be at the command of the person they're injected into, but for the rats, a computer took more direct control. "Pinky is series fifteen, but Inky is now *sixteen*!"

Scott raised an eyebrow "Sixteen? When did that happen?"

"When my brilliance made providence for it to happen!"

"Right." Scott sighed.

"Sixteen is a bit better at maintaining its own numbers in a living immune system, but I had to sacrifice a bit of tissue repair for the host. As you can see, Inky kinda looks like shit." An understatement.

Scott couldn't see, as he was still on the other side of the room. "I don't know. Whichever rat's been in the least fights." Scott simply wasn't playing along. Jonathan couldn't remember which had been in more fights anyway.

"Fine. I'll take Inky." Jonathan stood up straight, gazing down at the rats as were he a god. He positioned his finger over a button on a nearby terminal and announced sternly, "Round ninety four! Fight!"

He pressed the button and the nanites in the rats took control, acting as a nervous system, ignoring the hosts' weaker wills. The two rats looked around stiffly while the software did its best to identify the relevant items in the hosts' surroundings.

Wall, wall, wall, unreachable opening, wall, *target*! Inky's nanites were the first to come to terms with the tactical situation, and launched Inky at Pinky with no further hesitation. Inky's small but unnaturally strong jaw clamped onto Pinky's midsection, squeezing out an involuntary pained squeak.

Across the room, Scott winced to hear yet another such battle.

Jonathan grimaced. "Man, I have to get the object recognition routines polished up. At this rate, it's almost always just a matter of who sees who first." Jonathan fiddled the terminal interface and switched the nanite colonies into repair mode. Now in control of their own bodies again, the rats were free to whimper and cry out in pain.

But Inky didn't. Jonathan flipped a couple screens around on his terminal. "Oh damn! Inky died! The second I put them into fight mode! Inky won, and was dead the whole time! Awesome!"

"I'm sure Inky will find that to be a great consolation." Scott mumbled. Scott's dad wanted him to be an accountant, but no! Why waste his mind on work for calculators, when he could go into research sciences, and watch his egocentric boss mutilate innocent rats? Anyone need their taxes done?

Chapter 2: Hello Autar

Regan awoke. Her head leaning against the window, the first thing she saw was the side of the road whizzing by, a parade of dry vegetation. Since she left Kris', the view out this window had changed from lush greens, to this.

Yellowish brown bushes blended into the parched terrain, all the way to the horizon. This was the edge of the Yute desert. A half day's drive farther in would surround you with sand.

What a stupid place to build a city. Autar was looming ahead, the much hyped jewel of the future. The most recognizable feature of Autar was its four cornerstone towers.

The beige cornerstones were obscene engineering marvels, each tower being two hundred floors high with a footprint of three by three blocks. Between the cornerstones spanned four enormous bridges that connected the mid-sections of each cornerstone. The bridges were three blocks wide each and acted as a second layer of streets to develop on, a hundred feet above the ground. The bridges and the ground below bristled with monolithic buildings, each glistening with corporate pride.

Regan found it impressive but idiotic, and she wasn't the only one. Autar had its share of critics. The cornerstones were compared to towers of babil, and the bridges had gained the nickname of 'the square halo'. All of it seemed so unnecessary with all the open space around Autar. Defenders of the idea seemed clearly smitten with the difficulty of its construction, and sheer spectacle.

It was the kind of thing Regan's brother Harold loved. Just his luck that his company transferred him here. It did make it more difficult for Regan to go visit him though. Why did he have to move clear across Ayguola? And no where near a beach. An island nation, and Harold had to work in a landlocked wasteland.

Well, to be honest, this was less of a 'visit', and more of a 'unemployed-newly-single-broke-no-other-place-to-go' thing. It wasn't a new occurrence for Regan to go crash with Harold, but having to bus this far was new.

As the bus passed directly from wasteland to corporate obscenity, the shadow of the south bridge swallowed them up. Regan figured it wouldn't be long before they got to the bus terminal. She noticed a lack of anything that looked old. Not just that, but a lack of anything that wasn't founded by some huge company. Looking for a Ma & Pa pizzeria? Sorry, you'll have to make due with the nearest franchise outlet.

The bus pulled into its bay and the passengers sluggishly collected themselves, then poured out to wait for their luggage to be unloaded. Regan checked herself before disembarking. Her wardrobe had a habit of riding up in impolite ways when she was sleeping in public. A short miniskirt and a short tanktop made poor pajamas. After getting off, most of the passengers were still mobbed about the luggage hatch of the bus as the driver pulled things out and matched them to their owners.

Regan took this time to pull her portable terminal out of her carry-on duffle bag, and load up the city map. An ad that knew where she stood and that it was nearing dinner time, started playing to promote a restaurant half a block away. She muted it but had to let it finish before she could access the free map of the city.

'You are here' popped up with a red dot on the map. Ok, ok, now point to the note she had entered earlier of Harold's address. 'Plot a route?' Duh. 'Route options: Driving, Walking.' What, the ingenious little handheld multimedia ad-pumping device didn't notice she just got off a bus? Walking. A cute dotted line animated its way from her location over to the nearest cornerstone building. Harold didn't mention he lived in one of those behemoths. 'Estimated walking time: 30m:15s.'

She spotted her suitcase being hauled out of the bottom storage of the bus. She stepped up and gave the worker her baggage check tag. Yanking out the top handle, she was again grateful for the little wheels on the bottom. About half an hour worth of grateful, even if it would be a half hour that she'd be listening to the little wheels rattle against every little bump and dip on the sidewalk.

She started walking, terminal in one hand, luggage dragged with the other. She considered pulling the ear buds out of the terminal and listening to some music while she walked, but decided to take in the sights and sounds of Autar.

The sights and sounds of Autar were uninspiring on the whole. The city was populated almost entirely by nerds and suits. The vehicles on the street ranged in variety from 'sensible' to 'conservative'. Blue car, black car, silver car, black car, white delivery van, black car, grey car. Oh yeah. This was a party town to be reckoned with.

Looking at the businesses that lined the streets, she felt like she had walked into a movie with too many product placements. Well too bad for them. They'd get none of Regan's cash, as she had none! Haha! Outsmarting the big boys yet again!

Still, it might have been nice to have a bit of change to throw at one of the city trains that whizzed around. Look on the bright side. Regan didn't get her gams by taking public transit, and flabby thighs just wouldn't do these stockings justice. And her boots *were* made for walking after all. Walking, or kicking people. Multifunctional.

Darn, these were clean sidewalks. Maybe nerds and suits don't believe in chewing gum. Certainly they'd dispose of it properly if they did. Heaven forbid that the mighty Autar be defiled. It kind of made her want to spit on the sidewalk just to see if some tidiness cop would spring out of nowhere and give her a ticket. Probably not. They hadn't ticketed her for her dirty boots yet.

Speaking of tidiness, the tidy nerds and suits in the streets sure seemed to be checking her out a lot. Was she that much of a misfit here? Did she stink from being packed on a bus for so long? Heavens no. Regan looked at it more realistically. They all wanted to get her in the sack. Too bad fellas. Ladies? Fill out the application. Done right, the nerd look and the suit look could be pretty darn hot.

The southwest cornerstone got closer and closer. For some reason, Regan had expected it to be one huge three block wide wall with one door in the middle. There were three significant entries, with pompous staircases, and required ramps, as well as several smaller doors, and a smattering of storefront shops.

Regan consulted the all-knowing terminal, and entered the middle staircase. Inside felt a little like a shopping mall, but with less shops. A cluster of benches broke the middle of the space, and overhead hung an array of signs giving directions. 'Residential elevators: 5, 6'

Over in the back right corner she could see them. She dragged her suitcase over to number five, and looked at the directory sign. "Alright, what the hell floor is he on…"

The terminal spoke back in a chipper female voice. "I'm sorry, I didn't understand you. Please restate the name of your desired destination." They didn't miss a beat with this place, did they?

"Harold Grier." She considered also mouthing off at the thing, but the sentiment would go unappreciated.

"Floor forty-seven, apartment five." The corresponding entry on the directory throbbed with a soft glow. "Would you like an elevator to the forty seventh floor?"

Regan looked at the terminal. 4705. She knew that. "Yeah, sure."

"I'm sorry, I didn't-"

"*Yes!*" she spoke as clearly as she could, then muttered, "you silly bink.."

"Thank you!" The elevator door opened.

Regan stepped in and the door closed behind her. Another directory was waiting inside for her. "Next stop, forty-seven."

"Super." Regan replied, ignored. "So, you come here often? Wanna go grab a few drinks? Maybe a movie?"

"I'm sorry, I didn't under-"

"Shut up." It did. The nerd responsible for this thing at least predicted the need for it to understand *that* phrase. A steady feeling of acceleration pushed down on Regan gently for twenty-three floors before changing to deceleration. The doors opened, and Regan stepped out.

"Harold Grier's apartment is five doors to your-"

"Shut up." Regan guessed to her left, as going right would have involved a wall. 4705, there it was. She pressed the intercom button.

A moment later, Harold's voice came. "Regan?"

Regan replied. "Little pig little pig, let me in!" There was a slight delay, during which time she could almost hear Harold roll his eyes. Then the door clicked to unlock, and Harold's voice came though again. "Come on in."

Entering Harold's apartment, she found it to be exactly what she expected. Clean, organized, dull as heck. Harold came around the corner, and they had a hug. "Hey dork!" Regan said. She noticed that he still wore the cheap silver ring that she had given him years ago.

"Hey dorkette. The spare room has a small bed set up in it already. It's cluttered though. Come check it out." Harold was Regan's only living relative worth mentioning, and by far the more responsible and successful of the two, the ant to Regan's grasshopper. Among the populace of Autar, Harold was among the nerds. Generally quiet and professional, Regan is one of the people who enable his sense of humor to emerge. He has always been unquestioningly supportive of his little sister.

"I didn't know you had an apartment in one of these huge towers, Harold. You're moving up in the world, huh?"

"Hah. The cornerstones are Autar's slums. These things are more than half vacant. Money lives out where you can be visible and stand out."

The spare room was cluttered only by Harold's definition of the word. Yes, there were a lot of things in the room, but they were all neatly stacked, mostly in boxes, all against one wall. Regan wagered with herself that she could point to any box, and Harold would be able to list its contents from memory... but something else caught her eye first. She dropped her luggage to the floor, and floated over to her electric guitar. She picked it up and strummed a bit. It wasn't plugged in or anything, and all one heard was the tinny plucks, but it felt reassuring in her hands again.

"Help yourself to *my* guitar, Regan!" Harold teased.

"OH, pff. I'm gonna buy it back as soon as I have the cash, don't you worry! I'm gonna pay rent here too!"

"Uh huh."

"Besides, I bet you haven't played it more than once since you bought it off me." Regan said.

"Well, if I had an amp to go with it, I may have. You may as well stick to acoustic if you're going to keep selling your amp anyway."

Regan's only reply was to make a rock star sneer at him, while playing more tinny plucks. Harold raised an eyebrow. "I'll leave you two alone for a bit. Dinner's in an hour and a half." As he left, Regan was still playing a song in her head, performing for an imaginary audience, singing under her breath.

No sooner had she put the guitar down, than her little terminal beeped for an incoming call. The display read "Kris Taylor". Bleh. She was just beginning to enjoy herself. She ignored it for a bit, but it kept ringing. She stared at it for a second, and she could feel Kris staring dispassionately at her. She grabbed it up with aggravation, and answered.

Kris's face popped up, with just the expression Regan had expected. "Yeah," she said flatly, "I figured you were gonna take off with my jacket.."

Regan rolled her eyes. "For the last time, it's *mine.*"

"Mm. Whatever. It suits your whole 'street urchin' look better than anything I go out in anyway." Kris' comments often mixed insult with compliment. She was good at that.

"Look, you didn't call about the jacket. What the fuck do you want?"

Kris huffed a little. "Well. It doesn't look like you're on the road, or some cheap motel... I suppose you went to your brother's?"

Regan snapped. "*What the hell did you expect?*"

"Please. The theatrics aren't necessary."

"Did you think I was just gonna hang out around town waiting for you to call so I could come crawling back?! God, your ego must blot out the sun. You're a fucking chronic slut, Kris, I woke up to it, and I'm *sick* of it. If I had half a brain when I met you, I would have seen how-"

"Oh, calm down, I heard this rant when you left. Really. Don't-"

Regan hung up on her, and threw the terminal at the wall. It made a loud bonk, and bounced to the floor. She sat on the bed, staring at the terminal through closed eyes.

"Ah." Harold's voice came. "And I thought you were just here because you missed me."

Regan lifted her head a bit, face hidden by her hair. "Why didn't you warn me she was an evil slut when I moved in with her?" she said sulkily.

"Because I never met her..?"

"Bleh. You have an excuse for everything." Her voice was weak, and on the verge of crying. Harold sat beside her, and put an arm around her. "I guess you're all I've got now, dork." she whimpered.

"Ah, don't fret," he said, running a finger along a fret of the guitar, "Before you know it, you'll find some pretty thing that catches your attention, and you'll forget all about Kris, the evil slut."

"Yeah?" she sniffed.

"Yeah."

"Not a blonde this time." Regan's expression softened a bit. "Maybe with less ego? And HUGE... eyes?"

Harold smiled warmly. "Yeah."

"Okay."

They sat quietly for a bit before Regan spoke up again. "Got anyone like that at your work?"

"Yes, but they're straight and I'm sleeping with all of them."

Regan laughed and pushed her brother off the bed. "DORK!"

Chapter 3: AutarLabs

Regan awoke and gazed up at the ceiling while her mind caught up with itself. She was on the bed sideways and her feet touched the floor. She considered that to be a head start on the day and blissfully ignored the time.

She found she was hungry, and mysteriously just as unemployed as when she passed out. The first problem was solved easily enough, rummaging through Harold's kitchen. Harold had already left for work long ago.

The second problem seemed to have an obvious solution. She picked up her guitar and headed downtown to find clubs that might need a player. She was soon to find that live music wasn't as desirable here as it was in a couple of the smaller towns she'd lived in and so far, those that did have people play didn't seem to have an opening. It was discouraging but maybe it was for the best. She was probably rusty as heck anyway... she decided to get a little amp and practice before she went looking for much else in terms of gigs.

But an amp takes money too. Ick. She didn't feel like a service industry job and the guitar thing was really the only thing that went with her wardrobe. What good is having Kris's cool jacket if she can't work in it? Damned Kris. Okay, enough for today's two minutes of hate.

She looked at her terminal's city map. Harold's work wasn't that far away. She thought about going over, and casually mooching some money for an amp, but decided against it. She'd go visit though. That can't hurt. And if conversation happened to lead to her lack of an amp, she couldn't be blamed for that, could she?

There was the building. As close to the center of the city as the company could afford, it loomed with great self-importance. The peak of the building sported a slant that wanted to be stylish and original, just like all the other buildings with a slant on the top. The company logo stood out with a similar degree of flair in red light. "AutarLabs". Wow, what a creative name. Regan chose to blame that one on the suits. Nerds would have found a way to make a reference to some nerdy mythological thing like maybe Prometheus, or Icarus, but without the downer ending. As she got closer she called her brother on the terminal.

"Hey Harold! Mind some company?"

"Hm? Sure, I guess I can take a break. Where are you?"

"Out front, headed for the front doors."

A moment of silence. "Hey Regan, look up, can you see me?"

Regan looked at the building's windows. After a bit of scanning from window to window, she could barely make out a person in a lab coat waving, from the fifteenth floor. "Naw, I don't see ya, just some dork flailing his limbs."

"Yeah yeah. Hey, I'm just gonna finish something up here. I'll meet up with ya inside."

The lobby was oversized, and the dozen or so people hurrying across from one doorway to the next still left it feeling desolate and cold. There was that unsettling quiet that always seemed out of place but was always present in places such as this. Straight ahead at the far end was the reception desk. It was a large, authoritative command centre, staffed by a lone girl who looked abandoned there in her oasis of furniture, in a desert of an otherwise stark room.

As a personified contrast to the entire building, Regan strolled across the floor, casually taking in the room. This place was almost certainly staffed by 100% uptight, busy, fidgety sorts. The girl at the desk was cute. Blonde, big glasses with thin frames. She reminded Regan of Kris, except without the evil. The girl watched Regan walk towards the desk, patiently waiting for Regan to come within 'greeting distance'. Regan smirked as they looked at each other. Was the receptionist flirting or did Regan just stick out that much here? Regan chose to think flirting. Her gaydar skewed considerably to her whims, and often gave false positives.

"Hello, may I help you?" The receptionist said, perhaps seeming a little intimidated in the shadow of Regan's swell in confidence.

Regan slowly and casually leaned down on the desk, sharing a bit of a view down her top should the receptionist choose to look. Regan spoke just soft and slow enough so that the receptionist could choose to notice it or not. "Mmm. Yeah, I'm here to see my brother. He works here somewhere. Harold Grier...?"

"Alright, if you'll wait a moment..." the receptionist tapped a few buttons as she put on an earpiece with a microphone. Regan smiled softly in acknowledgment and tried to read her eyes. Pure professionalism. Bah. She was probably straight. Or just plain boring. Or both.

"Doctor Grier?" the receptionist said, staring blankly into her desk, "Yes, there's a young lady here, your sister, here to see you? Yes. Alright, I'll send her up." She took off the earpiece and turned her attention back to Regan. "Alright then, take this visitor's pass and head up to fifty-three. Doctor Grier will meet you at the middle cafeteria there. It's a non-restricted area."

Regan took the plastic card being handed to her, thanked the pretty but dull girl, and headed for the elevator. As she passed the desk Regan looked back and saw that the receptionist did not have a body below the desk, but instead a base labeled "RECEPTIONIST". Great. She'd been flirting with a machine. Oh well, it's not like it was the first time.

The pass card beeped happily as she walked into the elevator, again when she pressed '53' and once more when she exited the elevator. She was tempted to see what would happen if she dropped the card and went wandering, but she didn't want to get Harold in trouble. Much. If this was what it took to get to a "non-restricted" area, she wondered what sort of measures Harold had to go through on a regular basis. No doubt some sort of very polite automated fingerprint, retina, DNA, and prostate scan.

"Regan!" Harold called out, waving her over to the cafeteria.
"Hey bro!" She caught up to him and they got into line.
"I guess an early lunch won't kill me for one day." Harold said.
"It's almost two."
"Oh."
They made their selections as they went along, and were soon next at the cash register. The young man ahead of them was having some kind of trouble. He turned around to the mass of tables and meekly called across, "Doctor Coll? You didn't give me enough!"

The wiry Jonathan Coll leaned back in a chair with his feet on the table and yelled back. "Pay for the difference yourself, Scott! I'll get you reimbursed, don't worry!"

Scott turned back to the cashier, rummaging though this pockets. "Sure he will." he mumbled.

When Regan and Harold got to the cashier she found that Harold was paying for her as well, so she thanked him sheepishly. As they headed for a seat, Regan noticed that the wiry man and the man getting him lunch did not sit together. In fact, no one was sitting with the wiry man, and he seemed quite happy that way, pecking away at a mini terminal while absent mindedly picking at his lunch as if it were an inconvenience to have to eat. He stopped and looked at his assistant. "Hey! Get me some ketchup for this slop!"

Regan glanced at her brother. "Wow. HE'S a real charmer."

Harold rolled his eyes. "Yup. Jonathan-something. He treats the interns like his personal slaves. He's new. Supposedly a hotshot. Demanded some big salary and got it. He works in my division but luckily not my lab. I haven't had much exposure to him."

Regan shrugged it off, and gobbled a bit more of her passable casserole lunch. "So what is it you do here, anyway?"

Harold got a little excited smile and reached into his shirt pocket for a little flashlight, about four centimeters long. 'Mana' was written on the side. "Look..!" he pressed the button, and it turned on.

Regan stared at it intently for a few moments. "Oh. My. God! *You invented the lightbulb!*"

Harold laughed. "No, no. This is a souvenir from the project I was on a few months ago, fine tuning the mana drive."

"Mana drive, huh? Biblical. A city with four towers of Babel, a halo of bridges, and a mana drive. Who says scientists like playing god? Okay, fine. This thing has a mana drive. Whoopie. What's so great about that over a battery?"

"No, no. You see the power is actually being transmitted from a facility like ten blocks away from here. The flashlight just has a little receiver inside!"

"Okay fine. What's so great about that over a battery?"

"You non-nerd types, sheesh." Harold rolled his eyes. "The applications are enormous. Have you seen a single power line since you came to Autar? No! There are none! Darn near the whole city infrastructure runs off the mana drive; free energy flowing through the air!"

"Sounds hazardous to your health. This is better than a battery or power cords- why?"

"Sheesh, Regan, you just don't get it."

"Guess not!"

"Well, anyway, I'm on another project now. Researching using nanites for medical purposes."

"Nanites. Is that like a robot nanny, like your receptionist?"

Harold stared blankly. "I can't believe we're related. *Nanites.* Microscopic robots. We're trying to get them to do things like assisting nerve functions and repairing or even *replacing* damaged tissue. One of the labs apparently made a remote controlled rat!"

"Thrilling!"

Jonathan headed back to his lab, leaving his less-dedicated intern to waste the rest of his break on having a break. Scott often wasted a lot of his break time socializing. It was things like that which left Scott out of the loop.

'When did series sixteen happen?' Scott had asked. Hah. Series sixteen happened while Scott was dashing home as soon as he was allowed, no doubt to get drunk and stare at the wall, or whatever it was that lazy interns did. He could be such a waste of flesh sometimes.

Inky and Pinky were healing nicely. Mind you, they still looked like hell, but the nanites were set to prioritize structural repairs. First bone, then muscle. That was all the nanites really needed since series twelve, really.

Jonathan's personal terminal beeped to life on a nearby counter. He picked it up and read the display. "Incoming call: L" As in Lancer. No doubt it was Mr. Book. What did that bloated troll want now?

Jonathan tapped the answer icon on the screen and as expected, the grey, tired visage of Mr. Book popped up in a window. Truly if there was ever a joyless face in all creation, this was it. "Hello, Book." Jonathan greeted him flatly. It was hard to fake enthusiasm while looking at Book's face.

"Coll. Any progress?"

"Inky won a fight while-"

Mr. Book cut Jonathan off "I'm not really interested in your rats, you know. We placed you there to get us a base-level fabricator."

Jonathan huffed. "What the heck for? The stuff I've already sent you can self-replicate if told to."

Mr. Book's face became even wearier, if it was possible. "Coll, your toys are useless for practical medial application at this stage. We need to get our hands on a base-level fabber if we're going to make anything we can use. Everyday practical applications. Your little projects might eventually be useful for wartime emergency medicine, but we need to see some results we can use now. There's only so much funding Lancer can keep off the books without something to feed our business sponsors."

Jesus, did he even take a breath in between all that? Jonathan had heard it all before and it was getting less interesting every time. He just felt lucky to have been spared the speech about the ways an organization like Lancer was vital to the nation. Hypocritical windbags. Jonathan wondered how big of a swimming pool Mr. Book had, paid for by his Lancer salary. "If you're feeling desperate," Jonathan said, "I might be able to pull a rabbit out of my hat."

"Then get on it, Coll." Mr. Book hung up without another word. Self important whale. Screw him. Screw Lancer. They want to see what his toys are good for? Maybe they want a taste of that hypothetical wartime Mr. Book alluded to. This could be fun.

Chapter 4: There was an Incident

Regan had resisted hinting to Harold about money for an amp for three days now and she was proud of herself. An amp might be a moot point anyway. Positions for guitar players seemed sparse at best whether she had her own amp or not. Maybe today she'd look for some lame waitress job or something. That's assuming that all of those choice positions weren't already nabbed up by flirtatious vending machines.

She wandered to the kitchen, flipping on a terminal while she nibbled, and browsed over to a newspaper, with the intent of heading for want ads. However, the headline on the front page caught her eye before she flipped past.

"4 Violent Unexplained Deaths" The article went on about how four bodies were found, three of them seemingly bitten and brutalized by the fourth person, whose cause of death was still undetermined.

"Lovely," Regan thought, "I guess every city's gotta have its freakazoids."

Regan finished her little breakfast, picked out a handful of places to apply for menial jobs and two clubs she missed yesterday. She slung her guitar over her shoulder and headed out.

The closest she got to a guitar job was a 'maybe later down the road' from an assistant manager who seemed to be being more polite than anything. On the 'crap-job' front she got a few 'the manager will be in on-', and a lot of 'not at this time' responses.

It's not like she was *expecting* to fall into a multi-million salary job playing guitar in the first week, but it would have been nice. Between today's discouragements and the breakup with Kris in the back of her head, she felt the need to visit her ever-supportive brother again for lunch. She punched him up on her mini terminal.

"Hey Regan!" he soon responded, obviously multitasking with work.

"Hey Harold. Whatcha up to?" Regan said with wistful melancholy.

"Oh, I'm at work, so I'm... you know.. working."

"Yeah. Have ya done lunch yet? Mind if I pop in again?"

Soon enough, Regan and Harold were sitting down in the cafeteria again with lunch paid by Harold. Although it wasn't by any means the biggest contribution Harold had been making to Regan, standing there while he paid did make her feel the most like a mooch. This job thing had better happen soon.

"Hey," Regan mulled while idly forking her food, "That jerk isn't here today." Not that she missed him.

"Jonathan Coll? No, he quit this morning. No real notice. He just said he quit, and left."

"I'm sure the interns are devastated."

Harold raised his eyebrows for a second. "Well, two of them certainly are, but not over Coll. That thing on the news... the deaths? Did you hear? Two of them were interns here."

"Shit! Really? Did that happen here?"

"Yeah. Well, in the lower levels somewhere. A whole wing has been taped off by the cops. It's got a lot of people rattled. Lots of dumb rumors running around. So how's the job hunt? Wanna apply for intern? I think there's an opening." He said jokingly.

"Ugh. I doubt I'm qualified." Regan said, missing or ignoring the tactless attempt at humor.

Harold sighed sympathetically. "It's going that well, huh? Well, don't worry, it takes time. Something's bound to pop up."

Regan left AutarLabs and headed towards home. The failures in finding a job nagged at her with self pity. It's thick stuff, self pity; no wonder it makes one walk slower. It had nothing to do with Kris. Nothing.

The early afternoon sun came down starkly overhead, making sharp shadows which weren't all that dark, except compared to the shafts of light that managed to sneak between buildings. For all its cleanliness and technological perfection, Autar only seemed to feel less and less familiar the longer she was here.

Even the streets were clean. Unusually clean. Drop a sandwich, pick it up, and still eat it clean. No doubt some technical wonder kept any offending dirt away. Even the alleys looked clean.

Regan couldn't help but stop and stare for a moment down one of these clean alleys when she saw a homeless man in one. It seemed quite unlike Autar to have any homeless. He looked out of place, way back down that clean alley.

No. He looked a bit too out of place. He was leaning against the wall, not standing straight and facing away. Regan ventured down the alley timidly until she got close enough to see a smear of blood along the wall. She broke into a jog. "Hey, man! Are you alright?"

The man turned around when he heard her. His head was bleeding, a part of his skull caved in. He raised his bloody hands towards Regan. One of the hands had two fingers hanging limp, nearly ripped off. Regan's first reaction was repulsion, then concern. "Hey, just stay there, I'll get help." She was reaching for her mini-terminal but the man staggered forward, ignoring her suggestion to stay put.

"Just hang on! You'll just aggravate the-" she looked into his eye for the first time. This was not someone who was in pain, or wanted help. His expression was hollow except for a slight frown on his brow, and clouding of his eyes. Regan stepped back.

"I said stay there."

He ignored her request, and walked forward at an unsteady pace. She could have run but being so close and looking this thing in the eye, her instinct chose "fight". Without thinking, she swung her guitar as hard as she could.

A splash of blood from his previous injury hit the wall when the guitar impacted his head, and he was forced against the wall. He didn't seem very bothered by it. He corrected his step and continued forward, grabbing the stem of the guitar with both hands and snapping it in two.

Regan still had her hand on the head of the guitar. She pulled it back, splintered wood on the one end marred by blood from the creature's hands. She looked at the shard of guitar, and looked at the thing advancing on her. She stabbed the splinters into his abdomen. That didn't really bother him much either. After dropping his part of the guitar, he reached out to grab Regan's head. She skipped back out of the way then ran to the mouth of the alley, getting about five meters between them. A few other passers by were now looking at the man as well. He walked towards them bit by bit, the head of the guitar still sticking out of him.

Regan called the police on her terminal. A message came on that sounded recently (and hastily) recorded. "At this time, emergencies throughout the city have unfortunately risen beyond expected numbers. We cannot respond at this time. If this is in regards to a violent death, or an untalkative assailant, we can only advise that you avoid the assailant, and not confront them directly. We will be addressing incidents systematically. Please leave a-"

"Yeah, wonderful" Regan said, disconnecting. She saw another person leaving a frenzied message anyway on their own terminal.

Down the street, a scream was heard. In the other direction, a storefront window was smeared with blood. Wide eyed, Regan gritted her teeth and muttered "Just wonderful."

Chapter 5: Cavalry

Regan called Harold while walking home, crossing the street often, or even walking in the street to avoid incidents where there had doubtlessly been attacks. There were more and more of them and it was becoming rare that there was not some blood to be seen somewhere, if even just a humble smear from a wounded hand across a door.

One of the more staggering displays of gore was a large pool of blood that almost spread across the street with significant large splatters up the building it was next to. In the middle were several bodies, some of which were moving. She dared not get closer. It was impossible to tell if the movements were living people in the last throws of death or dead people in the first groggy motions of becoming one of the legions which were spreading across the city. The red dragging footsteps that led away from the pool were even less inviting to investigate.

Screams came from random directions. Distant, lonely, desperate calls of fear or despair as the living became a rapidly rarer sight.

A man came by running for his life, terrified. He bumped into Regan. He wasn't wounded, but was not alright. Regan felt the need to say something to him before he ran off but she couldn't think of anything helpful.

Finally Harold picked up one of Regan's calls. "Regan! Are you okay?"

"Yeah. I was gonna head home. How about you?" Regan's casual answer surprised even her. She felt like her mind was working on two separate levels. Outwardly, she was handling everything cool and relaxed, while inside, she was ready to scream.

Harold was understandably tense. "I'm fine. We've been advised to stay indoors until this blows over. Are you closer to home, or here?"

"Home."

"Okay, go there, lock the door, and keep an eye out."

"Yeah, that's pretty much what I planned." Regan was quiet for a moment, wishing her brother was by her side. The noise around her was creeping closer constantly. "Stay safe."

She disconnected and kept going. Regan considered calling Harold back just to have someone to talk to, something calming. She saw some of the dead wandering out in the streets. Some in groups. This wasn't about to get any better.

Shortly after, she could hear a commotion ahead. Yelling, shooting. As she neared the next intersection, she could tell the battle was less than a block to her left. She stood at the corner of the building, and peeked around it.

Just over half a block away, half a dozen police officers were firing pistols and shotguns into a crowd of dead that continually ambled towards them. Now and then one of the walking would fall, only to be trampled by the one behind it.

The chaotic battle and the moans of the dead struck her. There was no denying what these lost souls had become. There was no other word but 'zombie'. It was just too unreal. This sort of thing just doesn't happen.

Regan was trying to decide if she should go talk to one of them to ask for information or just stay out of the way. Her train of thought was derailed when a door to a building between her and the police crashed open, and more zombies started pouring out. They weren't fast, but they had a steady persistence to them.

"*Hey cops!*" Regan yelled over to them, "Run over here! You're gonna get cut off!" Only one heard, but he then saw the growing group forming behind them, and alerted the other officers.

Regan started crossing the intersection as she watched the officers begin running towards her. One started firing at the zombies in the way. Regan dropped to the ground to avoid stray shots.

The zombies were closing the open path between Regan and the police. Hoping against the obvious, Regan watched as her view of the officers became obscured by the mob. She heard more shots being fired. A frustrated yell. More shots.

Less shots.

A scream.

One more shot.

A cry of hopeless anguish.

A vivid scream that ended with gurgling blood.

Regan was still lying prone on the pavement, staring forward at the churning mob. The sounds of combat were gone, replaced only with deathly low groans and a silence beyond sound.

She saw some of the zombies looking around. They'd spot her soon. Time to quietly leave. Once she made it out of view, she ran until she couldn't hear the moans anymore.

Some time after her hands stopped trembling, she heard a sound she hadn't heard in the city before. A deep hissing, overhead. She looked up to see a large aircraft. It looked only slightly more aerodynamic than a small house. It was compact, but even from the ground it was easy to tell that it was big. It bore no tail, just stubby stabilizer wings with turbines on them. It passed under the southern bridge and just kept going, despite Regan's waving.

It looked like it was planning on landing somewhere in the next block or two, so she ran to go meet it. As she got closer, Regan began seeing other people who were also heading for the aircraft.

Once she got closer to the thing parked in the street, it was rather daunting. Its bulk took up more than three lanes, leaving very little space for its side fins and turbines. A mob of people was already forming and three soldiers were guiding people into a cargo door.

Regan went up to one. His uniform seemed a little unusual though she couldn't put her finger on why. His shoulder didn't bear any markings to identify his unit.

"Hey Mister soldier guy!"

The soldier didn't even really look at Regan, keeping his attention on the mass of people. "Miss, just get aboard the airlimb, we'll get you out of here."

"Airlimb?"

"Yes Ma'am. Helicopters aren't cleared for flight in the middle of the city. None are nearby anyway. We were nearby when things erupted, so we're using our four airlimbs to get people out from as deep in the city as we dare."

"*Four*? There's a lot of people in here! When's there going to be more help?"

"I don't know about that Ma'am, I'm just doing what I can."

"What about AutarLabs? My brother's there!"

"Aut-" he flinched, momentarily glancing at Regan. "I personally don't know what order we're evacuating where Ma'am, we're just doing our best."

Regan stepped back, and pulled out her mini terminal, and called Harold. It rang.. and rang.. finally it picked up.

"You've reached Harold Grier, I'm busy at the moment, so leave a message and I'll get back to you."

Regan gave a frustrated sigh. "Harold, I wanna know what's going on there. Have you heard anything about being evacuated?" Regan paused for a sigh. "Aw fuck it, I'm coming there. Call me when you get this." She stuffed the terminal away with an extra "Fuck it!"

This caught the eye of the nearby soldier. "Ma'am, if I heard right, I wouldn't suggest going to AutarLabs."

"Why the hell not?" She snapped.

"Well, aside from the attacks all over the city, we've had reports that AutarLabs is having especially strong creature-presence."

"Creature?! Call a duck a duck already, we're dealing with zombies."

A passing evacuee piped up, "I think they prefer living impaired."

Regan gave him a vicious glance as he slunk away.

"Regardless Ma'am," the soldier continued, "I really don't think you stand much of a chance unless you come with us now."

".... and my brother...?" she quietly said to herself. She looked down the street. It was mostly clear, how hard could it be to find Harold? She patted the soldier on the back. "Hey man, thanks, but I'll catch the next bus." and she ran off.

"Ma'am! Get back here!" He took a few steps to chase her but saw she was determined. He decided to stick with the crowd who were more cooperative.

Chapter 6: New Reign

As Regan got farther from the airlimb, its sounds, and the people, she began to realize that the city had been undeniably, fundamentally changed, and it would never be the same again. Despite distant sounds of the airlimb taking off, sporadic gunfire, and the occasional sounds of the odd lurking, groaning zombie, an oppressing quiet managed to weigh so heavily that it seemed to slow Regan's stride.

Night had snuck up and few lights were on. Many were damaged. Others just had no one to turn them on. Cars sat silently in the streets here and there and no people could be seen, not even panicking ones.

The gore which in daylight had stood out bright and alarming had now sort of blended in with the city. From immaculate in the morning, the evening bore dingy bloodstains and smears from desperate panic. These weren't stains on a sparkling city. The blood was now part of it. This was Autar's blood. This was just the way things were now.

Regan found herself staring at the blood and occasional body so intently that she forgot momentarily about the escape she had just recently refused. With her heart pounding, she forced herself to think of the brother she aimed to find. Focus.

A flicker caught her eye, and she looked up to a streetlight that struggled with some malfunction. A few blocks further down she could see a digital advertising screen showing a mix of static and some computer error message. Regan imagined some control room somewhere, maybe half shot up, maybe being ripped apart by zombies.

She turned a corner and stopped in her tracks. Just before the next intersection the street was filled wall to wall with a mob of zombies, very similar to the group that had claimed those cops earlier. This group was closer, and she could see them a little better. Many were badly injured, missing limbs, chunks out of their torsos or heads. The injuries would be incapacitating if not fatal to humans, and crudely displayed the vitals of these freshly claimed. The variety of people who had been taken into the mob included brutalized children, and more police officers. How many of the zombies' injuries were from gunfire, and how many were inflicted while the victims were still living?

Regan realized fully that these monsters were recently people. Ordinary people with lives of their own. All that had been taken from them. They were dead, but not resting, their bodies being puppeteered around in cruel dispassion to what those people meant. Revulsion, pity and anger washed over Regan, and forced her to stare.

They were headed for her slowly, as if they just happened to be ambling in her general direction. It was more than enough to justify a detour. She picked a street and walked quietly out of view of the mob, hoping not to attract attention. Safe from their gaze, she ran for about a block and a half.

She paused to rest, leaning against a building to catch her breath. Across the street there was a church. A crude sign was strung across the closed doors. 'Evacuated' She wondered if they were alright, or if they were part of the mob she just ran from. Did they toss holy water at them?

A familiar sound approached. An airlimb passed overhead heading the opposite direction she was. She considered trying to wave it down and just get out. But they'd never spot her, and she had a brother to find. She hardened her resolve and started walking again.

Less than a minute later she heard the crash echo from behind. It was too much of a coincidence; it had to be the airlimb. Her first reaction was to run and help but then she realized the mob was between her and the sound. She could only hope that if the people on board were alright from the crash and had a clear path to the outside. It was about this time she realized how hard it would be to eventually find her own clear path out. It's not as if she'd find her brother, get a happy 'game over' and get magically teleported away.

She cursed her stupidity. For all she knew Harold got out already on an air- *damn*, he might have been in that crash!

Fear of the zombie mob left her and she began running again. A building she could see ahead housed a mall. If it had an entrance on the other side, it might lead out behind the mob and she could get to the crash.

She burst into the ravaged mall and ran down the hall. Ahead there were a dozen or so zombies scattered across the hall but her fear and logic couldn't catch up with her. She picked out the weak spot in their haphazard blockade. As she passed a deli she picked the small folding menu board off the ground. Its top handle made it a good weapon if swung so its panels were angled to cut through the air.

The menu impacted the jaw of an unsuspecting zombie with a distasteful crack, knocking him out of the way. Regan's recovering target and the others nearby turned their attention to her. They began to follow her but she was already running away, further down the mall. The menu was awkward to run with and striking with it made her hand sort of sore, so she dropped it and kept going. After turning a corner she saw the glass doors of the exit she was hoping for. It was there alright, but it didn't lead behind the mob. It went straight into the thick of it. She ran close enough to get a better look and rested, hands on her knees, checking things out.

Nope. They were packed thick through the street and up against the glass like the world's worst mosh pit crowd. Hundreds of them. She'd have to go back and around somewhere else. She was still catching her breath when she heard the glass start to crack. Damn, they noticed her. Her body wasn't too happy about running again but it reluctantly obeyed. She made a mental note to pace herself in the future. Outrunning these guys wasn't a big deal unless you've been running a lot, which she had.

She turned the corner and saw where she had hit the zombie before. That thin barricade of zombies wasn't so thin anymore. The ruckus had apparently attracted more zombies out of nearby shops. About thirty more.

"Fuck, fuck, *fuck!*" she said in her gasps. Looking around, she picked a store hoping for a back exit. She ran through the shoe store and barged into the back. She pushed on the fire escape door and the alarm bell erupted furiously, a meter from her head. "I don't *need* this right now!" she yelled at the bell, and pushed on the door. It bumped something and then opened more. The mob was out there too. If the alarm hadn't gone off she might have heard the moans of the dead sooner, but as it was she barely dodged the grasp of one particularly bloody fellow. Closing the door was not an option anymore, so it was back to running.

She ran into a store across the hall, wondering how long she had until something caught up with her. As soon as she got to the store she saw it was already infested. Odd, nearly all the zombies had taken clothing off the racks and put some on. Almost all of them had chosen obnoxiously bright coloured shirts and she could swear one had a hair barrette clipped to a chunk of exposed brain.

Regan stopped to look at this in disbelief. She commented quietly, and stunned, "Never get caught dead in a Hawaiian shirt." She blinked, and headed to the next store over.

Well, it wasn't a store, it was a bank. And it looked empty. She ran to the back, but on the way she saw a dead guard. No, he used to be a guard. He was a dead zombie now. Well, that was an oxymoron. He was an inanimate zombie. And he had a head start on decomposition. Too bad he didn't have much for a head.

It looked like he.. it.. had been shot.. a lot. Judging from the wounds, and the assault rifle at his side, it could have been his partner. Autar liked their over-armed guards. Everything had to be bigger and better in Autar. At least it was good to see that with enough head trauma, these things would go down for the count.

Regan scooped up the weapon which she later learnt was one of many variants on the classic 'Fabrique Nationale Project 90', and headed for the back. No back door. By the time she was ready to try another store, zombies had congealed into a loose crowd out front. That wasn't the way. It looked like a last stand situation. She went behind the counter and leaned on it, aiming at the crowd. She glanced at her ammo. This was pointless. The generous fifty round clip had maybe fifteen shots left.

"Why am I hiding behind the counter? They don't have guns!" She stood normally. Aw heck, if she was gonna die, she may as well have fun. She used a chair (which nearly rolled out from under her) to get up on the counter and made her best heroic gun-toting pose. She paused, looking into their faces. They were people. They were innocent. They had families, some who weren't even in Autar and didn't know yet. Some had brothers and sisters. They were *people*. Were. They weren't people anymore. She choked down her pity, and summoned her bravado back.

"*Alright you bandito gringos! You aren't getting into my sa-*"

She stopped, and blinked. "My safe...?" She hopped down, and ran to the back again. There was the walk-in safe, door left open as if the bank were currently operating. She got in and hauled the heavy door shut. The simple interior control panel only had four buttons. Lock, open, lights on, and off. She hit the lock and heard the bolts sliding shut. Stunned in her new sanctuary of calm, she staggered back against the far wall, dropping her gun as she went. The safe was about the size of a cozy living room, but there was nothing cozy about the cold metal lock boxes that lined the walls. She slid down the back wall into a seated position, staring at the door. How much air was in here? The thought got put on hold as the zombies started scraping at the door. It was barely audible, but it was an inescapable, desperate sound. She may as well get comfortable.

Captain Harringer, in many ways a model soldier, walked into the cockpit of the unmarked Lancer airlimb. Its dark interior was lit only by status lights and control displays.

"Here, Sir." the copilot said, standing to give up his seat for Harringer, "Chief's on the line."

Harringer nodded and took the seat in front of a display with a waiting call. He tapped the screen to take it off hold, and the sullen visage of Mr. Book appeared.

Mr. Book turned his attention to the display. "Harringer, report."

"We just unloaded our third trip of evacuees. The other three limbs are at about the same progress. It's getting harder and harder to find survivors. Over the last hour, resistance put up by the infected has mushroomed. The harder we focus our forces, the thicker they counter. The more we take down, the more there seem to be to retaliate."

Mr. Book groaned. "It's probable that the infected you take down won't stay down very long, Captain. Do what you can, but don't risk any of our boys. There's all kinds of reasons that we can't afford that."

Harringer nodded. "Sir, you realize there's no way we can get a significant number out of Autar."

Mr. Book grunted. "Of course. But it will be significant to those we *do* get out."

"And out of curiosity, how do we hide our involvement?"

"That's my job, Harringer, Don't worry about that. There's going to be more than enough confusion flying around to bury this operation in."

Chapter 7: Broken Bird

Once or twice the sounds from the other side of the safe's door stopped, but whenever Regan peeked out, the zombies were still in the area and the sound of the door opening attracted them. She'd have to be more patient and wait for them to wander farther away.

She took off her jacket and curled it up for a crude pillow. She sat back down, when her terminal rang. It was amazing that the signal got through the safe. Hoping it was Harold, she rifled though her 'pillow' to find it.

The display read 'Incoming: Kris Taylor.' Lovely. Just who she wanted to hear from.

Regan answered sourly. "What do you want? You can skip tormenting me today. I'm *kinda* having a bad day already."

Kris smirked. "Oh, such venom! I'm calling to see if your whiney ass is alright. You're not on the list of evacuated people."

"What? How can you see such a list?"

"They're posting em on the net for family n stuff. Have you seen the news? This is all anyone's talking about. They're building some kinda wall thing, and-"

Regan bit her lip and rolled her eyes. "Ya *know what*? I haven't had a whole lotta time for TV today, what with the *undead massacre* and all!!"

Kris huffed. "Yeah yeah. Well you're alright, so I'll just-"

"Hey wait!!" Regan interrupted, "See if Harold's on that list!"

Kris turned her head to another screen unseen by Regan. "Nope. He's not with you huh? Well just get out, you'll probably meet up. I'm sure this list is still being added to, and-"

'Connection Lost' suddenly replaced Kris's image. It shortly changed to "No Network". Well, there went trying to call Harold again. She lazily tossed the terminal and watched it spin across the floor. She stared into nothingness, letting her brain catch up with events. The things she'd seen today. Even here in her little sanctuary there was a bloody smear across a few of the safety deposit boxes.

She stared. After a while it occurred to her that they probably didn't have time to clean out the boxes. Hmm. The owners must be insured. Or dead. And it didn't seem like anyone was coming back for it. Maybe she could loot a little. Just for something to do. She stood back up and tried one. Locked. She stood back and grabbed the salvaged P90 and took aim. She winced and squeezed off a single precious bullet. The locking mechanism was quite nicely brutalized. She also learned in the process that she should hold the gun a bit more sturdily, according to the twinge of pain in her wrist.

A recorded voice came from somewhere in the ceiling. "Security has been compromised. Authorities are on the way."

"Yeah, I'll hold my breath for *that*!" She pulled open the drawer with some effort. The damage to the front made it difficult. Inside was a set of very old, but not exceptionally valuable looking jewelry. Someone's heirlooms probably. She stared at the necklace and other bits, and thought about all the lives that had ended today. Lives. Not just statistics on a list, or filled body bags, but people. People with heirlooms and families, and a world of concerns that were all cruelly made irrelevant today.

She slid the drawer shut again and went to lie down. She didn't need their heirlooms. She thought about checking other drawers for things that didn't carry emotional baggage, but right now her ammo was probably a lot more valuable in practical terms than a fistful of cash.

Regan awoke, not really remembering falling asleep. She looked around, remembering where she was, and everything that had happened. She felt her eyes burn with approaching tears but pushed them back. She had work to do, and a brother to find.

She put her jacket back on and collected her things. Her mini terminal might be useless for communication now, but it still had city maps on it. Who knows what else might be useful. The pain in her wrist from yesterday's recoil was gone but she remembered to hold the P90 a bit better. Like she'd seen in movies. The way the soldiers in the background hold them, not the way the star holds it.

She hit the button to unlock the vault and leaned against the door to open it, slow but silent. At first glance there were no zombies in the area. She began by stepping out slowly, then hopped around the corner to check behind the door. She'd seen that in movies too but her little hop turned out more cute than typical hollywood heroics. No zombies there either. Maybe they all just died overnight. That happened in one of those old movies too, didn't it?

Not this time. Once she got near the front of the bank she saw a few wandering aimlessly further down the mall. One of them was one of the hawiian shirt lovers. He'd found himself a fishing hat too. He was quite plain to see out in the open. Not like his friend rummaging through a large bin of plastic lawn flamingos as if it was full of candy. How many others might be hiding? She went the opposite way down the mall. In the far end of one of the shops she passed she saw one a zombie with a pair of underwear on his head. It gave a new meaning to those 'Inspected by' tags.

She made it to the glass doors that had yesterday been swamped with zombies. The street looked pretty clear now, so she stepped out and got her bearings. Where had that airlimb crashed? She got to the next intersection. From there she could see a great distance down the street. The mid-morning sun seemed to be entirely ignorant of the massacre yesterday, and the dead things walking the streets. Its light reached between the buildings and flooded around her. Almost to say 'Its not so bad.' Except for the reality around her. Blood drenched streets which had mostly dried were starting to stink, and yelled back to the sun, 'Oh yes, yes it *is* that bad.'

Straining her eyes against the sun, Regan saw two zombies wandering around oblivious to the sun and unfortunately NOT conveniently bursting into flames. The alley nearby had several more, protected by shade. So sunlight wouldn't keep her safe, but when she had the option, she'd stick to sunlit routes.

But what was that building far in the distance? It was far enough that it faded a little into the colour of the sky. It wasn't super tall but it was wide enough that she couldn't see either side edge from where she stood. She shrugged it off. It's not like she knew every building. She continued on to the next intersection. Looking down the street, she could still see the building. Was it wider than a block, or was the perspective and street layout just playing tricks on her?

The next intersection revealed two things of interest. To her right about half a block away there idled about two dozen zombies. They didn't seem very motivated but more were joining them from a nearby building.

More importantly to her left, buildings showed great scars where the crashing airlimb had slid in yesterday. It had apparently then bounced a little towards the middle of the street, where it now rested. Its back end was more or less shredded, with chunks of metal littering behind it. Streaks of black served as evidence of there having been a fire. It had probably burned through much of the night.

She approached the back end carefully. It was facing her approach anyway, and the ripped open end made an obvious entryway. Standing in the jagged threshold, it didn't look like there had been anyone on board. There were no signs of blood in the immediate area and nothing to suggest there had been a mass of people riding. The airlimb was either empty when it went down, or the passengers all evacuated safely. Or were in the back half and were shredded. No, there would have been signs of that.

The door to the cockpit beckoned her ahead. The floor was slanted up a bit. Was the pilot trying to pull up desperately to save the cockpit from taking the worst of it, or was it just the way it happened to land?

The door was unlocked and slid aside. There on the floor lay the body of the pilot face down, and in military fatigues. A relatively small mark of blood on one of the edges of the dash said to Regan, 'He shoulda buckled up.'

Regan stepped up slowly to the pilot, her P90 trained on his head. She nudged him with her boot and stepped back. Nothing. She pushed him over. He had a small wound on his forehead, but it was enough apparently. He was dead. Just plain, old fashioned dead. It lent a different mood to the blank stare in his eyes. Regan couldn't force herself to close his eyes. She just stepped back and slumped in the co-pilot's seat. She leaned forward, resting her head on her arms with the P90 dangling in her hand in front of her face.

At least she knew if she gave up and blew her head off, she wouldn't turn into one of them. Is that what passed for a 'comforting' thought now? She smiled a little at the absurdity while forcing back tears again. She felt a little weak for having to, but dammit, having your city overrun by the dead is pretty bad. She could justify a tear or two.

No time for it now though. She had work to do and staring at her gun gave her a good idea. She was on a military vehicle. She was low on ammo. She slipped back to the section behind the cockpit and started going through the lockers she had passed on the way in. Bingo. A full clip of ammo. And another, and another. She then turned to a larger locker that was built more like a trunk, and lifted the lid. There were at least six boxes of ammo that were marked as '500 rounds'. That would keep her going for a while!

Below the boxes was a large package marked 'AP MASS IMPACT ACCELERATOR'. Before she got to open it, she had visitors. A mob of zombies was closing in to the rear open end of the airlimb. She wasn't going to be able to get out the way she came in. This was probably the same mob she ignored from the intersection. Lovely. She grabbed a duffle bag from one of the lockers and dumped in the clips, and one of the boxes. There was some other stuff in the duffle bag. Whatever it was, it was flat now. No time to be gentle.

The mob was now boarding the airlimb. Regan's first thought was to go out through the cockpit window, but then she saw the regular personnel side door not far away. She ran the few meters to it then turned to the mob. "Not today morons!" She whipped the door open. On the other side were four zombies hanging around, who took notice immediately. "Aw, ruined my snappy escape." she thought. No matter. The few rounds she had in the gun when she found it were now less precious than they were two minutes ago. Taking aim, she fired a round into the zombie furthest to the right. SPAP! in the head. It staggered but didn't go down. She fired again and missed, overconfident. Another round sent it down. By this time they were closer, making the lineup tighter, so she fired on the next one in line less discriminatingly. She yanked on the trigger four or five times. She didn't know how many hit and how many missed, but the result was what was important. It was down. She took her opening and ran.

A dead zombie just looks a lot like a badly mutilated human. Running past her first kill, she muttered "I'm sorry."

Chapter 8: Nesting

Dusk was sneaking up quickly. Regan's voyage to AutarLabs was taking a lot longer than before the outbreak. She now had to make the effort to avoid the zombie mobs by taking wide detours.

She was tired and hungry when she came to a city park. It was quiet and peaceful. If there were signs of killings, they managed to be hidden or absorbed into the grass. She bent over to pick a blade of the grass. She was nearly surprised to find that it was real grass and not some amazing uber-mod grass substitute.

Not far off sat a stout little building made of large bricks and painted thickly with white. A small door on one end was marked as 'WOMEN', and doubtless the men's was on the other side. On the side of the building facing her was a small concession stand, closed up tight. She didn't want to fire off a round needlessly so she looked around for something to pry the metal shutter open with. Nothing presented itself offhand.

Remembering there were some odds and ends in the duffle bag she grabbed, she went into it to see what bonuses she had nabbed with her ammo. A bottle of pain killers, some fancy goggles, and two military ration packs. She decided to make due with the rations tonight and deal with the concession stand in the morning.

The washrooms looked big from the outside and seemed like they might make good overnight shelter. She took note that the door into the women's washroom swung inwards only, and the cement potted plant outside would make a good barricade to hold the door shut if she dragged it in. It might not stop a zombie if it was very determined, but it should stop 'casual' zombies. Even then, the ruckus should wake her up with plenty of time to grab her gun.

The park had several sports fields, so as it turned out this was no mere washroom, but more of a locker room. There was a lot of space, lockers Regan was happy to loot, a massive shower room, and of course the standard plumbing facilities.

Satisfied that the locker room was secure, she set up her little barricade and made a crude bed out of people's abandoned clothes. In the process she found a few other little useful items and stuffed those in her duffle. The little locks of the lockers surrendered easily to the butt end of the P90 but most of them weren't even locked.

She settled back, and tried to relax. So, this was the end of the second day after the end of the world. (Or Autar at least) The locker room was a bit cozier than the bank safe, and it was 'in a good neighborhood'. She hadn't seen a zombie in the park, at least not yet.

Having the time to examine some of her loot, she put on the goggles she had confiscated. Of course she was familiar with the notion of VTag equipment, but not being military, she never had a chance to play with it before.

A translucent display came to live in front of her eyes, complaining about not being associated with any VTag network. Regan fumbled with the buttons on the side of the goggles' frame and started browsing the goggles' interface. It wouldn't let her join a network that was apparently in the area without a password. Fine, she'd start her own. She left the default name 'New VTag Network'. The option for 'private' came up in the process. Sure, OK, private sounds good, whatever.

Once she was on her network of one, she managed to figure out how to place an actual VTag. The middle of the display in the goggles sported a little crosshair. She lined it up to one of the sinks, and hit the appropriate command.

Pop! A friendly, circular icon appeared on the sink. It reminded Regan of a lifesaver. Text below it waited to be named but Regan just left it at the default 'VTag01'. Now no matter how she wished to move, the sink would appear to have the icon and its text pinned on it. She leaned her head so that a corner of the wall was in the way, but the display still faithfully tracked the position. Through walls, through her hand, through the other side of the planet if need be.

Still wearing the goggles, she looked at the two paperbacks she'd salvaged from the lockers. They were trashy things, but they beat staring at the ceiling. She flipped to the first page of the first one. After half a sentence, Regan rolled her eyes and dismissed it as crap. She put the book down in her lap and used the goggles to put a VTag on the book, and labeled it 'This sucks'. She tossed the book against the wall, but the VTag remained where the book had been, hovering just a bit above her lap. Alright, so VTags don't track moving objects. That's nice.

She pressed another button, and suddenly the wall rushed at her. She yelped in surprise then laughed at herself. It seemed the goggles also operated as binoculars. After toying some more she managed to get the game of zooming in and out.

After picking through some of the more mundane items she'd obtained, she thought it would be wise to examine her gun a bit more. She discovered the safety. She wouldn't have known where to find it before. Lucky for her it was off when she needed it to be. She also found out how to switch it from single shots to full-auto. It hadn't even really occurred to her that it might have a setting like that. She was firing single shots up until now, and that had been enough so far. However she now had a pile of ammo and access to more, so she flipped over to full auto.

There was some other little plug that came out on a little wire but it wasn't labeled, so she left it alone. On the front end just under the muzzle there was a laser sight built in, but it didn't seem to be working.

The need for sleep came calling. She settled in and glanced at her door barricade. She left the lights on for safety, but dragged the sleeve of someone's pullover over her eyes.

The solitude began to creep up on her again and she missed her brother. In all the fun of setting up a safe spot for the night and toying with the VTag goggles, she'd lost focus a little. She wasn't even sure she'd find anything at AutarLabs. For all she knew Harold was out and safe, or worse, got killed somewhere. Either of those scenarios meant she was risking her life for nothing.

Harold was the only thing in the world that meant anything to her. The only real, stable thing. The rest of her life was just flakey jobs here and there, a couple crappy relationships... nothing worth remembering, really. But Harold was always there supporting her, even in her stupid moves, while he tried to sneak in advice. Or being an ear to whine to, or letting her crash at his place and mooch. Well, it was time for her to make an effort for him. He'd never needed help before, and now was her chance to do something meaningful.

Resolve pushed her hopelessness aside, and sleep finally claimed her.

Although morning came, the locker room had no windows, so no new light reached in to wake Regan. She awoke on her own and looked at her watch. Quarter to ten. That was the earliest she'd been upvalor in a week. She wasn't in the mood to waste time, but she had a perfectly good shower room here and she didn't know when she'd get another chance. It wouldn't take long. Her clothes could use a wash too, but she didn't have the patience to watch them dry, nor did she really want to run around in someone else's jogging pants. She'd put up with her unwashed clothes at least another day. They weren't that bad all things considered.

Once she'd put herself back together, she dragged the cement pot barrier out of the way of the door and swung it open. A zombie was standing about four meters away and Regan yelped. The zombie turned to bear down on her but she managed to fumble for her P90 and pepper it with bullets rather quickly. It fell to the ground but kept coming, dragging itself along with its arms, leaving a trail of blood on the path. She aimed at its head and finished the job.

Well, it almost seemed a fitting way to start a morning after sleeping in a bathroom.

She stepped around the body and headed towards the concession stand. She'd already made noise with gunfire, why not open it the easy way? She fired on the latch to the rolling shutter that covered the front and pushed it up, having to force the damaged metal a bit. The door finally came loose, rolling up into the ceiling and shedding forth mid morning light on a colourful treasure trove of junk food. She climbed over the counter and attacked the nearest bit of chocolate. With the bar hanging out of her mouth, she examined the rest of the inventory. Oh, look, a door. If she had walked a little bit farther around the corner outside, she would have seen it. To add insult it wasn't locked. She could have been munching junk food last night instead of her selection of rations and nutrition bars. Yeah, that would have been healthy.

With her duffle bag now stocked with a fresh water bottle and some goodies on top of boring 'survival' food, she was ready to head out again. This spot turned out pretty good. Before she left she got out the VTag goggles again. She erased the VTags she'd made while experimenting, and put a Vtag on the little building. 'JUNK N SHOWER'. Onward.

As he packed his equipment onto his new little boat, Jonathan Coll couldn't help giggling to himself when he thought of what he'd done. Such little effort, such huge effect. Too bad they don't give out a Pulitzer for this kind of thing.

Killing Scott was simply too much fun. He seemed so surprised! What an classical invention, the knife. The simplicity of the method was an amusing contrast to what happened to Scott after he died. A heavy dose of immune suppressant let the nanite chaser do its work all that much easier.

Coll was a little disappointed how easy the other killings were as well. He figured if his toys were going to really take the town nicely, he'd have to plant a few more seeds in different areas.

Simple math told him that the spread could potentially be very quick, being based on a doubling exponent, but he knew in practical terms that people weren't about to line up to be chomped efficiently. They may as well have though. Panic had spread so quickly.

Ditching Autar was a matter of timing. Leave too soon, and he wouldn't have been able to plant an optimal number of seed zombies. Leave too late, and the town would have been locked down. Being officially evacuated tended to leave a record.

As it turned out, he felt he had found the optimum time. Surely he'd be presumed dead, and with Scott being taken out of the picture, there wasn't much chance of getting named in this mess.

Except maybe by Mr. Book. That would have been sweet, if that useless hunk of lard could have been in Autar for the party. He won't speak up though. He has his own butt to keep safe from blame. Oh yeah. Ole' Book's gonna want Coll dead, no doubt. To heck with hiding from the cops, it was time to hide from Lancer.

Chapter 9: Crown of Thorns

Evading the larger mobs was becoming routine to Regan and not all that difficult. It's difficult to overlook a couple hundred walking corpses, even at a block or two away. Also, they weren't exactly quick to swarm someone who stayed mindful of an escape route. It would have been very handy to be able to put VTags on as many zombies as possible, but of course the tag would just hang there in the virtual air behind the zombie as it shuffled along.

No, the large mobs weren't much of a problem. It was the lone wanderers hiding in the obscure little nooks, or small groups like the one milling around behind a parked van Regan had just passed. Yes, *they* were a threat.

A bloody forearm which had begun to stink whipped around Regan's neck from behind. In reactionary panic, she yelped and tried to push the arm away. It was inhumanly strong. She felt it tighten enough to start strangling her. She heard at least one other shuffling up from behind.

Regan fought off the panic and trembling enough to bring up the P90. Maybe she could fire a burst into its shoulder to weaken its grip. Firing in such a sloppy manner would be risky to her too, but she only had a split second to think about the risks.

Or less. The zombie holding her bit at the back of her head. Panic crystallized into rage. She bent forward and pulled the zombie over her, onto the ground in front of her.

She hopped away, aware of the threats still behind her, and turned to face them. There were a total of three of them. She took a moment to quickly check her wound. The bite mostly got hair, but she was bleeding and it stung appropriately. Now that she was facing her opponents and had some space, it was little effort to send them down with her powerful little rifle. The one that bit her was getting up. She fired a burst into his head to put him down for good. The other two continued forward until they met the same end.

She stopped and stared at the one who had bit her, while she touched her wound again. Ow. Lovely. Does this mean she's infected? She dropped to her knees. Fucking lovely. It ends just like that. And for all she knew, Harold had gotten out anyway. That's fine, that's fine, we can just leave Regan to die in the ghost town. Nobody would give a damn except maybe Harold anyway.

She slumped down, posture and optimism melting until she was flat on her back, staring at the azure sky; ready to become one of *them*. What was the difference now?

The midday silence surrounded her. It pressed down on her and her three zombie buddies. The silence may as well have been six feet of dirt.

A sound interrupted Regan's self-eulogy. Distant. Gunfire? She sat up, and looked towards the sound. That building she noticed before far off in the distance seemed to be the source. Wasn't that building in a different direction before? She pulled out the VTag goggles and put them on to make use of the zoom feature. The building had some kind of structure on it. She zoomed in closer, closer. The smaller structure had a man in it, and the man had a big gun. It was mounted into the building somehow and he was firing it down at the ground. She couldn't see the target from where she sat, but it was obvious he was defending himself from zombies. He must be stranded on that building and..

No, wait... he stopped firing, but his body language.. he's very casual about it all. She needed a better view.

Regan looked around and saw a building with a glass elevator that reached up nice and high. It looked zombie-free. The lobby was visible to the street thanks to the glass panels that made up most of the ground floor so she felt safe rushing to the elevator. She pressed the button and stood back. The elevator *doors* were not glass, and could have been hiding a nasty surprise. They weren't.

She got in and pressed the top floor. As she went up she looked around through the goggles. The Vtag 'JUNK N SHOWER' caught her attention as she looked around, even though her haven itself was obscured by another building. She turned to the building she had come up here to investigate. The tops of surrounding buildings were mostly out of the way now.

There was a very good reason why that strange building seemed to be everywhere around the outskirts of Autar. Because it was.

It was a wall, and from where she stood it looked like it circled the entire city. They had built it all in the few days since the initial outbreak. She had heard of military engineers building much, much smaller walls quickly for the threat of floods and such, but this was a very different scale. This would hold a lake if it needed to.

So. They had already given up on reclaiming the city. They just didn't want the zombies getting out.

The wall had many of those small gun posts. Why not just bomb the living snot out of Autar? Not that she was complaining. She got to live, at least until she started craving brains. Her wound stung less now. Was that good or bad?

Either way, she was feeling a little less apathetic. She may as well finish her probably-pointless trek to the lab. As the elevator went back down, she heard noises above her. There was a zombie on the roof of the elevator. Frig, was it there all along?

She watched the ceiling and got out carefully when she reached the bottom. No need to stir up a fuss when she can just walk away. As she left the building she looked at the elevator from the outside. There were at least four of them on there.

They took notice of her and began throwing themselves against the glass. A considerable smear of blood blotted against the glass as they struck again and again.

A crack sounded. A few more strikes later, the glass broke and three of the four tumbled like wet laundry off the top of the elevator, onto the ground. They started picking themselves up, caked in blood and broken 'safety glass' bits. The fourth trudged through the break in the glass, and fell behind the other three with the unpleasant crack of bone.

Regan was a safe distance away by now, but she didn't need them following her and becoming a problem later. She had the ammo to spare, so she took them down.

How easy it was becoming, to kill the dead. Easier to forget they were people ever so recently.

She took a moment to imagine their names on some list somewhere on the net, while family members wondered how to hold a funeral.

Chapter 10: The General

With yet another detour while evading a mob, and another small scuffle, Regan was finally at AutarLabs. Well, she could see it, anyway.

The building was surrounded by zombies. That in itself was not a huge shock, but they were standing in a crude formation. Nearly shoulder to shoulder and five zombies thick.

The front of the building had about fifty rows. Each row had five zombies in a line. Multiply that by four sides of the property, plus lots of strays just wandering around. That equaled to a lot of rotting people standing around.

From a safe distance of two blocks down the road, she used the VTag goggles' magnification to look for a weak point in the barricade, but found none. She did find another odd thing however. The barrier also surrounded a large, open area in front of the entryway. The kind of concrete front yard you might expect a co-operation to grace with a fountain of some gaudy abstract stature.

AutarLabs didn't choose to have anything there, but they had something now. Right in the middle stood a large zombie.

This big fellow wasn't quite a zombie. It was twice the height of a person. Zooming in closer revealed that its form consisted of random body parts and gore held together by seemingly nothing more than will. It stood like a General behind his troops, staring forward without any noticeable eyes.

It all seemed to have some kind of purpose.

The only feature the General had besides the random mish mash, was a loose cable hanging out of its side. It didn't look like a power cable. She zoomed tight on the suspicious cable and raised the P90 to aim.

No good. The gun was so magnified through the goggles that it was impossible to even know if she even had it facing the right way, if it wasn't for the fact that she could feel it in her hands.

She looked around the building for hints about how things were inside. A few windows had lights on and one caught her eye. She counted what floor it was on. Thirteen, fourteen, fifteen. It was Harold's lab. At least, it was the window he waved at her from before.

She zoomed into it as tight as she could. She couldn't see activity, but she couldn't exactly see a lot inside other than the ceiling. He could be just a couple meters away from the window and be obscured thanks to Regan's viewing angle. On the plus side, there were no signs of violence that she could see.

That was it, she needed in there. She felt a bit more like she hadn't just wasted her time. Now she just needed to get past the General and his troops.

She zoomed back in on the General's suspicious cable. She sat back and lifted the goggles onto the top of her head, and stared at the P90. She was still getting to know the weapon. She had taken long enough to figure out how to switch it from single shots to fully automatic firing, and she still didn't know what the little cable on the bottom was for.

A lightbulb turned on over her head. She felt like an idiot. She pulled the little cable out and found it plugged in quite nicely into the mysterious little socket on the side of the goggles. She put the goggles back on properly.

The goggles displayed 'wait....' for a moment then popped up with 'Accept weapon targeting data feed? Y/N' Regan giggled at her stupidity, not having tried this before... but then, she didn't have a need to.

Now when she aimed a handy red icon waved around in front of her. She zoomed into the General. The aiming icon was shakier the more she zoomed in. The minor unintentional movements in her aim counted for more at long range, but she could deal with it. She aimed at the cable sticking out of his side. It must be important. She switched to single shots.

She fired and missed. She quickly fired again and hit the cable, severing it. It fell to the ground. The other end wasn't attached to anything. It wasn't important. However, shooting it off was not entirely without effects.

She zoomed out a bit to see that the General had turned its eyeless head towards her. She zoomed out more and saw about thirty zombies headed her way. They weren't moving faster than a brisk walk, but they were determined, they were focused, they were following orders.

She switched to full-auto and targeted one of the approaching zombies. It fell easily enough, but the moment it did, another from the formation started towards her. She shot it, and again it was replaced. She debated just mowing them all down until she saw stray zombies coming from various directions to fill the gaps.

The General..!

She zoomed back to him, and traced the severed end of the cable, and visualized where it might be leading inside his body. She fired. The General's body jerked back a little for a split second, and then the mounds of flesh moved and churned, putting more of itself in the way of Regan's attack. It was using its flesh to defend whatever that cable belonged to and the P90 wasn't getting through. Of course it was hard to tell even through the scope, but repeated rounds just seemed to hit like pebbles sinking into mud.

Small groups of zombies that she hadn't noticed before were joining in from most directions. Directly behind her still presented a clear path, and if she didn't take it now, she's be swamped soon enough. The zombies were still a fair way away but she had seen how these openings had a way of disappearing quickly. She pulled herself together and bolted. Looking back over her shoulder for a moment, she saw Harold's window. She'd have to come back but she'd need a little help. She knew where to get it, too.

Making her way though the city was slowly becoming routine. The aggravations of dodging groups of zombies and staying sharp for the stragglers was no less hazardous, but she was getting a sense for how they behaved in general.

They didn't tend to pay close attention to her if she was far enough away, unless she made a big sound. That wasn't the kind of thing she wanted to bet on though. Their random ambling around made any non-secure places a risk to linger in. It was starting to make a bit of sense. At least it had a pattern. They liked to be near others. They ambled around and if they found other zombies, they'd stick together for a while, often creating these big mobs. If they instead found someone alive, well… yeah. Chomp. Welcome to the club. It was all very heartwarming.

Regan felt her little head wound. She didn't want to be in the club. It had been quite a while now. Did she manage to avoid getting infected, or did a small wound just take longer to convert you?

Some aspects of their behavior were a little beyond her. Many of them seemed attracted to truly tacky things. As she traveled, she spotted a mound of bodies, some motionless, some shifting. Sticking out of the mound were about two dozen pink, plastic, flamingo lawn ornaments. Zombie art. Wonderful.

She made it to her destination, the crashed airlimb. It was much as she left it, minus the mob that chased her away.

The two zombies she'd gunned down were still there on the ground, but they looked like they'd been decaying for ages, not overnight. Even the skeletal structure appeared to be rotting. Exposed bones were much thinner. The head and rib cages seemed far more collapsed than her shots would seem to account for.

Regan decided to keep clear in case they were somehow diseased. This precaution felt a little silly given the bite on the back of her head, but it didn't hurt to keep clear of them.

She went back to the armoury compartment, and uncovered the container she had seen before. 'AP MASS IMPACT ACCELERATOR'. She knew AP meant 'armour piercing'. Hopefully it would apply to fleshy armour. She pulled the dull-green metal container out to get a better look at it. About a meter long and thirty centimeters wide, it had little wheels on one end and a handle on the other so it could be dragged along like luggage.

Ignoring that for now, she opened the little latches on one side and flipped open the lid. To her dismay, it wasn't assembled and ready to go. It was in about seven large pieces and had a sub-compartment of at least thirty little bits and pieces. And no instructions.

She looked around the rest of the armoury for any kind of manual, but nothing useful could be found. A little label on the lining of the case pointed to the edge of the lining and said 'AMMUNITION'. Sure enough, by lifting the edge Regan saw six large 'bullets', a couple centimeters across and about twelve centimeters long.

That would have to be enough, since no more were to be found around the airlimb. She tinkered with the parts a bit, but it was soon apparent that it would take a long time to figure out. It wasn't safe to dawdle here if she couldn't keep her guard up.

She threw some more P90 ammo into the box just because she was here again, and closed it up to drag it back to her little locker room fort. To 'home'. Before she left she tried an experiment with a spare visor laying around. She turned it on and got it to access the network she had created before. With a little toying around, she was able to see though the second pair of goggles using her first set. She left the second pair on the floor, positioned to watch the entrances to the airlimb, and packed some extra goggles into the metal case.

Chapter 11: Rally

The sound of the case's wheels going down the middle of the street attracted some attention here and there but thankfully no mobs. The stragglers that took a liking to her were spotted soon enough that she dispatched them at a safe distance.

She made it 'home' to the locker room and checked to make sure she didn't have any unwanted pests settle in while she was gone. She dumped her cargo on the floor near her little 'laundry bed' and took out one of the spare visors and some duct tape she had found, then went to the concession stand outside.

She set up the goggles to her little network, and taped them to the wall inside the concession before picking out a 'meal', and returning to the locker room and barricading herself in.

Well, the experiment worked. With her main visors, she could view the other two she set up. The interior of the crashed airlimb, (which currently had about five zombies roaming around it), and the concession. Ah, she could now keep a close eye on her precious treasure hoard of junk food. If she didn't get out of Autar soon, she'd have to raid a grocery store or something. Artificially cheeze flavored food stuffs just aren't a balanced diet.

But then again, the infectious bite on the back of her head was probably a bigger worry. That thought slowed her down for a moment, and self pity wrapped itself snugly around her again.

She curled up on her haphazard bed and closed her eyes. She didn't *feel* like she was turning into a zombie. She looked okay in the mirror and the wound didn't seem especially bad from what she could see through her hair, but she didn't know anything about how these zombies worked. For all she knew, some mysterious growth was developing around her vital organs at that very moment, preparing to choke her from within or hijack her brain.

What about Harold? She had no idea where he was, and her best hunch was vague at best, behind an army of corpses. Why did this have to happen?

Things weren't all peaches and sunshine before the zombies, but needing a job sure seemed like a small problem now. Things were great! She was with the one person in the world she could trust, and things... things were great.

Then this mess. Even that bitch Kris would be welcome company now. What's worse? Being alone in a city full of people who don't care about you, or being alone in a city where they just want your body? And which was which?

She realized she was crying and sat up, mentally scolding herself. There was work to do. She violently flipped open the lid to her new 'AP mass impact-' thingy, and tried to focus on the puzzle of making it work.

One component was clearly a battery of some sort and it conveniently came with a charger, so she plugged it in. The indicator on it showed it as dead, and she may as well start charging it now.

One part looked vaguely like a muzzle, another featured what looked like a brace for on the shoulder, and one had an assembly for a trigger. She laid those out in logical positions on the floor, and then looked over to the five other chunks and the mass of other little pieces.

Hey. No problem.

Regan awoke with an imprint on her face from the part she fell asleep on. She sat up, and looked at her progress. Most of the big chunks were together, kinda. Some still needed little parts matched up in between them.

The battery was charged now, too. She grabbed a nearby bag of junk food and had breakfast while staring at her little project, remembering where she left off.

This wasn't good. Her best case scenario was Harold being trapped in AutarLabs, and here she was playing with a jigsaw puzzle.

Well, the *best* case scenario would be that Harold was out, and safe long ago. But then that would mean Regan went through all this for nothing.

In that case, the best case scenario would be that she had dreamt all this, and would wake up in Harold's guest room with her biggest problem being her lack of a job.

For that matter, maybe she should just wish that Kris wasn't a bitch. Then she wouldn't have even come to Autar. Regan allowed her idle thoughts to stray further on Kris. The hate she had for Kris was now almost a comical distraction compared to her current situation, and it made the work go faster. It beat letting herself get trapped in hopelessness again.

About an hour and a half after she woke up she was convinced she had the weapon put together right. She pulled the lining of the case out to get at the ammo and dropped three slugs into the weapon's ammo chamber. It only held three. That left three in the case. There was some kind of paper showing under one of them.

Regan pulled it out. It was a booklet labeled 'AP MASS IMPACT ACCELERATOR: MANUAL, MAINTENANCE AND ASSEMBLY'

"*Fucking hell!*" She kicked the case across the floor. Ok, spilt milk. She had a big 'AP' gun, and a big zombie to shoot with it.

She slung the hardware over her shoulder, and gathered her usual traveling gear including the P90 and the remaining ammo for the AP weapon.

She stepped outside, and considered testing the weapon. She aimed it at the ground ten meters ahead of her or so, and flipped a switch onto 'standby'. A light on the battery came to life, and an ominous hum built up, fading to silence after about four seconds. A little green light came on.

She raised it to her shoulder, double checked her aim, and pulled the trigger.

A sound that could only be described as both dull and sharp erupted. Regan was tossed onto her back and the weapon slipped free, and slid back another couple meters with an odd rattling sound.

"Oh - kay. Note to self. *Recoil.*" She'd remember to have a better stance next time. She should have figured. The lesson the P90 taught her the first time she fired it came to mind. She sat up and looked at where she had aimed. Yup, there was a hole.

A very tidy little hole, actually. The ground around it looked 'swollen' around it, having been pushed around by the impact. She got closer and looked down the hole. It was deep enough that she couldn't see the slug. Maybe dirt had caved in behind it, she couldn't tell. Either way, it should do the trick.

Chapter 12: Assault

On the trip to AutarLabs when she felt safe enough, she flipped through the AP weapon manual. She found out that it could hook into the visors the same way the P90 did, thankfully. She'd never be able to aim the monster at any decent range otherwise. Finding the manual late was better than never. She hadn't even thought as far ahead as aiming it.

Her position from before was not an option now. It was casually littered with zombies who may have very well been remnants of the group that had been sent after her before. She spotted them long before she was near and they didn't take notice of her. If she wanted she could have taken them out easily at this range, but that would have alerted the rest and she'd be running again before firing her new toy at the General.

She snickered to herself, half with confidence, and half *at* her confidence. It was not long ago that she was cowering in a bank vault while local authorities fled, and/or died. Now here she was planning this attack like she was Rambo or something.

Focus. There's a task at hand, and she needed a new perch. About half a block away she saw a building that looked like it would have a clear shot at the General's position. She entered it carefully, mindful of her blind corners and any little sounds that might be waiting threats.

This small, three story office building had no lights, its power cut off. Only the setting sun's dusky light lit the way through the various windows. It was a gloomier, tighter space than she'd been forced into before.

Along the stairs, there were minor signs of blood. Of course these days, 'minor' meant less than a body's worth. Debris littered the stairs as well. Paper scattered, trampled and stained. An office chair with a bent leg. There had been struggles here. Desperation still hung in the stale air. Regan almost wanted to scream, just to shatter the oppressive silence.

Regan made it to the roof, once again in an open space with no hiding spots for ambushes. But it provided no relief from the stairwell experiences.

The roof itself looked like it had been a final stand for some poor souls. The stench of drying blood was enough to choke on. Handprints along the ledge in one corner told the story of someone pinned down, grabbing desperately for any help. Regan's imagination put herself there, under a few zombies. Smearing her own blood, trying to scream while her throat was ripped out.

Yeah. Nothing like an active imagination to eradicate your confidence.

She closed her eyes for as long as she dared, and tried to relax with a deep breath. The stench of the blood wasn't so horrible after you got used to it. So why was she shaking?

She gripped her new toy.

FOCUS.

She tuned out the rest of the world and efficiently set up her sniping position. Her brother was alive and there wasn't time to let other theories get in the way.

She hooked her visor up to the mass accelerator gun and zoomed in on the Autar Labs grounds. Yup, the General was there, pretty much as she left him; surrounded by an organized barrier of guards.

There was another activity going on though. There was a small group of zombies walking away from the building, one of them carrying a computer case. What the heck? Were the zombies looting?

The small group was let past the guard lineup and Regan just watched as they disappeared down a nearby street. Regan tried to figure out the relevance of this, but there were no further answers being supplied here.

Another similar group was coming out of the building. Whatever.

Regan took aim at the General and checked the slugs in the accelerator. Using the ledge to steady her aim, she lined up her shot to where she had tried to penetrate with the P90 before.

The world faded away until there was only Regan's breathing, her finger, the trigger, and the target.

She pulled back on the trigger until that sound erupted from the accelerator again. This time she was ready for the recoil with her foot planted hard against the floor behind her. It still pushed her back from the ledge a bit.

She looked back to the General. The front glass of the building had shattered behind him and the General had a sizeable hole in his abdomen which was gushing blood and slowly sealing.

He was looking at her and so were about thirty of his guards, who were approaching Regan's perch. She remembered the blood smears in the corner. No no no, *No* thank you.

She took aim again, this time in a different area on his torso.

That sharp yet dull sound rang out again and again. More glass shattered and tile flooring inside was fragmented as slugs that wreaked their havoc on the General just kept going. He already looked pretty mangled but it was the one shot that could *not* pass though him that ended him.

Regan's final wild shot hit him just below the neck, making a dull metallic sound as it hit. The zombies approaching her stopped suddenly, as if stunned by the sound.
The General seemed to melt as if he had lost the will to hold his body together. The gruesome bits of him slid apart onto the ground, and he was soon just a pile of meat.

The zombies coming towards Regan and all of the guards took a stunned moment, and then started behaving like 'normal' zombies; wandering without purpose, some creating mobs.
Without their General, they were mindless. The group that was carrying a computer away as Regan began firing was now gone, lost in the rest of the zombies, their computer left dropped on the ground, case cracked open.

She waited on her rooftop for the aimless zombies to wander away. Some went into Autarlabs and some entered the building she was standing on, but by far the bulk of them eventually just went away to haunt other areas of Autar.

After about two hours of waiting for the zombies to thin out and meander away, the sun was getting close to setting.
In this time, two zombies had wandered up to Regan's rooftop. Regan had been very ready for them, and cut them down easily.
The gunfire attracted another to come up. Not wanting to attract any more, she tried another tactic. She stood in one corner with the P90 in one hand and used her other hand to drag the AP gun's bulky case.
When the zombie started getting too close for comfort, she ran to another corner of the rooftop. As the zombie tried to follow, it ended up walking more or less parallel to the edge of the roof.
Regan steadied her stance and swung the bulky case, bashing the zombie against the edge. Its upper body flopped over the edge, lower body still secure.
Not quite what Regan was going for, but she'd take it. Gritting her teeth, she grabbed the zombie's ankles and tossed him over the edge. She stepped back, looking at her hands, revolted that she had felt some of its skin. She heard it land.
Looking over the edge, she saw it slowly figuring out how to get standing again. When it got upright, it looked around side to side. Regan bit her lips trying not to laugh as it limped away in a randomly chosen direction.

In all the time since she had arrived, Regan hadn't spotted any activity in the window of Harold's office. She let out a deep sigh and decided the mob was about as dispersed as it would ever get.

She gathered her gear and started down the stairs. She spotted one more zombie along the way before she made it out, but since it lingered far from the stairwell, it wasn't difficult to quietly sneak past. She remained vigilant however. She didn't want to have to fire another shot around here. She also didn't need another wound to speed up her infection.

As she approached the AutarLabs property she came to the broken computer that the small group had been carrying. How many other computers had other groups taken off with before she arrived, and why?

She envisioned a van somewhere on the other side of town, with a zombie trying to sell stolen computers out the back along with a coat full of 'genuine' watches.

The stench here was stronger than anywhere she'd come across so far and it wasn't all coming from the General's nearby body. Sure, this huge pile of decayed meat was a significant factor, but so was his legion which had been standing on guard for who knows how long.

This place above any other in Autar, was stained.

Regan looked over to the General's shambled remains. It didn't show any signs of having being one giant being. It was now just parts of people, butchered. Sure enough, Regan could make out the shape of a computer tower, ripped open by one of her shots. Maybe the other computers were meant to be the cores to other Generals. Hopefully those plans were ruined at the same moment the other zombies returned to their normal, pointless selves.

Chapter 13: Hollow Chysalis

The AutarLabs lobby appeared much like when she first saw it, in some ways. But now the occasional aloof business types were gone, replaced by four zombies who seemed fascinated with something on the wall towards the far end. It was one of the slugs from the accelerator, and it was pretty mangled. That answered the question about re-using ammo.

Also thanks to the accelerator, little bits of safety glass were scattered across the floor. They crunched as she walked on them. She kept an eye on the little group of zombies to see if they cared. They still seemed content to stare and poke at the wall damage about ten yards away from Regan's chosen path.

She walked up to the reception desk. The automated receptionist was gone, ripped out of the floor. Pity. Regan was kinda looking forward to some 'human' contact. The elevator opened and even obeyed her button press to Harold's floor without a passcard, like she needed during previous visits. Luck again made up for her own lack of planning ahead. This also meant that zombies could have been riding the elevator at will, especially if they had been ripping off computers.

The elevator opened onto her desired floor. No zombies to be seen. She stepped through the doorway, and a yellow light flashed overhead while a recorded voice rang out.

'Security alert! Unauthorized personnel entering floor! Security has been dispatched!'

Once the surprise wore off, Regan rolled her eyes at the flashing light. She had imagined automated net guns, or tazers or something. After the automatic receptionist and Harold's other bragging, the flashing light was a bit of a let down. She slowly walked away from the elevator towards a posted floor directory, and the flashing light gave up.

Once the automated fuss had quit, the stifling silence of the hallway began to close in. The only sound was the ever so slight hum of the lights. Regan walked towards where Harold's office should be, checking door labels as she called out.

"Hello? Harold? Or anyone else with a pulse?" She held her P90 ready in case someone without a pulse decided to respond. It was becoming apparent that perhaps the entire floor was a desolate husk of former chaos. Disrupted or broken furniture and dividers formed barricades here and there, but the blood signs everywhere suggested that none of them were too effective.

It didn't look good for Harold.

She found a door that was labeled with Harold's name, as well as several other names. It wasn't an office she'd been looking up to, it was a lab. The chaos shown here was minimal compared to other rooms she had seen into. Pushing a fallen stool aside with her foot, she entered and figured where the window she was looking for was.

Sure enough, beneath it was a section of counter that was Harold's little corner. There was a picture of Regan. It was her grade twelve picture. It was a little embarrassing, but sweet that it was there at all.

There was a tape recorder with a note stuck on it that said 'play me'.

Regan held it, and looked at Harold's writing. Stared at it. At great length.

She didn't really want to hit play, but eventually her hand squeezed on the button, on no other impulse than the fact that it was going to happen eventually.

"Hello," It was Harold, and he sounded like hell. "This is Doctor Harold Grier. I've been wounded rather nicely by one of those things." Fuck. *Dammit*. Regan slumped to the floor, letting the recorder slide a short distance on the floor as it continued playing.

"I've lost a good deal of blood, and well, my crappy little bandaging attempt won't do much good. If you're listening to this, you probably have a clue that the nanite project here is the cause to this whole mess. I'm guessing that thanks to my wounds, my own blood has some of the little buggers." Wonderful. Regan was probably filled with them by now from her earlier bite.

"It seems to be operating much like a virus. How it's transmitted, I can't say for sure, but I could guess bodily fluids are a safe bet. Saliva, or blood from their wounds getting into the fresh wounds of a victim and replicating. Once the host has been overcome, they presumably take control, either by manipulating the nerves, or directly stimulating muscle mass."

Regan stared at the floor and touched the back of her head where she was bitten. Yeah, that's kinda what she figured too.

"But, now I'm kinda in a good news, bad news situation. The good news is that my immune system has been winning against the nanites, slowly but surely, according to repeated blood samples. The bad news is that with the amount of blood loss from my wounds, I'm pretty darn sure I'm not gonna make it."

Regan tried not to imagine how Harold looked at that point, but grizzly images forced their way in. His voice didn't help either, staggered with pauses for slow, painful sounding breaths. He also sounded tired. Very slowly slipping closer to unconsciousness due to blood loss.

"So now the question is... at the point when I die, will my immune system have enough *oomph* left in it to take out the rest of the nanites? I'm pretty sure I won't be alive long enough to test that... and certainly not conscious. Wouldn't that be funny? If I died, and my corpse defeated the nanites in me after? If you're listening to this, and see my peaceful corpse lying around, feel free to have a giggle for me."

Regan took another glance around her surroundings; just in the oft chance she missed something. There was no body. Just signs of his bleeding, and a discarded, heavily stained rag that had been a crude bandage. He was out there somewhere, walking, roaming, a corpse. A puppet for a bunch of tiny robots.

"*Little fuckers!*" Regan yelled. It echoed in the lab, mercifully covering up the recording as Harold gasped a ragged breath.

She stared at the recorder bitterly. He'd been working on nanites. Could he have in any way be responsible for this mess? No.. not directly at least. Harold's voice resumed.

"Oh. I don't know when or if this is gonna be found. If you can, and if she... if she made it out of this... my sister, Regan... Regan Grier. Um. I don't know. Tell her I love 'er. And. I don't know what else. Just to look out for herself. Regan, I'm not gonna be able to help you out anymore. Learn to stand strong, okay? Um.... Yeah, I guess that's it."

There was a click as his recording ended.

She stood and stared at the little device. Tears burnt in her eyes. She wanted to scream. Scream and scream until she passed out. Stand strong, huh? She was trembling, tense. Was this strength? What the hell kind of strength did he expect her to have now?

She saw his silver ring. He always took it off when working, and there it sat in the sill of the window, waiting for him to come back and claim it. His sister would have to do today. It was too big for her. She stared at it. If it irritated him so much to wear, why did he keep putting it back on?

Regan almost cracked a smile. It was like her. She irritated him too, but he kept putting up with her.

And now he was dead.

Worse than dead, actually. If she had gotten in faster, could she have done anything? Made him a proper goddam bandage for one? So her big rescue... all this effort was for nothing.

At least she knew now that whatever nanites that were in her own body were doomed, as long as she stayed alive. Now she could leave this city. This wondrous city of Autar. This grave. She could walk to the wall, wave down those snipers, and get out.

And leave Harold here to wander.

Bullshit.

She owed him. Hell, even if she didn't, she didn't have anything else. He was her whole family, and she wasn't about to just let these things use his body like that. Besides, since Harold was all she had, she was all alone now. She could be just as alone in Autar as she could out in the rest of the world.

She stared out the window, gripping his ring, staring across Autar's vast terrain. Finding Harold would take a while.

And then what? If nothing else, bring his body rest. She put the ring in her pocket and walked into the hall. This building was the logical place to start looking.

Around the city, the new wall stood to contain it. To contain the dead. Snipers sat in powerful gunnery, watching the outskirts, ready to destroy any corpses that tried to leave.

Around the wall, stretched the desert. Before Autar was built, it was merely a lifeless stretch of desert. Now it was home to death.

Around the desert, the world stared. Stared at this wall, stared at this dead city. Mourning, shocked, confused. Afraid that it could happen in their city, and wondering how, and why.

Time passed, and forgotten by the world, Regan searched.

And searched.

And time passed.

Chapter 14: Crown Keepers

The air around Autar was as still and silent as a crypt. No crickets were heard at night, and no birds in the day. Not here. Not for a little over two years.

The city had been left for dead, and left to the dead.

Occasionally, the smell of a crypt would wander out, carried by the wind. Decay, dust, and maybe a bit of rust, or chemicals. The soldiers of the quarantine wall would say "It smells like Autar tonight."

Around this city was built a wall. Thick and tall, it looked very much like a huge circular dam. On the north edge of the wall there stood a great metal door which led from the surrounding wasteland, into the wall's interior. No door on the north side faced the city.

On the south side an even greater set of doors, almost fit for a coliseum, faced inwards to the city. To pass through the wall into the city area one had to enter the wall from the north, travel the entire distance to the south end, then go through those doors.

The top of the wall was dotted with sentry stations, each with a grim looking gun pointing in towards the city. This has spawned the nickname of Autar's "crown of thorns". These 'thorns', were the ZS-103 'zippers'.

The zippers were designed specifically for the guarding of the Autar wall, and could deliver a *lot* of lead to a precise target. A zipper's floor mounting sported a sensitive system of hydraulics and a noise suppressor, allowing the gunner to pump 5.7mm hollow point rounds from a belt up to 1200 RPM, with luxurious ease.

Corporal Robert Parker was one such gunner. He leaned on the controls of his zipper, contentedly listening to the chatter of the night watch. He was younger than most of them, but his ability, likability, and level head tended to make him the unofficial leader of the watch.

Parker surveyed his edge of the city through the scope of his Zipper. Aside from the comm chatter, the night was silent

"I spy," hummed the voice of Richards, another gunner, "Something near the northwest cornerstone, and it's yellow."

"Yellow? Must be you, Richards!" immediately retorted another voice. Richards seemed to be heading up the game of 'I spy', and he was on the north side so Parker had given up on playing much. He kept scanning the lower area near the outskirts.

After hours since the last sighting, Parker saw something move. "I have motion in the south lower outskirts. I'm dropping a VTag on it...... Bam." Parker centered with crosshairs on the motion, and tapped a hotkey on his scope. A VTag appeared on everyone's display to show them exactly where he meant. "Someone help me out here."

"I'm with ya," reported Jerins, who manned the station to Parker's right. "Yeah, that's motion all right. Coming out from behind the rubble."

"Ok." Parker replied, "Major, you listening?" Parker hoped that Major Grant, the wall's CO, was monitoring things from his office as he often did.

"I see it." The Major replied. "Hold off a sec."

"Check." Parker, Jerins, and the Major watched intently while the other wall gunners kept radio chatter to a minimum. Finally, the source of the motion revealed itself.

"Yup. That's a zombie. Hey, another one wearing a hawaiian shirt." Jerins observed.

"Permission to open fire, Major?" Parker asked.

"Hold up a bit, Corporal....just wait for it......" The Major had predicted well. The zombie made its way forward and moved a sheet of metal out of the way revealing three more. "Ha. Silly twits. Let em come out into the open a bit more.... and.... alright Parker, you spotted it, Let em have it. Fire."

Parker 'opened up his Zipper', and sent a swarm of metal towards the small team of undead. The hollow points practically exploded against the zombies, shattering and obliterating them.

A few moments of silence passed. All else aside, these things were once human, and they were now at peace. Even the rowdiest of the team respected this. But respect only lasts so long. A haggard-sounding voice came from Jerins' com. "Arrrrrrrr... whassa mattaaaaa? Didn't you like my shirrrrt?"

Such was the duty of the Autar Guard. Keep the zombies at bay, keep the rest of the world safe. Of course, it's only a stopgap.

In the two years since the initial incident, no one had forgotten, but most of the world was happy to ignore Autar. Now and then the news would make mention of it and run footage of the soldiers who came out alive.

The zombies never stopped coming, and no cause was ever found. The officials in charge had decided surprisingly early to essentially give up on Autar. The wall had been built, the guard was in place, and there was no further threat to the public.

As time passed the debate about what to do about Autar began to fade into the academic.

Chapter 15: Understaffed

Captain Alisia Terone had been stationed at Autar for roughly a year. She had been posted to a team whose duty it was to enter the city and put as many of the zombies to rest as they could.

She had seen them interviewed on the news, they were heroes. That was what the public saw. Heroes doing their best to make things right in Autar.

The reality was a little different however. These missions were now regarded by superior officers to be token gestures. "We're doing something, we're fighting hard!" When Alisia joined, it was a whole four person team fighting hard.

Sometimes not so hard. She had suspected that less dedicated members had given up. The density of zombies never seemed to change, the city always supplying a consistent supply of resistance.

Disheartened members of the team would sometimes squeeze off more rounds then needed. When their ammo ran low it was easy to say "Well, that's today's work done. Let's go back."

On the other hand, distracted members tended to die. A cautious, well armed, well trained soldier had little to fear scavenging easy kills in the outer areas, but getting sloppy still ran you the risk of getting killed.

A member would die, get a medal, a burial, and an honourable mention on the news. The burial would sometimes be a coffin of bricks if the claimed soldier wandered into a mob of his new allies.

Alisia's mother would call her and fret for a while. A new member would be assigned to the team. The gung-ho ones burned out quicker than the sloppy ones. Some requested to be transferred out. This didn't get you a medal or a mention on the news, but no one seemed to mind.

Alisia survived by not being sloppy; by not being gung-ho. She survived by being professional, and not thinking of her missions as token gestures.

But the replacements gradually stopped coming. The team, which had become her team, seemed to be no one's priority anymore. The gunner guard kept the public safe, and that was enough for the brass. Quietly, her team became a team of one. One pretty redhead to show up on the news now and then wearing the Autar guard's blue camouflage, to be the token hero. Not that she liked it that way.

With or without faith from the brass, she intended to make her futile missions count. Every round fired from her rifle flew with the purpose to make the dead stay dead.

Today, a token of faith arrived.

"Major?" Alisia asked, coming to a halt before the Major's desk. The Major was a weathered man with a trim, peppered beard. His desk was a cluttered but organized array of papers threatening to overtake his keyboard. Alisia noticed a younger woman to the side of the room in a textbook attention stance. She was in the blue uniform. Her big blue eyes and chin-length, light brown hair reminded Alisia of a mouse.

"Yeah, Terone. I finally got around to arranging replacements for your team." The Major earmarked a spot in his paperwork, and turned his attention to the matter at hand. "Captain Terone, meet Private Tracy Kensington."

"Sir!" Private Kensington chirped.

Alisia glared at Private Kensington for a moment then slowly slid her stare towards the Major. "One Private? Please don't tell me that's it."

"For now it is," the Major calmly replied.

Alisia sighed. "I've been trying to expand the team for ... *ever*, and now I'm down to me and a little bitty Private? They're gonna chew her up in no time flat." Alisia's assessment made Private Tracy Kensington shift uncomfortably, but no one was paying attention to her to notice.

"Well, it's your job as her commanding officer to make sure that doesn't happen." The Major's tone had a distinct "That's the way it is" ring to it. Alisia stormed out down the hall, and before disappearing around a corner she turned back with a bark. "Private Kensington! Are you coming or not?!"

Tracy Kensington jumped in shock, darting her eyes between the Major and the Captain.

"I think you'd best get going, Private." the Major sighed.

Tracy caught up to Alisia around the corner, finding her leaning with her back against the wall, looking angry but calm. Tracy faced Alisia, and snapped to attention.

Alisia sighed. "Ooh-kay, kid. Rule number one. Relax." She looked up at Tracy, still at attention. "Relax was an order. At ease, and stay there." Tracy tried very hard to relax.

"Rule number two. I don't know if you were calling me or the Major 'Sir', but don't do it to me. Captain will do. Got it?"

"Yes Captain!"

Alisia sighed. "If that's out of the way, I wanna apologize about what I said in there. I'm not going to let you get chomped. I have had people die under my command, but in most cases it was because of excessive stupidity on their parts. Not to speak ill of the dead, but it's true. With only two of us, we're not about to split up so you'd have to be acting *really* stupid to get killed with me watching your back. Are you stupid?"

"Uh, no, Sir." Tracy stammered.

Alisia smiled to herself "You might be. You just called me 'Sir' again, after I told you not to." Tracy stood silent.

"Oh, lighten up a bit." Alisia revealed her smile much to the relief of the Private. "Alright. See me in my office tomorrow morning, and I'll brief you. Dismissed."

"Oh-six-hundred hours, Captain?"

"Holy shit no, Private! What do you think this is? The army?"

"Uh, yes.. Captain...?"

"We make our own hours, kiddo. We don't get no respect, but we get quite a bit of freedom. Now scram, will ya?"

"Uh, yes, Captain!" And with that, the bewildered Private wandered off.

Alisia breezed into her office fashionably late to find Tracy sitting in perfect posture, waiting patiently.

"Hey Kensington. That sounds kinda odd- can I call you Kenny?" Alisia sat at her seat, and threw her feet onto the desk.

"Uh- that's a boy's name.."

"Aw c'mon, all the cool kids have a nickname." Alisia teased.

"Wha... what's yours, Sir? Tracy cautiously inquired.

"*Arg*! It sure as hell isn't '*Sir*'! My nickname? You're not high enough rank to know that. So? Kenny?"

"Uh, alright Captain, if you say so." It beat the nicknames they handed out in basic training. Thus did Tracy Kensington come to be known as Kenny. It was something she regretted almost instantly.

"Alright Kenny, down to business. Fighting zombies. What do you know?"

"Well," Tracy started, "Hollow point rounds are generally used, but no grenades." She paused. "But I don't know why."

"Well," Alisia explained,"normal bullets make a hole and if you're lucky, an exit wound. Zombies don't generally give a rat's ass about that kind of injury, because for whatever reason, zombies don't need to rely on their organs to live. A hollow point reliably causes a big enough mess to actually break apart chunks of the target, removing their ability to move, or at least move effectively. A lost leg will take them out of immediate hazard, unless they're close enough to crawl and grab. Arms are good to take off, too. A walking torso with a mouth is pretty easy to avoid, but it's never bad to get the head too. Basically, you just need to disassemble them until they stop coming. Simple headshots used to work pretty good, but I've been having less and less luck with that."

Tracy took a moment to absorb the new tactics, and tried hard not to visualize it too vividly. "And grenades? Wouldn't that be ideal?"

"Yeah, they would, but for some reason they're totally off limits. I don't know why." This had been a standing order since the outbreak. "Ok, we have the basics of offense covered. Now for defense. If you go into hostile territory, how do you protect yourself, Kenny?"

Tracy responded seamlessly. "Avoid open spaces, stick to smaller areas when you can, use the environment for cover to be unseen, and become less of a target."

"Correct," Alisia chirped, "Now forget that entirely. Zombies don't use guns and they don't train snipers. The only risk to open areas is being seen. When you *are* seen, you want some space between you and the zombie. They're slow, but they're strong. You *must* debilitate incoming zombies *before* they get to you. Hand to hand is not impossible against a zombie, but just trust me that you'd rather not risk it. Their strength is also part of why you don't go into tight spaces. I've seen stronger ones break through some pretty thick walls to get at a person, even when a door was just a meter away. Oh yeah, most of em are dumb. So keep in the open and just keep your eyes peeled. Infra red won't help you because they don't give off any body heat."

Tracy studiously crammed the new information into her head. "Oh! What about infection?"

"Yeah, don't get bit. You get zombie slobber in your blood, and at best, we'll have to toss you into observation. Been there, done that."

"You've been infected?"

"Yeah, well-" Alisia was interrupted by her comm. She tapped the little device that cuddled her ear. "Captain Terone here."

"Captain, we have an interesting anomaly on the top deck." It was the Major.

"Oh?" Alisia put the comm on the table and turned it up so Tracy could hear.

"About fifteen minutes ago, random VTags have been springing up in a concentrated area."

"So? A zombie probably found some discarded goggles, and has been playing with the buttons." Alisia spoke of the hypothetical zombie as if it were a toddler.

"That was the first hunch of the snipers, but when they tried to track it down, they spotted a moving IR signature."

"I see. A zombie playing with a car maybe?" Alisia was stretching it.

"Well, possible, but not very likely. VTags *or* a moving IR signature are interesting enough, but both...?"

"Alright Major, we'll suit up ASAP, and go hunting."

"Very good, Captain."

Alisia tapped the comm off, put it back in her ear, and shot a sheepish smile at Tracy. "Giddyup!"

Chapter 16: Warm Welcome

The south doors lurched open slowly, spreading the visage of the city to Tracy Kensington for the first time. It didn't look this big from on top of the wall. Even from this distance the cornerstone buildings and their bridges seemed to reach towards you ominously. With 'boots on the ground', it was suddenly a lot less hypothetical. She was going in today.

Alisia stepped forward and made one last equipment check on the two of them.

P90s, chosen for the sheer volume of hollow points they could pump quickly, and the availability of salvageable ammo in the city. It also made a good smashing weapon in a pinch.

Custom Magnum Desert Eagles, donated by Magum Research after Alisia made a comment on the news that she was a fan of their pistols.

Good basic combat knives that didn't see much action, but were handy in a utilitarian way.

The most interesting toy was Alisia's one of a kind 'Bad Mojo'. It was a fairly bulky experimental weapon. Alisia wasn't quite sure how her team ended up with it, but she didn't complain when she inherited it from a retiring comrade. It definitely looked more like an experiment than a mass-produced weapon. It took two hands to aim its heft, and lacked any proper grip on the front end.

Using magnetic rails, the Bad Mojo hurtled a single projectile that shatters into an immense number of fragments. Technically it wasn't a grenade launcher, so it snuck by the 'no explosives' rule. The ammo was hard to requisition, so Alisia didn't use it often, but it was invaluable to break up a mob when she got cut off.

Satisfied that the rookie hadn't forgotten anything, Alisia turned to face Autar once again. To Alisia, it was a very familiar sight, even though she had never been in very deep. In an average mission, Alisia would go in far enough to find a few mobs of zombies and use up most of her ammo, then leave.

Today was different however. There was a much more specific objective, and it meant going deep. Corporal Parker, manning a tower zipper, was assigned to assist Alisia and Kensington; to keep an eye on them as much as he could and to assist with tracking.

Alisia started walking towards the city fringes, and Tracy followed. "Parker. You with us?"

"Yes Sir, ma'am. I see ya. You're still really close, and this scope zooms great. I can damn near see down your shirt."

Alisia discreetly flipped the bird over her shoulder.

"Anytime, Sir." Parker replied.

"In your dreams, *Corporal*."

"Aw, can't a guy dream, Captain? Hey Kensington, you're a Private, wanna fraternize later?"

Tracy turned around sharply, and made the rudest face she could think of, which in all reality just came out 'cute'. Parker remained silent, and smiled softly to himself. It might be worth making a point to talk to her later.

When Tracy turned around again, the city seemed suddenly closer. The sky seemed darker. It was not long before they reached the first of the buildings, which were in various states of disrepair. On the outskirts it was mostly factories, warehouses, and things of that nature. Instinctively, Tracy walked closer to the nearest building to not be out in the open.

Alisia continued down the middle of the street and noticed Tracy. Alisia whistled as if to call a dog, and pointed at the ground near her. Tracy understood and got back into formation.

"Hey Parker." Alisia asked, fiddling with her visor. "You still see that heat signature moving? My IR at this angle isn't really much help." While she did see many heat signatures, they all seemed still. Machinery and such still gave off heat, many still running on their own after all this time.

"No Captain. It's either gotten under some cover, stopped moving, or cooled off." Parker replied. "Most of the boys have their eyes peeled, so we'll probably see it if it pops up again."

"I hope we're not going in here for nuthin'. Hey, where's the nearest mystery VTag? Maybe if I looked around, I could get a clue.."

Parker was quiet for a moment before Alisia's visor showed a new VTag, flashing to draw her attention. "Over there," Parker's voice said. Right next to Parker's new VTag was one of the unknown ones. It was labeled simply "FW".

"Hey, Parker. Make things simple for me. Let me see *just* the unknown VTags, and the IR signature's last position."

"Right. Jussec." Soon, all the other VTags that the zipper snipers had marked disappeared from Alisia's view. There were about a dozen of the unknown tags. Most were labeled either 'FW' or 'GA'.

"Somehow they don't seem very random." Alisia observed.

"Captain!" Tracy called out.

"What?"

"I see dead people!" Indeed, Tracy had spotted a small grouping of zombies coming out from a hole in the wall of a nearby building. They were still fairly far off, so Alisia told Tracy to calm down. Tracy had heard that the zombies of Autar had a strange sense of style, and here was the proof. One sported bermuda shorts with black socks pulled up high by those little sock garters. His abdomen was nearly all gone, and as Tracy looked on, a small rodent poked its head up from inside and ran out, down the zombie's leg, and scurried off.

One zombie wore a bowler hat with a dead rose sticking out of the top. Another sported fashionable football padding.

All in all, once the group had cleared the hole there were six of them, one of which was swinging his detached arm in his other hand as a club.

"A nice warm-up for ya, Kensinton," Alisia said, "Go ahead, hose em."

Tracy aimed her P90 and let out a couple controlled bursts at them. Three of the zombies took chest wounds and staggered, but kept coming.

"C'mon. I thought I told you about this. Chest wounds don't matter to them. Try legs."

Tracy lowered her aim, and blew off a few legs. Soon enough all of the zombies were on the ground, crawling towards them.

"Nice shootin'. Normally I don't worry about ammo conservation, but today we might need it. We can leave em like this. They won't be a threat to us."

"But... Captain, they're in pain. Shouldn't we finish them?"

"Pain? I don't think they know what that is. Besides, look at em. If they were in pain, would they still be so eager to get at us?"

Alisia walked up to the nearest debilitated zombie, and kicked its head off with a hollow crunch. Its arms groped about blindly.

"Besides, I don't know if they ever *truly* die. They just stop moving and then rot."

Tracy looked down at the writhing mob of bones and flesh with pity, but she understood. "It's... like killing robots."

"Exactly," Alisia said, glancing back again as she moved on, "No soul, no feelings, no guilt, no problem. Some say that you're freeing their souls by 'killing' them. But who knows if there's anything to *that*."

Tracy seemed to like that idea so she ran up and cautiously kicked the head off one before catching up to Alisia.

Alisia smirked at the warrior mouse Tracy. "Don't get overconfident on me now. I have lots of experience at this. I can afford to be a bit cocky."

Amused mumblings from Corporal Parker could be heard through the comm.

"Pervert." Tracy said with a smile.

The two continued on into denser groupings of buildings. Tracy felt the streets were a little narrower. She looked around, and spotted several small lights, here and there. Was it was getting dark early?

"Captain, why is the power still going?" Tracy asked, "Why wasn't it cut off?"

"Autar's power comes from a generator plant somewhere inside the city. When humans evacuated, no one shut it down, and I guess the zombies haven't bothered to damage it."

"What kind of generator is it?"

Alisia shrugged "I don't know."

"There's no river for a dam and no windmills or solar cells. Is it nuke? They wouldn't build a city around a nuclear plant, would they?"

"I don't know. I asked, but it's classified for whatever reason. It would go a long way to explaining why we're not allowed to use explosives in here, but it doesn't *entirely* add up."

"How's that?" Tracy's interest was really piqued now.

"Well, if there were a nuke plant in here we'd have specific locations for where dangerous parts are and stuff. It would makes sense to not allow explosion near those areas, but why the entire city?"

"I don't know, why?"

Alisia looked at Tracy with a bit of irritation. "I don't know, Kensington. Why is the sky blue? Where do little zombies come from? What's the square root of infinity? Is Parker still looking at my ass?"

"Yes." Parker replied over the comm.

"Oh." Tracy said, "I'm sorry if I'm being annoying."

"Eh, don't sweat it," Alisia sighed, "You gotta learn somehow. But the bottom line is, there's some things I just don't know about this place."

Tracy nodded.

The rest of the trip to the 'FW' VTag was fairly quiet. They came across a skull with just an arm attached, dragging itself down the street. They ignored it and it ignored them. It seemed to be very intent on going nowhere in particular. Alisia had to fight the urge to do a 'hammer throw' with it.

They arrived at a building crowded between other buildings. The entrance was basically at the end of a short alley. As they walked towards it Parker piped up. "Ladies, I can't see you anymore. I'll keep track with IR, but I won't see anything sneaking up on you."

"No biggie," Alisia replied, "we're not that deep."

They looked at the three story building. It had large windows, most of which were broken, and a doorway with no door. It was plain that the 'FW' VTag was on the second or third floor. Alisia scanned around.

"This should be pretty easy to guard. Kensington, stay here and watch for anything coming towards the building. I regret not killing that skull-arm thing. It might bring trouble. I'll go in, check out the VTag, and be right out. Anything comes, double check to see that it's a zombie then fire away. I'll come running."

"Right." Tracy was proud that she was trusted on her own, and after proving herself against the group earlier she felt very ready for a five minute guard duty.

Alisia went in, checking her corners. The bottom floor was just two rooms. Just a small reception area and a main storage room towards the back. The stairs on the far side were easy to get to, and there was little to no risk of ambush along the way. She approached the stairs and checked upwards. All clear.

As she climbed the stairs, it quickly became apparent that the VTag was on the third floor. After a quick glance down the hallway of the second floor she kept going up. The top floor was an array of cubicles. Some partitions were knocked over but all in all, this floor was looking pretty good for being abandoned two years. The VTag glowed from a cubicle off to the left.

"Okay. What have we here?" Alisia made her way to it and saw five water cooler bottles, all full, and two cardboard boxes. She tapped the nearest one with the muzzle of her P-90. Nothing moved back so she unfolded the top flaps.

Canned food, junk food... beef jerky... non-perishables. "FW. Food and water. Well guys. Zombies don't need to keep track of food and water. It's starting to look more and more like our IR signature is a human."

"Where did they come from?" Tracy asked through the comm.

"Good question."

"A thrill seeker maybe?" Parker suggested. "Broke in, and looking for something to br-"

Just then, a shrill scream sounded across the comm. It was the kind of scream that gives you nightmares, ending with a rasp and a small gurgle on blood. The comm exploded into urgent questions from the many people who had been listening in.

"*Kensinton!*" Alisia ran to the nearby broken window, which overlooked the entryway.

In the corner, Alisia could just barely see Tracy's legs jerking as her body was forcibly yanked through a new hole in the press-wood fence.

"Fuck!" Alisia spat. She ran frantically down to the bottom floor, bumping the odd doorframe as she rushed. She burst out the front doorway.

Tracy's body lay in the corner with her upper half pulled through the hole. Alisia put together what happened. Tracy had sat down by the corner forgetting that she should stay in the open, and a zombie had tore through the fence. She didn't even get a shot off. Presently, the zombie kneeled contentedly on the other side of the fence, gnawing on Tracy's neck and shoulder.

"Oh my god..." Alisia breathed hard, drawing her P90 and looking at the red, runny mess that had been her subordinate.

She fired a controlled burst right into the forehead of the zombie, knocking it on its back. Alisia ran up over Tracy and kicked down the chunk of fence so that it fell on the zombie. She jumped on it, crushing the zombie below. It punched through, splitting the board in half. Alisia stood atop it and watched it fumble to grab at her legs.

"....you bastard."

She held the trigger down and the P90 sang the only song it knew, flooding its fragmenting rounds into the pitiful monster. Chunks of the offending zombie ripped off, ending its ability to fight back. 'click.' Empty clip. Alisia stared down at her decimated foe, silently catching her breath.

She spat at what was left of its face and went to Tracy to look her over. "Major? You there?"

"Yes, Captain. Report."

"Kensington's dead. She was taken by surprise. Looks like the first strike was a claw to the throat. It was quick. Fairly quick." Alisia's voice sounded tired suddenly. A mix of sadness and anger.

"Any bites?"

"Yes Sir. I'll burn them now."

"Proceed."

Alisia took out a small bottle of oil and splashed it onto Tracy's wounds. Poor cute little, mousey Kennsington. She then lit the oil on fire and couldn't look away as her hair, shoulder and face burned. The oil burnt out while Alisia tried not to cry, or be ill. The stench of the burning was just an extra insult to the way Tracy Kennsington's body was ruined. At least now, hopefully, the saliva wouldn't infect her.

Alisia did her best to sound alright. "Sir, can you send an extraction team? I want to proceed."

"Captain, you're alone now. I don't recommend it."

"Sir, if it is a human I'm tracking, then they could be in danger. I know my way around, Sir. I'm not in any real danger."

There was a long pause before the Major's voice came back. "Very well. Corporal, take care of Captain Terone."

"........"

"Corporal? .... Corporal Parker!"

"Uh! Yes Sir, Parker here." His voice was shaky. Tracy's scream was still resonating in everyone's minds,

The Major excused himself and logged off the comm.

Alisia's eyes fixed on Tracy's wound while she talked to her comm, "Parker, I'm going for the nearest 'GA' VTag. I want to know what they are." The nearest was on one of the bridges. Luckily, she wasn't far from a building that could get her up there.

It had a working elevator, with a (broken) window facing Parker's section of the wall. The zipper gunners liked to be able to see her as much as possible, for safety reasons.

Alisia took one last look at Kensington, and headed for the tower.

Chapter 17: A Visitor

Regan watched the little clip of video repeatedly. Someone in uniform had messed with one of her stashes. They didn't notice the visor duct taped to the ceiling, which alerted Regan immediately when motion was detected in its field of vision. The visor didn't get a terribly good look. The legs, even through the cammo pants, looked female and there was a glimpse of what looked like a P90. If the stupid duct tape hadn't slipped, she could have seen this person's face. In any event, they didn't take anything, but they ran off in a hurry, yelling.

This needed investigating. Regan knew the army had the city surrounded, but this was the first time she'd noticed any of them actually *in* Autar. Well, since the evacuation, anyway.

Regan headed out and made her way through her own little shortcuts and paths. A single scrawny zombie got in the way and she shot it once in the neck. The head fell off and the body groped around blindly. Normally she'd disassemble it a bit more, but she didn't want to waste time.

She made it to a rooftop and pulled out her favorite salvaged visor. She looked down to the FW VTag that had been violated. In hindsight she realized that she neglected to erase access to the army network from a visor she recently found, and this was what got her noticed.

Guessing the plan of her prey, she looked around through her visor for the next nearest tag to it. Looking around the space between the two VTags, she spotted some motion. The elevator in that building was moving!

Regan zoomed in, doing her best to keep a steady hand. Aha. Same cammo, same weapon. But this was the first Regan saw of Alisia's red mane. Alisia was sitting on her knees in the slow elevator, staring down out the window. She looked sad. This was the first live human Regan had seen in ages aside from tiny glimpses of the wall snipers.

Regan felt the need to go be sociable. This lovely redhead looked like she needed some cheering up, and Regan had many, many ideas on how this could be accomplished.

Alisia reloaded her P90 and sorted her equipment. She was having a bit of trouble finding good ways to carry the ammo she took off Kensington, and the effort only made her feel like more of a vulture. Some commander she was. She shouldn't have left such a raw rookie alone, even for a minute.

The elevator finally reached the top and eased to a stop. Alisia waved in the general direction of Parker and walked off into the building. She passed through the sullen quiet of its lobby and stepped out into one of the bridge's streets.

The limited, three-block width of the bridges left a bit more room for light to come in between buildings, and fewer nooks and crannies for the zombies to hide in. The daylight was still pretty good. No zombies were immediately apparent in the area. The bridges were higher than the zipper guns though. Only zombies that wandered to the outside edge needed to worry about being gunned down.

The GA VTag was about two blocks away. Alisia took her time. She hoped for something to pop out and start a fight, to get her mind off Kensington's bleeding throat. Did she burn the wound enough? Or was Kensington now a puppet, wandering about moaning? Would the extraction team have to shoot her to chunks to take her out?

How do you tell the family that? "Mr. and Mrs. Kensington? Yes, I was your daughter's commanding officer and I left her alone in a dark alley in Autar city, where a zombie ripped her fucking throat out, while I listened to her gurgling scream. Oh, and I left her body there and it came to un-life, so if you want the body for burial, we're sending it to you in forty-seven plastic containers."

Great. And just you watch, they're gonna outright disband the unit. Disband? What's to disband? There's only one surviving member! Why the hell don't they just nuke this damned place?

Alisia came to a strip-mall. The VTag was just inside the main doors. This would have been ideal, but in front of the doors was a gaping hole in the ground, with a view down to the lower street. A hundred stories down? Eep.

Edging sideways along the wall, Alisia tried to get to the doors. In places where the ragged edge of the hole was under the wall, it left only chunks of protruding metal to step on.

As she neared the doors, she saw the source of the VTag through a small clean spot in the otherwise blackened window. A handful of medium sized crates. One had a few P90 clips sticking out. "GA".... Guns and ammo? She kept going towards the door. It was opaque and had an auto-open feature. Unfortunately, since she had approached by the side and was so close, the sensor couldn't see her to trigger the door to open.

The trick now was to reach out and trigger the sensor above the door frame without losing grip and falling backwards through the hole. To extend her reach she waved her P90 out as best she could.

Finally she heard the door motors start. As the door opened, Alisia was treated to an up-close view of a dense mob of zombies. She panicked, and slipped.

Her P90 went tumbling just before she did. She screamed, desperately grabbing at anything but the outstretched hand of a zombie. She caught a chunk of the wreckage around the edge of the hole, but only for a split second.

Her other hand found a chunk of cable. Loose cable. She continued falling, dragging meter after meter worth of cable out of the bridge's innards.

An overzealous zombie stumbled forward trying to reach her, and fell forward, passing Alisia. She was at least being slowed by the cable. She watched the zombie plummet. Why the hell hadn't she just found a different 'GA' VTag?

Frantic hollering came though over her comm as she slipped down the cable, but she was too preoccupied to listen to it. The cable was also pulling other loops of cable out with it. The cable she was hanging onto finally ran out of slack, jolting her arm. Wrist, elbow, shoulder... none of them were happy at all, but at least she kept her grip.

She was now dangling, but not falling. Other cable that had been yanked free by the first one dangled and swayed around her.

"Captain!" Parker's voice came through the comm, cutting through the frantic mumbling of all the other gunners, most of which could see her dangling under the bridge. "Captain, what the hell are you doing?!"

Alisia looked down and up. She was more than half way to the ground. Still plenty to distance to get a person killed. She was suddenly very aware of her own breathing as she tightened her grip. The world felt light, and meaningless. Mortal fear has a way of being very clarifying. Suddenly, all the little unimportant things disappear. You're left with one simple, but huge, problem. The lack of control is almost liberating. You either survive somehow, and go back to the complicated mess of little problems... or you die, and have no problems.

She was snapped back to focused thought by the sound of a P90. Not close, but not far. "Parker! What's going on?"

"Captain, you're aware you're hanging from-"

"I *know*, I know! I think I might be able go down safely from here."

"We can get people there to-"

"Not before my fucking arm breaks off, you can't!" Alisia reached for a looped dangling cable with her free hand and pulled on it. One end was giving more slack, still feeding more cable from the bridge's insides. The other end seemed secure.

"Okay. Okay. The cable I'm on is out of length, but I think this other one can get me down. The loose end goes all the way to the top. By the time it comes out I'll have more than enough."

She wrapped the second cable around the wrist that *wasn't* screaming at her, and held her weight on it to give her sore arm a break. Cautiously, she released the first cable.

She pulled the loose side of the second cable until she had about ten meters more of cable to climb down. "See, Parker? I planned this all along. While I was brushing my teeth this morning."

"Sure, Cap."

Alisia chuckled nervously and made herself busy with climbing down, pulling more cable free as she needed it.

Then the secure end decided to come loose. "Oh shit."

Suddenly she felt weightless and sickly. Down, down, down. How far did she have left when she started falling? Why was she still gripping the damned cable?

After a second or two that felt like forever, she felt herself impact in some shallow water, and the world seemed to bob up and down. Cabling continued to land around her, so she tried to guard her face while losing consciousness. The water lapped up against her face, getting deeper. She knew that if she passed out with her face underwater, it wouldn't matter that she's survived the fall.

The world went black.

Chapter 18: Good Morning

Alisia, much to her surprise, awoke.

She was dry, she was warm, and there was no particular pain. As she awoke, she realized she was having a little trouble breathing. There was some kind of weight on her. And strands of black soft hair laid carelessly across her face.

There was a corpse on top of her. A fresh one. No... it's warm? This girl's alive? It's the IR signature! It *is* a human. Next question, why is this human on top of her?

Alisia felt that there was a hand near hers. With as little motion as possible, she felt for a pulse. Yup, she's alive alright. But, she just woke her up. Alisia went for her gun on instinct, but she was unarmed. Alisia froze in panic.

The girl on top of her sat up slowly. Her black hair dragged along Alisia's face as the stranger began to pull herself up. The girl's hand pushed down on Alisia's shoulder softly for some support to rise. The stranger's eyes were closed. She rose up to a straddling position and reached her arms up, up, up.

Her short tank top slid up as well, threatening to reveal a bit more than Alisia cared to see. As the stranger eased her stretch, she slowly opened her eyes. Regan smiled as seductively as she could.

"Good moooorning, sweetie." Regan purred.

"Who the hell are you?" Alisia asked.

Regan leaned forward, hovering over the new found object of her affection, running one of her hands up Alisia's abdomen.

"I'm your new friend." Regan smiled sweetly.

"*I'm not this friendly!*" Alisia pushed Regan's hand away and clumsily tried to worm free. Alisia got off the mattress, falling a few centimeters to the tile floor.

Alisia got a good look at where she was. It was a large public washroom that Regan had converted to a surprisingly welcoming living space. This corner was a little bedroom of sorts. To the left, the wheelchair stall had been converted to a kitchenette, and the other stalls used for storage. One of the sinks had a plant growing out of it. Further down was the entrance to a large shower room, racks of clothing, and beyond that, a barricaded entrance.

Alisia backed up against the wall. "You- you rescued me?"

"Yeah. I'd been watching you. When I saw you dangling over my rain-catching pool, I came running. Good thing too. I had to clean out that zombie that fell in before you."

"The shots I heard.."

"Yup, that was me. You're lucky, you know. I almost drained that pool last month. I constructed it under that hole to gather rain, but I never use it. There's enough bottled water around for one person. Anyway, I scooped you out, and brought you home. Do I get to keep you?" Regan advanced, and pressed against Alisia.

Alisia was stunned by Regan's outright, unabashed advances. "No, you cannot 'keep' me. I'm here to get you out of Autar."

"Hm?" Regan seemed suddenly a little detached. "No, we can't do that. I have business here."

"What? What possible business could you have here?"

"I have to find my brother."

"What? You.. must realize he's dead by now... it's a miracle *You're* alive."

"He's not dead, he's undead." Regan seemed suddenly serious.

"You know this?"

"By his own voice, recorded for posterity. He's one of them now."

"When did this happen?"

"During the evacuation."

"..... We still have to get you out." Alisia picked up her comm, which was nearby. "Major? Parker?"

Regan laid down on the mattress and did her best sex-kitten pinup pose while smiling at Alisia.

After a few moments, Parker's voice came through. "Captain!? You're alive? I don't believe it! There's a team headed your way to-"

"Don't bother, I'm fine. Speaking of teams headed in, did they get Kensington out?"

"Yeah, and she's not infected."

"Thank god. At least that's something." Alisia had plenty of complaints about getting members for her team, but she wasn't about to complain about how fast the Major could put a team together when someone needed to get out.

Just then, the Major broke in. "Captain! Good to hear you! Report!"

"I was rescued by my objective, Sir. I'm here with her now. She's apprehensive to leave."

"What? Who is she? What's her name? Why doesn't she want to leave?"

Regan slipped a comm out of her pocket and joined in. "Hello boys," she teased, "My name's Regan. Regan Grier. Thank you ever so much for sending this *incredible* specimen to come play with me. She's wonderful."

"Uh... huh?" Parker's full attention was now at Regan's command.

"But," Regan continued, "I don't plan to leave Autar until I find the thing that uses my brother's body, and bury them both."

"Grier......" It was audible that the Major was typing and pecking away at his keyboard. "Yes. Yes, I have your record. Not surprisingly you've been declared dead. Brother... brother.... Yes, I have it. Doctor Harold Grier. Oh my, quite a brain.."

"Yes," Regan sighed, "AutarLabs. Big stupid genius."

"You know that AutarLabs employees of his importance were implanted with trackers....?"

"....*What?*" Regan seemed both ecstatic, and infuriated. "You mean he's been running around with a tracker in him all this time?!"

"Correct, if we had his electronic signature, we could even put a VTag on him."

Regan dug into her pocket, and pulled out a card with a logo, a name, a barcode, and a magnetic stripe. "Would an AutarLabs ID card work?"

"Absolutely."

Regan grabbed a nearby visor, and pointed it at the card. "There ya go, read the barcode."

"Sorry," the Major said, "We need the mag stripe too. You'll have to bring the card here."

"Damn." Regan weighed her options. She could send the card back with this redheaded goddess. But then she didn't know if she'd get her precious momento back. Also, if she went back with this yummy creature, she could get more time with her, and maybe make her understand how much they were destined to be together. Yes, that's the way it must be. Besides, going to the outer wall isn't like she's *really* leaving Autar, and it *is* to find Harold. "Alright."

"You'll come with me?" Alisia hoped.

Regan smiled her most evil, seductive smile. "To the ends of the earth."

Chapter 19: A Day Out

The south gates slowly opened before them. Regan dragged a small cart of personal possessions behind her and looked about with mild curiosity as they entered the bay. It was big enough to hold a small jet plane if needed.

The gates closed and clamped tight behind them. The back wall had three features. A bed-sized machine, a garage-sized door, and a normal sized door. They all looked sturdy as heck, and probably airtight.

The Major's voice came out on a PA system. "Welcome back, Captain, and welcome to the Autar wall, Ms. Grier."

"Thank you sweetie!" chirped Regan.

"Ms. Grier, we're going to have to go through your possessions, and irradiate them to kill any infection that may be on them." the Major's voice stated plainly.

"That's not really necessary, but do what ya gotta."

"Captain, if you would sound off the items and place them in the irradiator?"

"Yes Sir." Alisia held out her hand to Regan, to get the handle of the cart. Regan gave it to her in a manner that let Regan stroke Alisia's hand, while she did her best to stare down into Alisia's very soul. Alisia rolled her eyes, and took the cart.

She wheeled it over to the bed-sized machine and opened up the side, revealing a large empty space. After taking off her jacket and throwing it into the irradiator, Alisia pulled out Regan's P90 from the cart.

"One FN-P90, personalized with stickers and paint. Six mostly full ammo clips." She placed them into the irradiator, unaware that Regan was slowly coming up behind her. Alisia then pulled out a small bundle of clothes, announced them, and tossed them in. This continued until she came to the last item.

"One small cardboard box." She failed to notice the writing 'toy box' on the other side of the box and opened it, to list off the items inside.

Alisia looked down upon the most dazzling array of plastic perversities she'd ever seen, complete with batteries. Regan chose that moment to delicately caress Alisia's shoulder, brushing down the strap of her shirt. Alisia froze.

"See those two?" Regan whispered in her ear, "We can share them. I like the blue one."

Alisia neared panic. Her breathing became a bit labored, and Regan mistakenly took it as a positive sign.

"Captain?" The Major's voice interrupted the horrified trance.

"Uh, personal effects, Major." Alisia stammered, "Toothbrush, hair brush, that kind of thing."

"List them off, Captain."

Alisia hesitated enough for Regan to step in. "Oh, Mr. Major Sir, a lady has to have *some* privacy."

"*Oh!* Oh, right, my apologies. Load them in, Captain."

Alisia slowly closed the box's flaps as if she were handling a landmine. She shook it off and then lifted the cart itself into the irradiator. She closed it and turned a dense handle, locking the thick lid into place. "That's it, Major."

"Very well, Captain. Hit the showers. Report to my office when you're ready."

Regan bristled with excitement at the mention of showers, and her eyes darted between the smaller door and Alisia. "Ooh! I should put my clothes into the irradiator!" She excitedly began taking off her jacket.

"*Halt!*" Alisia sharply commanded as if calling drill. "Ah, I mean, there's a smaller irradiator in the showers for that. Let's go."

Regan skipped ahead, turning periodically to make sure Alisia was keeping up. Regan opened the door, and stepped in to the three by one meter shower room. Seeing the irradiator box in the far corner, she rushed over, preparing to strip.

"Have fun!" Alisia said, stepping back into the main room, and reaching for the door.

Regan whirled to face her, and all the joy was lost. "But-" was all she could get out before Alisia's grinning face was obscured by the closing door, which made a satisfying *'foomp'* as it sealed. Alisia leaned her back against the door and slid to a seated position at the base.

The doorknob rattled. "Aleeeeesha...." came a sing-song voice from inside. Alisia let out an exasperated sigh before replying. "Put your clothes in the irradiator and let em nuke while you take your shower."

Regan put on her most 'innocent' voice "But.... don't you need to be clean too?"

"Yes, but I can wait."

"Don't be silly!"

Alisia needed to think fast, or this could go on for a while. "The... the irradiator in there is only so strong. Your stuff has been in Autar for a long time, so I want to make sure they get good and nuked."

"Oh. I see." Alisia heard the appropriate sounds for Regan to strip off her meager clothes and put them in the irradiator. The hum of it started up and soon, the sound of water. A few moments passed.

"Oh, Alisia!" sung Regan.

"Yes?" Alisia's voice sounded like that of a tired mother.

"I guess I should scrub well, huh?"

"Yes, Regan."

"Hmm... what should I scrub first?"

"Whatever!"

"Aleeeeeesha....?"

"*What?*"

"Guess what I'm rubbing, I mean.. *scrubbing*, now?"

"*I don't care!* I'm going to check on the main irradiator." Alisia jogged off before Regan could come up with a comeback. Of course she didn't need to check on the main irradiator, but at least it didn't hit on her. She sat by it for a few moments when she heard banging from the showers. Alisia ran over.

"What's going on?"

"Alisia, the door's locked! Let me out!"

"You're clean now, Regan, this room's dirty. You have to leave through the other door."

Regan talked softly, forcing Alisia to lean nearer to the door. "Speak up!"

"I said," came Regan's sweetest voice, "I'm still aaaawwfully dirty."

"*Just get out of there* so I can finish this up! I don't want to be out here all day!"

"Ach, Fine. You're just no fun."

Alisia heard the sound of the inner door opening and closing. She opened the outer door, and was a little surprised to find that Regan wasn't still in there waiting for her.

Meanwhile on the other side, Regan met a handful of the wall's male compliment, all of which seemed very interested in Regan, with her micro-skirt and all-too-small tank top. Regan took delight in their attention. She had no interest in them, but enjoyed the mental torture she could inflict.

She put her leather jacket back on ever so slowly, arching her back much more than needed. As hard as she tried, she didn't quite slip right out the bottom of the tank top. Ah well, the tease is often better than the show.

"So.... boyssss... What can you tell me about our little Alisia?"

Just then, the men's superior officer came by, and assessing the situation, ordered them all away. He looked sternly at Regan. "Sorry to have let them *trouble* you, miss." He left, leaving no room for reply.

Regan felt like a puppy that had just been swatted on the nose, but her disappointment was cut short when the shower door began to open. Alisia stepped out, eyeing Regan with great suspicion.

"I was good." Regan said in mock innocence. "Let's go see your boss guy, and get my brother's tracer tagged."

After a short distance, Regan yanked Alisia into a tight side-hall. Alisia was less than surprised. Regan leaned in so very, very close. Alisia could feel the warmth of her breath, and was paralyzed with a brand of fear never found in combat.

"Are you finished?" Alisia snapped nervously as she broke free, and continued down the hall.

Regan lagged a bit. "Not nearrrly" She hummed to herself.

With Alisia still storming ahead a few meters, they soon entered the Major's office. Regan tossed the ID card on the desk and sat down. "Heya Mister Major, Sir! Here ya go! Now stick a VTag on my bro, so I can go find him."

"It's not that easy, Ms. Grier. I'm going to have to do a little research to match things up. Get proper authority from the parent company of AutarLabs, etcetera, etcetera."

"What? What a gyp. How long?"

"About a day or so, depending how fast various people get back to me."

"Pffft. Well, then I'll just go home and wait, then."

"What? You're going back into Autar?" Despite the fact that Regan had been living in there since the evacuation, it still seemed odd that she'd want to go back now.

"Well what else am I going to do?" Regan said, absent mindedly scrolling her eyes over to Alisia's body.

"Well," the Major said, "I can assign you some quarters and you can stay here until we're ready."

Regan mulled this over, pretending to have some hesitation, all the while imagining 'accidental' situations she could get into involving Alisia. "Yeah, OK, fine."

Alisia cringed visibly.

"I don't suppose, Ms. Grier, that you could spend some time answering some general questions about your experiences in Autar?"

"Eh, sure, what the heck."

"Good," Alisia cut in, "In the mean time, I'll take care of a few things."

Regan turned to Alisia with pleading eyes. "You're not staying with me?"

"Sorry," Alisia replied unsympathetically, "I have things to do." She left the office, feeling Regan's eyes pawing at her back.

Chapter 20: No Means Ow

It was a relief to be rid of Regan for a bit. Being with her felt like being pawed by a lazy panther. The advances, the innuendos, the occasional uninvited touch.

Alisia was enveloped enough in her thoughts that she almost walked right into Corporal Parker, who also seemed to have his head in the clouds.

"Oh!" Parker jolted back to reality, "I, Sir! Sorry, I..."

"At ease, Parker. My fault."

"Uh, sure." Parker seemed to be slipping back into his own mind.

"What's up, soldier?" Alisia asked, carefully weighing her speaking tone between compassion and the detachment befitting rank.

"Sir, uh, Captain... I'm just kinda shook up about Kensington."

In all the fuss with Regan, Alisia had nearly forgotten about Tracy's death. She suddenly felt guilty about letting it slip so far from her mind. "Yeah. It was senseless. I shouldn't have left her."

"Oh, no, no, Captain. I didn't mean to say y-"

"Of course not." Alisia paused. "I was just saying. I shouldn't have."

Parker sighed. "You made your call, it just didn't work. I just... this is going to sound stupid, Cap.."

"Stupid's OK, Parker. Speak."

"I talked to her a bit before the mission, and I... kinda liked her. I mean, I hardly knew her, but she....."

His tone spoke volumes. Love at first sight? Alisia was cynical of the concept, but this silly Corporal was obviously affected in some way or the other. She really didn't know what to say about it. They stood there, looking at the floor for what seemed a long time. Finally, Alisia began to walk off with a soothing pat to Parker's shoulder as she left. Parker kept looking at the floor and leaned against the wall for a moment before continuing on.

As Alisia went about her business she suddenly realized she was hungry. She headed over to the mess hall. It was empty, except for a Private with KP duty tending to some little task behind the counter.

"Hey, soldier? Got any leftovers?"

The Private perked up and looked at Alisia. "Uh, Sir, yes. Want some?"

"I dunno, what is it?"

"......Meat.. something. You'd have to ask chef, he's not around."

"Sounds yummy. Yeah, hook me up."

"Right away." The Private disappeared into the back. Alisia wandered over to the juice machine and filled up two of those tiny glasses with OJ. She was looking down the counter for a tray, when she felt a presence.

Arms came around her and the heat and pressure of a body pressed against her back. So much for the vacation from Regan. One of Regan's hands slipped a pinky down Alisia's pants. The other hand snuck up under her shirt, threatening an even less welcome touch. A little purr escaped Regan.

"Hello Regan." Alisia grumbled.

"How did you know?" Regan's voice came back soft and light, ignoring Alisia's tone.

"Lucky guess. Could you let go please?"

A soft giggle came from Regan. "Hey baby, once you've had chick, you'll never want d-"

"*Please* stop talking now." Alisia almost yelled.

"Mmmm, what's wrong?"

"I don't like girls, I like *guys*."

Regan responded with a little mock disgust, but still in her soft seductive tone."Bah. What kind of lesbian *are* you?"

"*I'm not a lesbian!*" Yeah, now she was yelling.

Regan giggled softly again, "Not with *that* attitude you're not!"

Alisia's anger grew exponentially. Just then the Private came back with a steaming plate of 'meat' dinner. He nearly dropped it at the sight of Regan doing her damnedest to wrap herself around Alisia.

"Oh my god! Sir. I, sorry. Uh-" and with that he handed Alisia the plate and rushed back into the depths of the kitchen, face blushing.

Alisia snapped. Her elbow flew back into Regan's ribs. She turned around, nearly in the same motion, and threw Regan to the ground in a textbook maneuver. The maneuver did however send dinner flying, mostly all over Alisia.

Regan landed on her butt and looked blankly forward in shock. Alisia stood frozen, rigid with anger but also surprised at the magnitude of her own actions. It was a little rough, maybe.

Regan swung around while fumbling to stand, and began to run. Even if she was in the right, Alisia suddenly felt awful. "Regan!" she called, but Regan didn't stop.

Regan ran all the way back to the quarters that the Major had assigned her, pushing over a couple soldiers along the way just to blow off steam. She blasted into the room and slammed the door as hard as she could. Her body suddenly felt limp, and she collapsed to the floor sobbing.

"That stupid bitch!" thought Regan, "*Stupid straight bitch!*" She chose to blame straightness, ignoring her own inappropriately strong approach.

Though the tears had started before she made it out of the mess hall, she only noticed them now. They fell in front of her with wet slaps against the polished cement. She wanted to sit there and cry forever, but she was eventually forced to accept that her knees were sore. She dragged herself up onto the bed, knocking over a couple beer bottles that she'd emptied shortly after her talk with the Major. The male soldiers were ever so co-operative in helping her find a few necessities. She quickly emptied another. With some of her own possessions here, it almost felt like her home in Autar. The tiles were cement instead, her plant wasn't here, and she didn't need to barricade the door. The urge was there though.

She curled up on the bed, and obsessed over Alisia.

Regan sat up and looked in the nearby mirror. "Shit, look at me, I'm fucking hot!" she thought with self admiration and an alcohol head rush. "I mean, *really*. I don't care *how* straight she thinks she is, *look at this*. I mean, *damn*! I'd do me!" She flopped back and tried to think of evil plots to seduce the lovely Alisia. The gears in her head ground away. When she managed to grind away all her lusty tension, the alcohol commanded her to sleep, where she dreamed.

Chapter 21: Unattainable

Alisia was in the middle of cleaning her P90, but her mind was elsewhere. "That crazy bitch." She thought. But the moment after thinking it, she felt a little guilty. After all, Alisia was perhaps the first live human Regan had seen in a *long* time.

Who knows? Maybe she had some kind of psychological reaction and bonded to her or something. She might need some serious help. Living in a dead city, alone? She had to be nuts to begin with not to evacuate. Alisia wrestled with irritation and pity, then realized that the parts to her P90 were about as clean as they'd ever get.

She put it back together and cursed Regan under her breath again. Her dinner still felt sticky on her, even though she'd changed her shirt already. She headed for the main showers.

Regan lurked the halls, mind filled with... a mess. That's all there was to it. Being among living people again was difficult. Thankfully there was only the occasional soldier passing by. She couldn't stop herself from suspiciously eyeing strangers in the hall to make sure they were really among the living.

Just when she was about to head back to her room she spotted Alisia far down the hall, carrying a towel.

Regan grinned like a fiend. Towels usually implied all kinds of fun things. Regan discreetly followed Alisia and was thrilled to see her walk into a door labeled 'WOMEN'. Looking around for witnesses, Regan realized that no one would think it strange to see her going in too. Playing it casual, but with nerves rattling with anticipation, she walked over to the door and opened it.

This side of the main women's washroom was all stalls and sinks. Further down was a doorway to a changing room. Regan silently crept near it and heard the sounds of Alisia getting ready for the shower. Then she heard bare footsteps softly walking away. Regan peeked in and saw no one. Alisia had left through the far doorway, into the showers.

Regan continued forward, stopping for a moment to admire the neatly folded pile of clothes that Alisia had left behind. She defeated the childish urge to search for her unmentionables and headed on in search of the grand prize.

The sound of water began and a chill ran up Regan's spine. A mildly insane grin was plastered on her face. A few more steps forward... The main shower room was divided by occasional frosted glass walls. One such frosted panel stood fifteen meters or so across the shower room, and obscured the finer details of Alisia as she showered.

Regan's first instinct was to run over there and open up with the crudest innuendo she could muster, delivered in the sweetest possible voice.

But for some reason, she couldn't force herself any closer than the doorway. She was stunned by the beauty of the target of her desire.

Regan leaned against the wall, staring as her breathing deepened. Regan felt suddenly so helpless. Her usual overconfident thoughts were swept away by the idea of being curled up with Alisia and drifting into sleep. Regan slid down the glass and sat for a while, fighting tears.

When Alisia was done her shower Regan was already gone, unnoticed. Alisia dried off and got dressed. She couldn't find her dog tags though.

Chapter 22: ReEntry

Alisia walked into Regan's quarters since she wasn't answering the door. Regan was curled up tight on the bed asleep, still in her usual clothes, clutching the blanket like her life depended on it. Also clutched in her hand were Alisia's dog tags.

Alisia stepped closer, being careful to avoid the growing sprawl of beer bottles. She knelt down intending to take her dog tags back, but on getting that close she saw the expression on Regan's face. It spoke of anguish. She looked at the tags again. It would be hard to take them anyway, the chain was around Regan's neck. Alisia suddenly felt like she had intruded on something private.

She backed out of the room and slammed the door shut, following with a few loud knocks. She heard a startled mumble inside. That did it. Alisia knocked again at a more reasonable volume, and in a few moments Regan appeared. The dog tags were no longer around her neck. They looked at each other for a few moments in silence before Alisia remembered why she came.

"Oh, the Major says he got a lock on your brother's tracker. It moves around a bit, so he's uh.. still walking."

Regan, still groggy, was a little surprised at the news. "Mm, alright then. Stick a VTag on it and when this headache clears up, I'll go in."

"It's already active."

Regan looked Alisia up and down. "Uh.. well, thanks." She went back in and closed the door on Alisia. Alisia stood in front of the door for a moment as if there was something else to be said. Nothing came to her, so she left.

A handful of hours later, Regan walked into the bay of the south gate. She tapped her comm on. "Major? I'm ready to go. Open up."

"Alright, Ms. Grier, good hunting." the Major's voice replied.

A sound came from behind her. Alisia hopped off the irradiator, where she'd been sitting and waiting. She walked up beside Regan, facing the gates as they opened.

"Come to see me off?" Regan asked.

Alisia scrunched the corner of her mouth, adjusted her belt, and huffed. "Nah." She paused to adjust her eyes to the sun. "I'm coming along."

"You don't have to, you know."

"Well, the way I see it, I hauled you out of there, so you're my responsibility." The truth was that this was a military operation, and Regan was a guest.

Regan stared at her for a moment, trying to squeeze out every drop of meaning out of her words, but Alisia just stared forward at the city. When the gates finished opening, Alisia leisurely stepped forward. Regan kept pace and followed.

The last time Regan looked at the outside of the city like this, it was new. Brimming with people and hope. Now for the first time, she saw it like other people did. A shrine of ruin, a phantom of disaster. It was a unique flavour of dread that never found her while she was inside.

"Corporal Parker, watching your six again today, Captain." came through the comm.

"How ya doin today, Parker?" Alisia responded.

"It's okay, Cap."

In relative quiet, the two walked into the city. The sun was intense today, and cast bold, stark shadows. As they passed between buildings, the shadows seemed to swallow them up, especially as they neared the shade cast by the south bridge. Compared to the blinding brightness they had left, the shadows felt like midnight. The tracker's VTag was floating ahead.

As they drew deeper into the outskirts, a mob of two dozen or so zombies rumbled out of an alley. "Enemy contact!" Alisia called out. For the number that were there, Alisia felt justified in pulling forth her 'Bad Mojo'. She aimed the bulky weapon, and was deciding on where in the group to place the fragmenting shell when crackling erupted behind them.

Sustained fire from Parker and two other zipper operators shredded the zombie formation. A dusty squirming pile was soon all that remained. Regan looked back at the speck far away that housed Parker. "Nice one, boys!" she exclaimed.

"Happy to be of service, Miss." Parker grinned.

"Hey, what's that?" Regan said, pointing at the Bad Mojo.

"Magnetic Rail driven frag grenade launcher. All cold kinetic damage, so as not to violate the 'no explosions' rule."

"40mm?"

"Yeah,"

"What's this no explosions business?"

"For some reason, we're not allowed to use explosive devices in the city."

"Hm. I have a few nasty things squirreled away that I've never used.. maybe a good thing I didn't... what would happen?"

"Don't know.. only the higher-ups do."

"Hm. Can I play with that?"

"No."

The next while was pretty quiet. The bridge shadow had them, not to mention the taller buildings doing their best to rob any glimmer of sunlight that dared to squeeze by. The brightness of the sun behind them felt like another world.

"Hey, Alisia, got any non-fragmenting bullets?"

"No, what for?"

"Eh, I have a stockpile nearby. I wanna pick a couple up."

"Whatever."

A block to the side or so, Regan opened up a dumpster and jumped in. After a little bit of rummaging she came out with fresh ammo that would fit into the handgun she procured at the base.

Chapter 23: Rest

For some reason, Regan seemed pleased at the general location of her brother's VTag. It seemed she had something planned. "This'll be easy." Regan said. Alisia didn't see what was so hard about blowing away one more zombie.

It wasn't long before they snuck up on a group of four zombies mulling about heedlessly in the end of an alley. One of them was carrying around a pink plastic flamingo, a popular item among the zombies. There had been a factory in the city that made them, and for whatever reason the zombies seemed fascinated with them. Another wore fisherman's hip-waders. Another had T-shirt that said 'I'll sleep when I'm dead'. The last one was pretty plain, as zombies go. What he *did* have though, was a glowing VTag superimposed on the base of his skull. Here was Harold Grier.

"Ok, say when." Alisia said, aiming her P90.

"Don't hit Harold."

"Huh?"

"Just don't. Blast the other three."

"Ok."

Regan took aim and gave the word. The three others were torn down. Harold drew his attention to the girls and began walking towards them.

"Let's go." Regan said, turning around.

"What? Aren't you going to finish him?"

"Exactly. Finish him good. Not like that." Regan pointed at the felled zombies, still squirming and making horrid sounds. "We're going to do this right."

The two of them walked about half a block ahead of Harold, who mindlessly chased them as fast as he could go. Poor Harold was unlucky enough to not only be a zombie, but to be one of those really, really slow zombies.

They soon came to a factory. Here, Regan knew she'd have to get Harold a lot closer or he might lose sight of them and lose interest. As Harold got closer, Regan leveled her P90. "Sorry bout this bro." She fired a burst, and the fragmenting bullets took off his left arm. He moaned, and Regan's face showed a bit of pity. She took aim again and took off the other arm.

Those arms used to hug her not so long ago. Look at them now; rotten, discarded meat in the road. Harold kept trudging forward. Now his only weapon was his teeth.

Regan let him get close, then quickly grabbed him into a headlock.

"Ew." Alisia said. Regan dragged Harold into the factory, and Alisia followed, P90 at the ready. They came to a large room with a massive metal door.

"Alisia, can you open that?" The effort of keeping hold of Harold as he struggled and tried to bite was no small feat.

Alisia opened the metal door and saw inside a small metal room with blackened holes along the walls, ceiling and floor, and fine grey dust in the corners. Alisia now understood the plan and stepped aside.

Regan was struggling a bit with Harold. Even 'perfectly armless', a zombie had considerable strength. She tossed him into the small room and stood back. Harold flopped around a bit and began to stand. Regan pulled out the pistol and loaded the non-fragmenting rounds.

"Rest, Harold." She fired once into his chest, where once, a good heart pumped. Harold staggered back and Regan slowly closed the door with a resounding thud. Regan leaned back against the door. Soon, scuffing sounds were heard against the door and Regan winced, and pointed at a large red button over to the side.

Alisia went to it, and after getting a nod from Regan, pressed it.

The sealed metal room rumbled violently as it flooded with flame. Regan slumped to the ground. After a minute the sound subsided.

Regan got up and opened the door. A wave of heat escaped, and a bit of grey dust. She stood there for a while to let the room cool down. When she thought she could stand it, she stepped closer and knelt by the freshest pile of dust by the door. She used her finger to sift through the dust and found what she was after. The bullet she shot into his heart.

"Let's go."

They walked in silence through the growing shadows of the city, eventually coming to the park near Regan's 'home'. She led Alisia over to a spot by a tree that had gone fairly undisturbed. The grass here had been cut in the last month or two, unlike the rest of the park that was wildly overgrown.

A foot wide hole had been dug there. Regan walked up to the hole and tossed in the bullet from Harold's body. She shoved dirt on top of it with her hands and stomped it down. Alisia stood nearby, not wanting to interfere. Regan pulled a silver ring out of her pocket and tossed it on the little mound of dirt, and stepped back.

"..... it's done."

Only a few quiet moments had passed when an uninvited guest appeared from behind. A lone zombie staggered towards them.

Regan bristled with anger and charged it, with only her leather-gloved fists at the ready. Alisia called to her, but Regan would not hear. Possessed by rage, Regan proved too fast for this lone zombie. A wild swing knocked it back, and a second blow knocked it down. It tried to get up but Regan kicked and kicked as she screamed and cried. After a some lucky essential blows broke enough brittle bones, it was no longer able to fight.

She staggered back and looked at it. Her fist had a smear of its blood, her boot was a gory mess. Her eyes blurred with tears.

"Did I say it was over?" she called to it. No reply.

"*Did I say I was finished?!*" She yelled. It laid motionless, save for the twitches and writhing all zombies made in defeat.

"*GET THE FUCK UP!!*" Regan stared at it and caught her breath while Alisia just stared, stunned.

Finally Regan stumbled back to the little grave and sank to her knees, suddenly feeling so tired. She was still trying to catch her breath. Alisia knelt down beside Regan and put a hand on her shoulder.

"It'll be okay now." Alisa said, almost as a question.

Regan put her hand on Alisia's. Her breathing eased a bit. "Thank you."

They sat there for a while, quiet and still.

At length, Regan took a deep breath. "Alright. Let's go. I can leave the city for good now." They got up and began to leave. Regan looked back at the grave with a little smile.

"You goof. You and your stupid nanites. Look where it got you."

Alisia stopped suddenly. "Nanites?"

"Yeah, you know, the stupid little robots that make the zombies move?"

"......... what?"

"What, what?"

Chapter 24: Nanites, DUH.

"So," Alisia said, speaking through the comm to the Major, "It seems that AutarLabs was working these microscopic little robots, and these little suckers were organized from a separate computer, run by some kind of customized A.I. or something."

The Major paused in consideration and responded. "So... what, you're saying that this whole thing is caused by a crazy A.I.? Why? How?"

"Well, not sure how, but Regan's brother was in the middle of figuring it out when he died. Some interns were killed without explanation and then bam, shit hit the fan."

"All this time... and Regan Grier knew about these things all along?" The Major was a little stunned.

"Yup." Regan said, "I didn't think it was a secret!"

"So there is no biological infection," the Major mulled, "which is why we never found any virus or anything."

"And if you think about it," Alisia added, "when we burn wounds, that'll destroy any nanites. Any of them that are recognizable at that point might just walk away before we get any zombie flesh under a microscope."

"What a fine mess. There's going to be some heads rolling over this muck-up. So what we need to do is unplug the AutarLabs computer running the A.I." The Major said, starting go get excited, "And this could be all over!"

Parker joined in. "I've just put a VTag on AutarLabs."

"Regan, you up for this?" Alisia asked.

"That easy, huh? Sure, why not?"

AutarLabs was quiet. They carefully made their way in, and met no resistance.

"If this A.I. were so important, you'd think it would protect itself by having a lot of zombies around." Alisia said.

"Don't jinx it!" Regan said. "You should have seen the guy I had to take out to get here the first time after the breakout."

Their exploration through the darkened halls continued without incident. After covering a few floors around where Harold's lab had been, they finally came to an important looking set of doors. They looked at each over and nodded. Alisia wore a nervous smile of anticipation and gripped her P90 tight.

Regan stepped forward and kicked the right door open. It swung open and bounced back, slamming shut.

"Too much gusto." Regan said. "Did you see any zombies?"

"No," Alisia said, still aiming at the door, "But I saw computer towers."

The two calmly entered, cautious for any sort of trap. Regan had been here about two years ago, but she was looking for Harold, nothing else. It was a large room, lit even worse than the halls. Row after row of server towers stood dark and dead, except for one desktop machine. Its lights glowed faintly from atop a desk in the corner of the room. They carefully crept over to it as if it would jump out at them.

The screen was on but blank, so Alisia wiggled the mouse, and sure enough a display popped up. Alisia sat down in front of it. It was some kind of list. At the top, it identified this machine as 'Server 0001'

"It's a server list. There's hundreds.." Alisia mumbled to herself. The list in fact went well into the thousands. "Whatever, let's just shut it down." She reached over to the machine's tower but found no power button. "The hell?" She dragged the tower forward. On the back there was plugs for a keyboard, a mouse, and the monitor. That's it.

"Uh, Regan, this computer apparently runs on pixie dust."

"What are you talking about?" Regan leaned in, and saw that where a power plug is usually found, there was a smooth metal plate. "Hey, and how can it be monitoring servers if it's not plugged into a net connection or something?"

"Well, it could be internal wireless network stuff... and maybe a battery? A... really good battery? Two years?"

They grabbed the case off of the desk and plunked it on the floor. Alisia found a screwdriver nearby and opened it up. They weren't terribly familiar with computer innards, but one part was labeled 'Airnet wireless LAN adapter'.

"There ya go. That's probably controlling all the nanites." Alisia said. "That list must be the separate nanites it's controlling."

"Naw," Regan hummed, "There's gotta be millions of nanites in a single zombie. Maybe it represents groups of nanites, like maybe those in one zombie."

Alisia looked at where the power supply should be. There was a similar sized device, which looked very sturdy and polished, with only plugs leaving it to supply power to the machine. The word 'Mana' was embossed on it. "I guess it *is* a battery. Whatever." Alisia tapped on her comm. "Major? I think we have the nanite server. Permission to bash it?"

Regan spoke softly to herself, searching her memory. "Mana.. mana...?"

"Bash it?" The Major eventually came on to answer, "Why not unplug it?"

"There's no plug. Some kinda battery." Alisia put her finger on the mana box and aimed her visor at it.

"Sure, whatever."

Alisia and Regan stood back, and Alisia leveled her P90 at the shiny little box. Another voice jumped onto the comm.

"*Captain! Stop!*" The voice was not familiar. "Captain, this is General Westmore. Do *not* destroy the mana box."

"Sir?" Alisia was surprised to hear the Major's superior officer jump in. Short, unnecessary introductions were made. Since the start of the mission, the General was quietly monitoring events from his own office, wherever that was.

The General decided that events warranted filling Alisia and Regan in on the big bad secret of Autar. First, all others were cut out of the conversation, including the Major.

"Captain, thanks to you and Ms. Grier, we've been able to piece together some things. This A.I.-controlled nanite thing has taken advantage of Autar in order to power itself. You've noticed perhaps that many things in Autar have power without any noticeable power lines?"

"Y-yes Sir. I'd kind of assumed it was something like geothermal... or maybe some kind of automated nuclear reactor, but how is the power getting into this computer?"

"The city runs off of something called a Mana drive. One of the reasons Autar was expected to be the new way for urban planning, is that it can send power though the air, to be received by devices like the one in front of you."

"So.... with this, it's like you're pulling power out of the air... I've never heard of this."

"It was still in testing phases. It's a government project, but some trusted companies such as AutarLabs, were given receivers for field testing purposes. The drive also is connected to standard power stations in the city which supplied power to a lot of areas in conventional wires. Until now, no one imagined the Mana drive was related to the zombies."

"So, if we unplug the mana box from this computer, the nanites will lose their control, and hopefully, all the zombies will collapse?"

"....no.." Regan said, staring at the monitor. "These servers. This list is over four thousand long. They're servers just like this one. They're all doing the same job. We'd have to find them all. Dammit, I think I saw a couple being delivered shortly after the outbreak. The zombies did it."

"What? Christ, we should just get out and nuke the damned city!" Even as she said it, Alisia remembered that explosions were not allowed.

"That would be nice, Captain," the General said, "But there's a problem with the Mana Drive. Just as a circuit can have feedback, so can the mana boxes with the drive."

"Explosions might damage a mana box, and cause feedback..." Alisia thought out loud, "So what happens? The drive blows and we have some fallout to deal with? No worse than nuking the city... lots of desert around here, who cares?"

"No, Captain, not fallout. Let me explain. After Autar was taken, smaller-scale tests of the Mana drive took place. One of them suffered a critical failure. There was no explosion, but two hundred or so people in the building died on the spot. No apparent cause of death. We assume that somehow the drive spat its explosion out in the same way it transmits energy to the mana boxes, but was strong enough that it reset the neural functions of everyone nearby. Their biological functions were just... 'stopped'."

Regan and Alisia pondered it. It could be an even worse weapon than the 'neutron' bomb. "Ah, Sir," Alisia feared to ask, "You said this was a small scale project that blew..? How does that compare to Autar?"

"If the eggheads have their math correct, a blowout of the Autar Mana drive could easily blanket the country."

Regan rolled her eyes, and Alisia slumped into a stunned heap. "Serious? And this could be triggered if we nuke the drive? Or even shoot a mana box?"

"That is the speculation, correct."

Alisia thought about how close she was to firing at the mana box sitting in front of her. "Holy fuck."

"SOOOoooo...." Regan called out, "If we shut down the drive properly, *then*, will everything shut down? The zombies collapse in the streets, whoopie yay?"

"Sounds about right." The General said. "Come back to base, girls. I'll meet you there and we'll get organized."

Chapter 25: Fix

The two arrived back at base, tired and anxious. In the south bay, Regan headed for the decontamination shower without pestering Alisia at all. Regan stopped by the door, jacket half off, shoulders slumped. She turned back to Alisia.

"I... could just leave, you know."

Alisia paused a moment. "What do you mean?"

"Well... Harold is buried. It's what I was staying for..."

"Don't you want to stay, and see if we can beat the zombies?"

"......they're not exactly my highest priority." Regan slowly turned away from Alisia's stare, and trodded into the shower.

Alisia suddenly felt a little of the weight of Regan's crush. Logically, the crush was just because she was the first person Regan had seen in years... logically. Right?

An hour later they found themselves waiting in a board room. It was one of the nicer rooms on base, but still fairly spartan with its concrete walls. The chairs and table were a bit nicer than standard issue, at least. A few maps of Autar hung on the walls. Word had just come in that the General's helicopter had landed.

Soon, a soldier opened the door, taking a quick look around and saying nothing. He backed out and the General entered. His weathered face bore concern, but he still forced a welcoming smile. His white hair had long ago retreated to the rear flanks of his head, and his dark blue track suit said 'I'm too old to dress up for every damned emergency.'

He stopped just after he stepped in and turned to the soldier. "That'll be all, Corporal." The General closed the door and made his way to a seat at the table. "Good day, ladies."

Alisia saluted. "Sir! I'm prepared to organize an assault team on the mana drive. Some people I've pick-"

The General raised his hand, to stop her. "Easy, Captain. This is a very sensitive issue. We can't have more people in on all this than need be."

"What?" Alisia popped out, with a face that looked like a confused puppy, "But we're talking about getting rid of all the zombies here!"

"Yes, but we're also talking about leaking info on the Mana drive, a potential future threat, not to mention AutarLabs' partners who are unfortunately very valuable to us."

The girls sat back in mild disgust. "Money." Regan said.

The General sighed. "Well... yes, that's what a lot of it comes down to. Besides, it's not like the zombies are putting anyone new at risk here. The wall and defensive gunners do a good job."

Regan fiddled with the strap on her glove while glaring at the General. Alisia looked lost in her own thoughts, staring at the tabletop. The General sighed, and put his hands flat on the table. "Look. You two know all there is to know now. You've proven your ability as well. If you think you can, you two are welcome to try to unplug the mana core."

"Solo, hm?" Alisia said. She leaned back, and looked at Regan. Regan had obviously decided to go in with or without the General's blessings. She looked back at the General. "Fine. We go in the morning." The sound of Regan's leather gloves clenching spoke volumes.

"I expected as much. When you disable the core, call me and I'll mobilize a bombing run. If all goes well, this time tomorrow, Autar will be a crater surrounded by a charred wall." The General smirked to himself. "At least we get to have some fun with some bigger ordinance." he thought to himself. He stood and prepared to leave. "Oh, and Regan," he said, "Unless you have any objections, I'd like to consider you a civilian consultant. We can work out the details later, but given the nature of the work it should pay pretty well."

Regan nodded, almost obliviously. The General left, rejoined by his escort, leaving the girls sitting alone in the board room.

"A crater..." Regan whispered, earning a curious expression from Alisia. "He said Autar would be a crater. I mean... that's great... but... it's been my home for so long... and there's no other place like it. It sounds stupid, but I think I'll miss it."

Alisia got up and put a hand on Regan's shoulder. Regan took it and held in just under her chin. Alisia began to regret her action already, but to make it worse, Regan gave Alisia's hand a soft kiss. Alisia retracted her hand, perhaps a bit rougher than intended. Regan sat there, head hung low, just gazing at her lap.

"Regan..." Alisia uttered, "it's just that... well, you know... I..." She shut herself up, realizing that her words would fix nothing.

Chapter 26: Ponder

Regan sat in the deep windowsill facing Autar and set a guitar in her lap. The guitar was borrowed from a soldier. She saw him with it and asked. He gave it up with very little fuss after a little suggestive smile. No biggie.

She leaned back and put her hand over the strings. Her fingertips dangled down to the rim of the hole, where she felt the inner roughness of the wood. It felt familiar, safe, and for that matter, accepting. She tapped the outside gently with her nail to hear the hollow sound it made. It was the only sound in this area of the wall.

She looked out to Autar, glistening in the moonlight. You could hardly tell it was infested with walking corpses, and this made it easier for Regan to see it as the city she moved into long ago. It was home. What would life be like after tomorrow? Move to some random city and look for a job? It's just such an alien concept compared to the life she'd been living. Maybe she's be better suited to run off into the hills and live off the land. Less zombies, too. It sounded easy. But boring as hell.

Regan looked down to the guitar as if it would reveal answers. She plucked a string softly and listened to it fade into the silence. Slowly, Regan plucked out some old melancholy tune. The notes floated about, washing away the tension but leaving the hopelessness.

But the notes brought footsteps. Quiet, nearly silent footsteps, but Regan heard them coming up behind. She stopped playing and looked out the window. The footsteps stopped maybe five meters away or so. She could feel who it was and she desperately wished that Alisia would come closer. But she did not.

Alisia stared at Regan's back, wondering what to do. This silly little tarzan girl. She felt responsible for her, pulling her out of her... 'habitat'. It would be good to be her friend, but the lesbian thing was just too much. Well, no, not the lesbian thing unto itself. It was just that the lesbian thing was aimed right at *her*, and so strong. If Regan would just give it up so she could relax. Well, maybe she'll get the message.

Alisia turned away and walked off slowly. She decided that she needed a drink. She wasn't much of a drinker, but it felt like a situation where you're supposed to want a drink, so she headed for the base club.

It wasn't really much more than another conference room with a fridge, a couple cheesy posters, a stereo, and a volunteer bartender. It was quiet there. The bartender was the only other person there at the time. She ordered a glass of red wine and made herself at home at a small, secluded table in the far corner. She took one sip when Corporal Parker happened by. He stopped dead in his tracks.

"Uh, hey Cap, don't see you in here often."

"Hey Parker." Alisia replied, partially lost in thought.

"Cap? Uh, if you don't mind me asking, is something wrong?" His tone went quieter, taking his cue from Alisia.

Alisia looked at Parker. He wasn't a bad guy, so she decided to tell him. "It's Regan," she started.

"What? The girl from Autar? Is she OK?"

"Yeah, yeah, it's nothing like that. She just.. comes on so strong."

Parker blinked. And blinked. And blinked. "....comes on...? Uh, are you two....?"

"*God no!*" Alisia exploded, quickly restraining herself. She could just see Parker's imagination running full steam. "No, no.. she wants to, but I don't play that way."

"I see. So uh...." Parker struggled against his dominant thoughts to find something helpful or appropriate to say. "So... has she... uh.. then what..."

Alisia looked at the poor male with pity. "Soldier, you've seen far too much porn for me to have this discussion with you."

"Yes Sir, uh, Captain." Parker stood there still a little stunned.

"..... Dismissed?" Alisia said. Finally Parker snapped back to reality, and wandered off blushing.

Regan sat, holding the guitar, imagining if Alisia had approached. Maybe put her hand on her shoulder again. That was nice. Regan felt the need to relieve some tension and headed back towards her quarters. On the way she ran into Parker, who seemed unusually distracted to talk to her. He did prove useful however, in that he revealed Alisia's location. Regan thought for a moment about the effects of alcohol and decided that Alisia plus alcohol equaled hope abundant.

Regan found Alisia and sat down next to her with a confident smile and bedroom eyes. "Hey 'leesha. How's it goin'?"

Alisia's face looked a bit nervous, but if she knew the extent of what was going on in Regan's head she would have fled outright. The bartender came over and Alisia said she was buying for Regan. Regan took this as a great sign until Alisia mentioned "You can pay me back when your first cheque comes."

"Huh? Oh, I have money. You think I only ever scavenged bare necessities in Autar? There was a lot of money lying around. I popped a few safes out of boredom, not to mention cash registers, so I'm pretty well off financially."

"What? You looted safes and tills?"

"No one complained." Regan said, bringing her beer bottle to her lips.

Alisia couldn't argue the logic, but it still seemed wrong. About an hour passed by while Alisia asked about Regan's survival tactics and useful experiences with the zombies. Regan downed beer after beer, and looked for some key of wisdom that would help her win Alisia. Regan failed to notice that while she had drunk quite a bit, Alisia was still at the top of her second glass of wine.

Alisia was talking about the uses of her "bad mojo" gun when Regan lost all interest in talk.

"Yew drunk enough yet?" Regan slurred.

"Drunk... enough for what?" Alisia asked, still innocent of Regan's intent.

"So's I ken getcha inna my room, an' MUUaaaaaahhhhh....."

"...... no, I'd have to be a lot drunker."

Regan looked up at Alisia, (since Regan was slowly slumping over against Alisia's shoulder), and eventually mumbled "Hm. Keep drinkin." She rested against Alisia fully, wondering how much they'd both had to drink. "Wine's more powerful th'n beer," Regan falsely thought to herself, "She's gotta be plashtered!"

Regan snuggled into Alisia's side a bit more. "Hey! I know what. I'm gonna drink yew under the table...... yesh! Great idea. I'll get under th' table, an' yew get yer pantsh off!" With that, Regan fell asleep.

Alisia sighed and stared into her wine for a few moments, as if it would tell her how to handle Regan.

With patience and time, Alisia finally guided Regan back to her quarters. Alisia slumped Regan down onto her bed to find that Regan wasn't letting go of her arm.

"Jush shtay a minnit, k, 'leesha?" Regan's eyes were glazed over in a mixture of drunkenness, sleepiness, and tears. Alisia knelt down beside the bed and Regan held her forearm like a teddy bear. "Thanksh, 'leesh." Regan mumbled, squeezing Alisia's arm.

It wasn't long before Regan was passed right out. Alisia carefully removed her arm, careful beyond fear, not to graze Regan's chest with her hand. She headed back to her own room and went to sleep.

The next morning, Alisia awoke with the sinking feeling that something was wrong. It only took a glance to the side to see what had happened. Less than an inch from the side of her head was the side of Regan's head, upside down. At some time during the night, Regan had come into her room and made herself comfortable on Alisia's bed. Alisia decided not to blow up. Not yet.

".....Regan?" Alisia looked around a little more, and saw that the teddy bear that was usually at the corner of her bed was now under Regan's arm.

"Good morning, 'leesha." Regan replied. She was close enough that Alisia could hear the vibrations of her voice.

"Yeah, uh, what the hell are you doing in my bed?"

"Oh, don't worry, I was good. Kept my hands to myself." Regan innocently replied.

"Did... did you miss the part where I said I wasn't a lesbian?"

"Nope!" Regan pecked Alisia on the cheek and sprung up, headed for the door. "Gotta go get ready! Big day!"

"*I'm locking my door from now on!*"

Alisia pulled herself together and stepped out towards the showers. Who should be out in the hall, but Corporal Parker. He stared wide eyed at Alisia as she came out. Alisia looked at him with mild irritation and for a moment, there was silence.

"She..." Parker stammered, "...out of your room...."

Alisia rolled her eyes. "Yeah, that's right, Corporal. Last night, we got drunk and did it. Yeah. Hot and slippery all night. I'm kinda surprised you didn't hear the screams from your quarters."

"You... you're kidding me...!"

Alisia narrowed her eyes at Parker. "Geez, what do you think?" She said, walking off for the showers.

Parker blinked and turned to yell out after her. "*I think you're a mean, mean woman, Captain!*"

Chapter 27: Pit

By mid morning Alisia and Regan were deep into Autar. "General? Can we get a VTag on the target?" Alisia asked into her comm.

"Well ladies, it looks like Regan's already beat me to it." The General responded.

"Let me take a wild guess," Regan said, "it's a VTag I set called 'PIT'."

"Bingo."

"Ok, I give up you two, what's the pit?" Alisia said.

"It's the surface access to the mana core." The General offered, but was interrupted.

"Surface access!? Just how deep is this thing?" Alisia blurted abruptly, forgetting the General's rank.

"Well, the specs I have show about six floors." One could hear a smug grin on the General.

"Wonderful."

"Oh, at ease Captain. With cement walls over a meter thick, there won't be any surprises."

"Have you seen it these days?" Regan asked.

"Do enlighten us Ms. Grier." The General's voice mimicked the expression on Alisia's face.

"Well, last time I was there, it looked a lot like a huge empty swimming pool, with about fifty zombies mulling about."

"Lovely." Alisia mumbled.

"Captain, is this going to be a problem?"

Alisia thought for a moment. "We'll see when we get there, but we can probably handle it."

As the target VTag got closer, zombie encounters got heavier and more frequent. Alisia was glad she had packed extra ammo for this trip.

"I've never seen this many aberrations at once." Alisia said, referring to zombies which had taken on inorganic parts, or whose parts were in the wrong order.

At that moment, one decided to lunge out from around a corner. It had a pair of arms in place of a spine, and two extra arms on top of that. Regan leveled her P90 and shot its legs out from under it. It collapsed but kept coming, walking on its four available arms. The girls glanced at each other and relieved the determined creature of its walking arms.

"No worries," grinned Regan, "It's perfectly armless!"

Alisia looked around for immediate threats. There were several groups visible at the time, but nothing coming their way at the moment, so she took the chance to reload.

"Anyway," Regan said, checking her clip, "this area always has all the weird ones. I saw one once that looked like it was trying to do an imitation of a squid. A pile of arms, a head, and it was walking on its elbows."

"What? Was it any good in combat?"

"Good for me. While it was trying to get at me it tripped up three other zombies."

"They're not bright..." Alisia glanced towards the target VTag.

"Now and then, I see one doing something a little smart. Like trying to operate an elevator. I always made sure to nuke those guys fast."

"Why?"

"I was always worried that one day one would sneak past my alarms, and get me in my sleep."

Alisia tried to imagine that possibility, trying to go to sleep every night. Now and then Alisia was stunned by the idea that Regan had lived in this mess for two years. What does that do to a person, being alone and in mortal danger all the time? What kind of person would choose that? "Well.. we only have another few blocks to go."

There were a lot of wide open areas. Expensive corporate buildings wasted a lot of front space, making the wide downtown streets even wider. They worked at avoiding the zombies as they went, in an effort to conserve ammo.

They soon came to a block that was totally surrounded by a cement wall, almost five meters high. Outside the wall there stood a sparse, wide forest of pink, plastic flamingos. Regan kicked one up into the air for fun. "Damn crazy zombies."

"Let me unlock the gate." The General called in.

"Why?" Regan said, "There's lots of holes in the wall."

"Yeah, but look," Alisia pointed, "The zombies are using the holes to get in and out. If we open the gate and charge, they might not be around the gate. We can meet less resistance." The gaps in the wall had enough slow, ambling traffic to make it nearly impossible to peek inside without attracting attention.

"I have the commands for the entrance. It's in the bottom middle of the pit." the General said "So when you're about three seconds away from it, give me the word."

"Check."

They walked up to the steel gate as its red light turned green.

"Thank you General."

"When you're ready, ladies."

They double checked their rifles and stared for a moment at the gate. "Alright. Open up." The metal doors rumbled to life and began to drag apart.

Before them was the cement yard that hosted the pit. The pit sat fourteen meters wide, descending in beveled layers. Alisia mentally prepared a simple course to the man-hole-like hatch in the center. Forward, down, forward, down, and so on.

There was a denser concentration of zombies than they could have expected. The most space between any zombies was less than an arm's reach.

"That's different." Regan said softly. Already, a handful of them had turned their attention towards Alisia and Regan. "There's gotta be a thousand of em...!"

"Crap! No time to talk about it" Alisia slung back her P90, and brought the bad mojo forward. "*Charge!*"

Alisia fired a first round into the wall of zombies ahead. The sound was both dull, and sharp. Quiet, but you felt it through your body. At the same time, a hole appeared through the mob like a wave of rotting flesh being splashed out of the way. A dozen zombies went flying and uncounted numbers fell before them.

"*Holy fuck!*" Regan screamed in delight, "*Yes! Harder!*"

Regan P90'ed those zombies lucky enough to be missed but were still in the way. They ran into the mob. The bad mojo soon beeped, ready to be fired again. At this time, the horde was all around them except the rear. Alisia took aim and fired. Again, the sea of death parted before them.

"*Yeah baby!*" Regan's wild enthusiasm was a stark contrast to Alisia's silent professionalism. They ran forward, starting down the first beveled slope into the pit. They were now below the highest level of zombies and the gap behind them finally closed up, sealing the easy exit. They now felt thoroughly surrounded by the mob. Even the sky seemed at risk of being swallowed up.

They continued forward, blast, charge, blast, charge. Regan pegged back lucky ones with her P90. Alisia sometimes joined in with hers while the mojo recharged its capacitors.

A fallen one grabbed Alisia's leg as she took aim, but Regan took care of it before Alisia even noticed. "Sorry, buddy," She thought to herself, "She's mine."

They slowly got deeper and deeper in towards the middle of the pit. The terrain made it clear that they were getting closer to the bottom, even though the density of the zombies made it nearly impossible to see. Alisia blasted into the pit, and suddenly the manhole-sized hatch was revealed.

"General! *Now!*"

"Opening!"

The hatch began to open as they ran towards it. Regan used P90 fire to keep any curious zombies from getting in.

They reached it and quickly clambered down the ladder inside. As Alisia went down, she noted the thickness of the hatch. About fifteen centimeters thick. "Close it, General!" It started to scrape closed. Curious zombie faces began to peer over the rim, but a bit of lead made them reconsider. The hatch closed with a satisfying 'thoom' but it soon came to Alisia's mind that they were also trapped in.

Regan screamed in victory, hopping off the ladder to the floor of this small cement room.

"Report!" the General jumped.

"We're in, Sir. We're fine. Regan just got over excited." And almost as if to illustrate, Regan hopped up and down, grinning like a demon.
"Good work, ladies. The path should be pretty clear for a while. I've opened the appropriate hatches."

Nearby, the only way out of the room was an industrial elevator. They got in and pressed the only button. The doors closed and they started going down. Regan eyed Alisia, smiling, still breathing heavily from the battle. She cornered Alisia, pressing up close with her thigh up onto Alisia's hip. "Do you feel as hot as me right now?"

The General jumped in. "Really? I don't have access to the core's readings from here. I hope it's not spilling any heat or radiation."

Alisia thought quickly. "Uh, no Sir, I'm sure it's fine. We're just a little heated up from the running." Regan smiled into Alisia's eyes and leaned forward. Alisia grabbed her by the jaw and paused a moment. She considered kissing Regan and then tossing her on her ass, but she didn't want her sardonic sense of humor to encourage the poor girl. "Get your mind on the mission." She tried her best not to smile, but whether she was successful or not, Regan was still happy.

The elevator stopped and opened into a dark, empty hallway.
"I kinda expected to see zombies." Alisia said quietly. Regan hummed in agreement. She seemed to be more focused now. They moved forward with caution. Most of the doors were closed, sealed by electric locks. The General left the irrelevant doors alone. Alisia called door numbers now and then to confirm their route with the General.

Soon they were at a clean, steel-door elevator. Alisia pressed the button and was greeted with a sharp, annoying buzz.

"Damn." The General said. Through the comm, Alisia could hear him tapping on his keyboard. "That goes almost all the way to the core. Fine!" A clink was heard down the hall. "I've opened up the stairs. Five floors to go." The girls had their reservations. A complication was just another chance for something really bad to happen. Of course there was always the chance of the elevator failing and dropping them, too.

As they went down, the General's signal became progressively worse.
"General, this cement's starting to make it hard to hear you. I'm dropping a repeater."

"You have what, two? Will that be enough by the time you get to the bottom?"

Alisia reconsidered. "Hmm. Alright, I'll hold out." She put the signal-amplifying device back in its pocket.

The stairwell only went down one floor. "Next one's across the complex. Convenient, eh?" The General smiled, "It's gonna be like that for the rest of the way down, I'm afraid. Back and forth."

It was another uneventful stroll across a long hall, past locked doors, to another stairwell. They passed the elevator and tried the button to the same result as before. They continued to the next set of stairs, and after descending, the static was worse. Alisia dropped a repeater. Three floors to go.

The quiet and the lack of opposition was getting on their nerves. "You'd think there would be some guards here." Alisia said.

"Zombies aren't exactly great strategists." Regan replied.

"Well, maybe not, but I'd think that the A.I. controlling them would be. After all, the top of the pit was probably thick with zombies for a reason."

"Good point. Maybe the A.I. can't open the top hatch, so it would have no way of getting zombies in here."

Alisia considered it. "Sounds good. I think I'll choose to believe that. The A.I. may be taking advantage of the core's output, but it's not controlling everything."

"And another weakness; It controls the zombies, but not very well. If you think about it, why shouldn't a zombie move as fast as a human?"

"Because the A.I. has a poor understanding of the... the physics involved?"

"Maybe. Same with the tactics. A computer program is a pretty specialized thing. I bet this A.I. has enough trouble just getting them to not fall down, let alone attack. It just can't handle advanced tactics."

"So far."

"All the more reason to blow Autar the hell up."

Soon they were on the floor above the core, the second repeater freshly dropped. They came to the elevator again and saw the problem. A cart was lodged in the doorway.

"That's disappointing. I was expecting some kind of deliberate evil." Regan looked inside the elevator. "Hey, now that we know it's safe, wanna get in here and get it on?"

"No."

"I mean get the cart onto the elevator, of course! It's only one floor down but it'll be nice to have a ride up after. We can use the cart to hold the elevator till we need it."

"Uh huh. Sure. You're forgetting, we're going to have to go back up without power and climb up that first elevator shaft."

"Feh." Regan pulled the cart into the elevator and turned to face Alisia. "Going... down."

Alisia stepped forward and lazily shoved Regan in. She pressed the button next to 'core'. The doors closed and the elevator began its short trip.

Only it wasn't so short. The last floor was deep.

The doors finally opened into another hall, except this one went in both directions in a curve, probably forming a giant circle. A door stood directly across from them, which clicked as they approached.

"In there, ladies." The General's voice was almost unintelligible through the static, despite the repeaters. "The core will have eight large handles near the base. Twist em ninety degrees counter clockwise and pull em out. You'll get a meter long device. Feel free to smash em once they're out."

"Roger."

Alisia and Regan looked at the door and then at each other. Regan spoke. "When we pull these, there will be no more power being transmitted. The A.I. servers will go down and the zombies will be dead. If the A.I. has any last line of defense, it will be in here."

"Yup. Ready?"

"Alisia. I love you."

Alisia sighed in exasperation. "Ugh. Shut up, already."

"I'm serious."

Alisia looked down, feeling like she'd just been hit in the head with a giant bag of marshmallows. "I... I know." She finally replied, humoring her.

"Good." Regan said, "Now I'm ready."

They stood to either side of the door and opened it. Alisia hopped into the doorway, and back out. Regan looked to her with an expectant expression. "Well?"

"..... dick all. No zombies, no giant robots. Just one big helpless looking core-thingie."

"Then why are we still standing out here?"

"I... I don't know."

They walked in and looked around. It was a large control room with convoluted terminal desks arranged in two circles around the middle.

In the middle of the room, the core protruded from the ground as a roughly domed shape, six or so meters across, and one meter high. It seemed to meet the floor in such a way as to suggest that the core's bulk was under the floor. Like an iceberg showing only its top.

Pipe fittings and cabling plugs of all sizes and types littered its steely surface. Many were not currently in use, and many connected to pipes and wires that led everywhere. To the surrounding terminals, along the floor into the walls, or just right into the floor.

"This Frankenstein powers the whole city?" Regan said with a tone of disbelief.

Alisia identified the handles that the General had been talking about, and pointed them out to Regan before kneeling down to the nearest one. She reached out for it, but Regan stopped her and grabbed it herself. No electrocution.

"Just felt paranoid all of a sudden. Let's get pulling." Regan pecked Alisia on the cheek, making Alisia roll her eyes, and went around the other side of the core to start on a different handle.

When the handles were twisted and pulled out, a roughly cylindrical mass of circuitry, strange containers, and simply unidentifiable components came out. They soon found that they smashed spectacularly against nearby terminal desks.

Regan was pulling the last one, and Alisia walked up to her. Regan stopped and looked up at Alisia. She slid the unit back in slowly before pulling it back out with a soft 'ooh'. Alisia rolled her eyes. "What are you, twelve?"

Alisia contacted the General and got further directions for one of the terminals. A few keystrokes later the room's lights flickered and died.

"It's over." Alisia said into the darkness. Regan pulled out a flashlight, and shone it at Alisia's chest.

"Oh, grow up." Alisia said, pulling out her own. "General?"

"I can see from here, Captain. Autar is dark. We have sightings of zombies collapsing en mass. I'm calling in the airstrike. Come on home, and we're out of here." Just then, the lights flickered back on.

"*What?*" Regan yelped.

"At ease, Ms. Grier. Short-term battery back-up. Three days, max. It's safe for us to bomb the city like this. It just means there will be zombies on the way out."

"Alright" Alisia said, "Let's get going. We might get some distance in before the A.I. servers boot up."

They took one elevator up, then the other. "Open up the hatch, General."

"Be ready, we're seeing zombies moving again."

"Figures. Let's do it."

The two surfaced. There were no zombies around. Not walking nor collapsed.

"Maybe they responded to some kind of buggy error, and wandered off... like to the nearest server or something." Alisia suggested.

A shadow rose from the other side of the wall. "I don't think so…" Regan said.

A creature five stories tall turned its eyeless head towards them. The thing walked on its four huge, thick legs, smashing through the wall at the edge of the pit area. As it drew nearer, it could be seen that its gargantuan body was made out of zombies. Each one acting like a muscle group, pulling and pushing when needed to propel the thing. The individual zombies moaned of their own accord, forming a dreadful symphony.

"Cute." Alisia pulled out the Bad Mojo, warmed it up, and let off a shot at the thing's head. The zombies that composed its head flew apart from each other. Some fell to the ground, some landed on this thing's back, and others caught a hold before flying off to be pulled back in. Without missing a step, the behemoth reformed the damage to the head and absorbed the fallen zombies- some of which walked to the thing, others had to be picked up.

"Um…Let's go."

"Yeah."

They fled north toward a hole in the pit wall. Luckily, there were no other zombies hanging around. It was small comfort though, as the creature behind them was gaining speed.

"You were saying something about a poor appreciation of physics?" Regan said, making a few pot-shots now and then while running.

"Silly me!" Alisia turned and fired the bad mojo again, this time at a leg. "Keep going!" The beast staggered. It was already conducting repairs as it fell, but it was forced to slow down for a bit.

They passed the north edge of the pit wall and ran like hell. The footsteps of the beast thundered behind them and it bashed through the wall. Alisia fired another shot at a leg, to the same effect.

"This way!" Regan said, pulling Alisia towards a nearby building. "We might be able to lose it!"

They ran though a ruinous building, going through doorways and holes alike. Alisia suspected that Regan knew her way around here. The sounds of buildings being hit by the beast resonated from behind them. The chase continued from one patch of buildings, through empty streets lined with half-functioning zombies.

"We can't keep this up forever!" Regan gasped.

"We just have to get clear of the tall buildings!" Alisia said. She fired her second last bad mojo round, and kept running.

Finally, the first sniper tower came into view. "When the thing gets to this position, we'll have some help." A minute later, the welcome sound of an echoing zipper rang out. Sustained fire met the thing's left front knee. It served to slow it down a fair amount, which was just in time. Alisia and Regan were getting tired, and the bad mojo was almost depleted.

It was enough for them to lure it into view of another zipper tower, and finally they felt like they would make it. Through the din of the beast, a helicopter was heard. They kept running, now towards that sound, finding it waiting in an open intersection.

Parker sat in the helicopter's side bay door, manning a zipper. They jumped on.

"Don't be shy, Corporal," Alisia said, "Let 'im have it!"

With the girls safely out of the way, Parker opened up and started chewing up the ammo. The beast was looking very troubled, but more daunting than the effect of sustained fire from multiple zipper guns were the hundreds of attack VTags appearing everywhere. The girls sat back and then noticed the General across from them.

"Nice going, ladies. Now that we have you, the tower snipers can leave, and we can go watch the fireworks."

The chopper pulled out of the area, joining about two dozen others in the air. Everyone wanted to see the show. Through the visors, the city was bleeding VTags.

They waited in silence, except for the droning chopper engine, and the distant clamor of the beast as it approached the city's outer wall and began ramming it.

"It... it couldn't." Regan said. But despite her hopes, the beast soon opened a gaping hole. It struggled over the remaining rubble, staggering into open wasteland. Regan looked worried, but the General grinned.

The comm began to announce: "Airstrike approaching in three... two... one..."

The bomber was already gone before anyone realized it was there. The sonic boom hit at the same time that a flourish of genius-bombs appeared over the city. For a split second they idled in free fall, then locked onto their assigned VTags. All at once the swarm of bombs all fired to life, streaking generally downward with white smoky exhaust trails behind them.

A forest of white flame erupted in the streets. Chunk by chunk, the great bridges collapsed, pulling, and being pulled by the various buildings. One building lasted so long as to remain until a connecting cornerstone building began to fall on it. From the air it all seemed to happen in slow motion. All of it being consumed by the convulsing pool of burning oblivion.

The beast was tossed forward by the shock, but still stood. It staggered and rose to its rear legs. The sound of hundreds of voices screamed into the air before the thing collapsed, all the bodies letting go. Soon, it was nothing more than a heap of rotting meat.

"No more servers," the General said serenely, "No more zombies."

Autar was still foaming in violence. The outer wall was crumbling, especially at the north and south doors, and where the beast had damaged it. At some places, entire sections of the wall were falling outward.

Most of the choppers began departing while a few remained to keep watch, just in case.

Regan looked out the window and watched as Autar grew smaller and smaller, eventually to be eaten up by the horizon. Now, even from a distance it looked like a mess, smoke rising high. She tried to remember how it looked when she first arrived, shimmering in the sun. A monument to omnipotent progress. But that image seemed so far away. Forgotten was the cynicism she felt when she first saw it. She couldn't see beyond the tragedy now.

The General stiffened up, paying extra attention to his comm. Alisia noticed the grim look on his face. "General? Something wrong?"

"Hm? No," he forced himself at ease. "Ah, I just got word my team lost. I'm out a hundred bucks." He suddenly snapped into a cheerful mood. "Hey kids, we should celebrate. Let's go back to my base, you can meet the wife, and we'll all get hammered."

Regan made some comment about Generals always making the best plans, but Alisia wasn't put at ease by his bravado.

Chapter 28: Post-Game

The General entered the officer's club of Yute central base with his wife beside him, an hour and a half later than expected. Regan was already half plastered. Introductions were made. Luckily, the General's wife chose to be amused by Regan instead of offended.

"I didn't think ya were gonna make it, Gen'ril!" Regan said, slapping him on the back.

"Oh, had to please the press a bit, you know. They're hard to get away from sometimes, and they're very interested in the two heroes. We'll have to have a talk about what's classified and what's not, before you two start basking in the limelight."

Despite the General's jovial tone, Alisia was still unsure, and just sipped quietly on her red wine.

"Relax," the General told her, sensing her tension, "With any luck, you can sell the movie rights or something! My retirement egg is largely funded by a book I wrote about my missions from way back." Alisia smiled politely. Regan sorted some pocket change and excused herself before wandering off.

"General, you didn't lose any sports bet today, did you?" Alisia asked. She didn't really want to hear the answer, but the question was bugging her.

He put down his stein and sat back with a grim face. "Ya couldn't just leave it alone till the morning, could you? I guess that's admirable."

Across the club, Regan smacked the jukebox, and started 'Rebel yell', with a small shout of celebration.

"She's got the right idea," the General said as Regan sat back down, fresh drink in hand. Alisia threw the General an expression that let him know she wasn't giving up. He slumped his shoulders and looked at the table for a moment before continuing.

"Shortly after the Autar back up battery kicked in, a transmitter sent a large encrypted signal."

Regan tuned in, finally picking up that something serious was going on. "What does it mean, Sir?" Alisia asked quietly.

"We don't know yet, but it's a safe bet the A.I. at AutarLabs had something to do with it." He thumbed the handle of his mug. "Could be some kind of back up, or a data evacuation. It's also been suggested to me that the A.I. could not have become what it is now without help. The signal may have been meant for someone connected to that."

"Then it would mean that Autar's fall wasn't an accident."

"Well!" the General perked up, and finished his beer. "Let's not worry about that tonight." The General's wife put on her jacket, and they got up. "Well, I have people I need to talk to. Major Terone, I'll leave you and Ms. Grier to try to have fun, alright?"

"Did you say 'Major'?" Alisia asked.

"Yew heard the Gen'ril," Regan said, slinging her arm around Alisia, "We're shupposhed to have fun!" Hidden under the table, Regan's hand crept along Alisia's lap.

"I'll be in touch, Major." The General said on his way out.

Alisia watched the General and his wife disappear around the corner as the drunken Regan slumped against her. "General!" Alisia meekly squeaked, "Don't leave me with her!"

Chapter 29: Fractures

"If we're going into town, you're not wearing those shorts. And pull down your tank top so you're fully covered."

"Yes, mother! Damn, Alisia, what's wrong with this?" Regan stretched, and slowly moved towards Alisia, who was well prepared to dodge.

"I will *not* be seen with you like that. Don't you have something else? Jeans or something?"

"Hm, I think so. I'm sure I have *something*."

Regan eventually showed up in the chopper bay with her usual attire, but with a *slightly* longer skirt.

Alisia gave the most supportive critique she could. "Well, hopefully you won't get arrested."

They hopped a ride with a chopper going to the Meston airport. It was an uneventful ride and Alisia was thankful that Regan left her in relative peace for most of the trip. They landed on the tarmac and were told to be back around 20:00 for a ride back. Regan looked at the airport. It was the most civilian, normal looking place she had seen in a long time.

They approached the door, and Alisia noticed Regan was unusually quiet. They walked through some back areas leading to the main halls of the airport.

Suddenly they were witness to the living stream of people that always seemed to populate an airport. Some hurrying, some dawdling, and noise, noise, noise. Regan trailed behind as Alisia was attracted to one of those huge, overpriced chocolate bars at a nearby shop. She flipped through a magazine or two while Regan stood silently nearby, looking around nervously. Alisia went to pay for the chocolate. Regan kept right behind her, close enough that Alisia bumped her when she reached for her money.

Alisia took her change from the counter, and had no more than dropped it in her pocket when Regan clutched her forearm tightly.

"Alisia..." Regan whispered. She now knew something was very wrong. Regan's grip, while tight, was trembling. Alisia moved them out of the shop and out of the flow of traffic.

"What's going on, Regan?"

"I... I can't do this."

"It's the people, isn't it?"

"Yeah." Regan's wide eyes roamed across the mob of people milling past. "I want to go back."

Alisia was a bit disappointed that the day looked to be ruined, but her concern for Regan overrode it quickly. They started back to the chopper bays. "What exactly is it?" Alisia asked.

"I don't know. I just can't." Regan was still firmly clamped onto Alisia's arm. They made it through the door and out of view of the public. They stopped, and Regan took a bit of a breath. The sound of the crowd was strong. "No. Further. Please." Regan's voice trembled. They walked farther in, almost to the bays, when Regan decided it was far enough and slid to the floor, taking Alisia with her. There they sat while Regan buried herself in Alisia's arm as well as she could. Alisia took pity and got comfortable. Regan began to cry quietly, lungs heaving.

"It's okay, Regan. We're safe, I'm right here."

Regan eventually became quiet. Alisia suggested she go ask around the choppers for an earlier ride back. After a little bit of convincing, they got up, but Regan was still glued to Alisia's arm. It was surprisingly easy to find another ride, and they were soon in the air. Regan fell asleep leaning against Alisia, and the stress on her face slowly faded into peaceful oblivion.

The city of Meston dissolved slowly behind them.

Back at the Yute base, Regan went to her new quarters, slow and weary. She felt like a fool. Not long ago she was swimming in a sea of walking corpses, and here, today, she was totally undone by a mob of stupid tourists. She could only imagine what Alisia thought of her now. She took off the stupid skirt and put on her regular clothes.

She then stopped, and looked at herself. Did this look upset Alisia? Alisia sure didn't dress like this. Who the hell does? Even out of uniform, Alisia was always needlessly modest in her attire. Maybe that's just the style she liked. Confidence and cunning swelled in Regan once again.

Soon, Regan was in Alisia's quarters, uninvited and alone, looking at Alisia's clothing. My god, it looked like some *girl's* wardrobe. A large pink pullover caught Regan's eye in particular. She grabbed the sleeve. It was soft. She imagined how Alisia must feel in it. Soon, Regan was in it. It smelt a bit like Alisia. She felt a bit like a freak, but it was so good. She wrapped her arms around herself, and imagined Alisia. She imagined she *was* Alisia. Perfect, and strong. As she caressed the fabric, her hand hit her obtrusive leather miniskirt, which Alisia apparently hated so much.

"Oh hell. She'll never know." Regan exchanged it for a pair of Alisia's cammo pants. She staggered back and collapsed smoothly onto Alisia's bed. She stared at the ceiling, still enamored with Alisia's pink pullover. "Would she like me better if I were 'cute'?"

She lay there for a while fantasizing soft, warm fantasies. She clutched Alisia's nearby teddy bear in hopes it would give her some secret to winning her over. Certainly that 'I'm straight' stuff was just some kind of excuse... please? Besides, no one's totally straight or gay, right? Right? She just had to work on the part of Alisia that might be open to it, no matter how small. Such a tiny shard of hope to grasp.

Regan suddenly decided that she needed to get out, to avoid being caught. She had more than pushed her luck. She put the clothes back as exactly as she could and headed for the door.

Just then, Alisia arrived. "Regan?" She sighed, "What are you doing here?"

Regan paused, thinking fast. "I... just came to give these back." Regan pulled out the dog tags that she had taken days ago. "I'm sorry."

Alisia, still mostly in the hall, took the tags. She happened to look past Regan for a moment and saw her teddy bear out of place. She looked at the tags again. She didn't really mind if Regan had them, but she didn't want Regan to know that. She glanced at the garbage can nearby in the hall.

"I don't need these anymore. These say I'm a Captain. I've been promoted to Major, remember?" Alisia reached the tags over to the garbage, 'accidentally' missing, leaving them on the rim. She moved past Regan into her room and sat down. "I'll be getting new ones soon. Was there anything else?"

Regan stood, stunned. She didn't think she was convincing, but you can't argue with results. She still felt that something odd had happened. "Mm, no. That was all. Just, uh.. thank you. For today."

Alisia smiled ever so slightly. "What are friends for?"

Wordlessly, Regan backed out and closed the door. She then spotted the dog tags. She considered not taking them... it's not as if she was digging through the garbage or anything. She picked them up and hugged them in her hand.

Alisia looked at her bear as if to ask what Regan did in her room, but the bear told no secrets.

Chapter 30: Old Chum

The next morning found Alisia and Regan on a teleconference with the General.

"Ladies, without question you two are the authority on fighting the creatures that lived in Autar. Since we doubt we've seen the last of these things, I've gone ahead and authorized the use of an airlimb to be the base of operations for a unit specifically for combating this new threat. Major, you'll be the C.O. of this new unit. Ms. Grier, if you wouldn't mind, we'd like you to stay onboard as a civilian consultant."

Alisia was blown away. Airlimbs were for the elite.

Regan nodded to the notion of being kept on as consultant. It's not like she was going anywhere without Alisia, or had anywhere else to go.

The General continued. "Very good, Ms Grier. In that case, I have a surprise up my sleeve if I can pull it off. Oh, and Major, you'll need a zipper gunner."

"I'd like to request Corporal Parker, if he'd accept." Alisia didn't have to think about it.

"Done. I'll send word to him tonight. In the mean time, your airlimb is already docked at Yute base. Familiarize yourself with it, and make it home. Have fun, ladies." And with that, and no chance for questions, he was gone, disconnected.

"Wow." Alisia said, stunned.

"Man, this will be like my third move in a row." Regan mused.

Alisia mulled the new position in her head while chatting with Regan on mental autopilot. "Moving again, yeah. I'm gonna have to move all my crud again."

"Why? You're a Major for crying out loud. Make some grunts do it."

By noon, the two of them and Parker were moved into the airlimb. For a mobile unit, the quarters were pretty roomy, bigger than their previous ones. At least the first two were. Parker was stuck with one of the ten smaller ones. "On the plus side, no room mates."

In general, the airlimb interior was dark and a little cramped. While well lit, most of the walls and fixtures were of a dark metal. No one complained though, being either too impressed with the slickness of the airlimb, or deciding the cramp was... 'cozy'.

This was Alisia's and Parker's first time on an airlimb. It was Regan's first time being on one that wasn't ripped in half. Remembering the fancy toy she salvaged from the last one she was on, Regan went looking in the storage lockers for something similar. Something to even the firepower a little between her and Alisia with her bad mojo. Alas, this airlimb wasn't currently stocked with anything besides rations and medical kits.

"These things are made for about a dozen troops." Alisia said, seeing Regan take interest in the storage lockers. "Some units can spend more than a week in the air, just waiting for orders. With this few of us, I guess we all get a lot of closet space.

"Hm." Regan wandered down the hall a bit. "Too bad most of my wardrobe's gone up in flames. I had some really hot stuff in Autar." She got almost to the aft of the airlimb, and saw the doorway to the two washroom/showers. One labeled 'men', the other labeled 'women'. "*Holy fuck! This thing has shower rooms?!*" That was definitely something that she didn't see on the last airlimb she was in. "Leesha, Leesha! Let's try out the women's showers!"

Alisia sighed, and rolled her eyes. "Don't say things like that. If Parker hears you, he's bound to have a stroke or something."

Regan giggled, resisting the urge to make a comment about stroking.

In the late afternoon, Alisia was called to the base Colonel's office to do some paperwork and other administrative garbage.

Alisia got back to the 'limb late. She was a little surprised to see a maintenance crew working on the airlimb at this hour. The General must really be excited to get things going. She made her way to her cabin, and on opening the door, saw Regan curled up asleep on her bed, clutching her teddy bear tight. Alisia's first notion was to yell at her, but it was late and she was tired. She walked over to Regan and nudged her. "Hey. What are you doing in my cabin, with my bear?"

Regan moved a bit and let out a satisfied little purr.

"You can get back to your own room now."

Regan sheepishly peered out at Alisia, and groaned meekly. Despite her disappointment that Alisia hadn't decided to just curl up, Regan dragged herself off the cozy bed, patting the bear on the head, and picked up her blanket. She toddled towards Alisia on her way out, sneakily planting a small kiss on Alisia's cheek. Alisia rolled her eyes. It could have been worse. Regan was soon in the hall. Alisia peeked her head out and spoke to her.

"You do realize we're not a couple, right?"

Regan just kept going, and made some kind of grunt. Alisia couldn't tell if it was an angry sound or a sarcastic laugh. Maybe both.

Alisia closed the door and quickly got ready for bed. As she slipped under the covers, she noticed it was still warm from Regan. Already nearly asleep, she reached over to the night stand to set the alarm, but her hand first hit a folded note, standing like a tent. It had Alisia's name on the front.

She dreaded to open it, but instead of the expected dirty, suggestive come-ons, it was almost all doodles. At the top, it read 'Alisia-' as if to start a letter, but the rest was filled with little drawings of Alisia, the teddy bear, little hearts, and things like that. At the bottom where one might expect a signature, there was a doodle of Regan. It was far away from the other happy doodles, and looked sad.

Alisia stared at it for a bit and imagined Regan trying to come up with words, but not knowing what to say. The sweet little 'note' angered Alisia somehow. "How dare you impose this on me?" she thought. She crunched the note and threw it in one motion, and turned over to try to sleep. She could still feel the warmth of the bed's previous inhabitant, and hated the fact that it felt nice.

Regan slowly made her way back to her own cabin, when something familiar struck her. A scent. A familiar scent. "No...." Regan thought to herself, "can't be." She continued to her room, and went to bed.

When Alisia woke, the events of last night were gone from her mind until she stepped out of bed and felt the crumpled note under her foot. Her heart sank. She picked it up and smoothed it out a bit.

Regan's crude little face was there. It was still looking at the other doodles, but it felt like it was watching her. She put the note in her nightstand drawer, and got ready for the day.

Alisia could hear the airlimb engines running. They sounded great, the airlimb must be nearly ready to go. She saw someone out of the corner of her eye and followed the motion to the cockpit/ops room. When she caught up, she was surprised to see a woman with blonde hair and glasses, making herself at home in the central control seat.

"Eh? Soldier? Who the hell are you?"

The woman turned in the chair to face Alisia with a smooth smile and bedroom eyes. "Captain Kris Taylor, reporting for duty as operations officer, Sir."

"Ah," Alisia said, almost forgetting that this Captain was now lower rank than her. "Well, I guess the General assigned you. Welcome aboard."

Just then, Regan appeared. She stopped in her tracks, and pointed at Kris. "*No! Demon! Back to hell with you!*" Regan stormed off, nearly bowling over the emerging Parker. Everyone just sort of stared back to Regan's door as it slammed. Parker and Alisia then slowly looked back to Kris.

"Hm." Kris said, "She really needs to get over it. Too bad."

"You... know each other, I gather." Alisia said.

"Yeah. We used to.. hmm.. be a 'thing'."

Parker huffed in disbelief, but didn't seem to mind the whole thing terribly.

"What?" Alisia said, "Oh... the General. You're his surprise for Regan."

"Your surprise is here, General." Alisia later said in a comm conversation.

"Ah! Yes, record shows that before the Captain enlisted, she and Ms. Grier were room-mates. Maybe Ms. Grier will take better to military life if she had an old buddy around."

Alisia considered telling the General everything. About Kris and Regan. And about Regan hitting on her. But then she reconsidered. The General was an old man, no need to give him a coronary so close to retirement. "I see. Ah, well, it seems they didn't part on such great terms. Hopefully I can smooth it out."

"Oh? That's a shame. I guess I should have researched it further. But Captain Taylor seemed eager to take the assignment. Can you handle it?"

"Oh, probably."

"Good, good. By the way, your unit is designated "AZU-1". Anti-zombie unit one."

"Cute one, Sir."

Alisia later went to check up on Regan.

"She's a *slut*," Regan seethed, "An evil, evil slut!"

"I thought that was *your* description, Regan."

"I'm flattered you think so, but no. I'm just.. aggressive. Kris is an ev-"

"Evil, evil slut. Right. Got it. Well, if you hate her, and I'm straight, we won't have to worry about her sluttiness."

"Yes, yes, again with the straight talk. Just promise me when you realize you're not, that you'll come to me first."

Alisia sighed. "Fine."

"We must also warn Parker." Regan darted her eyes around as if the evil Kris could pop out of the walls at any moment.

"*What*? She's BI??"

"Like an old airplane. Hell, she probably did half the base crew on her way here! *Damn it*, I knew I smelt her perfume last night!"

"Aren't you over reacting, Regan?"

"Listen to me." Regan grabbed Alisia by the shoulders and stared into her eyes with the intensity of fire. "She converted a girl in half an hour *without alcohol!*"

Alisia blinked.

And blinked.

"What?"

"You heard me."

Alisia shook her head, accepting the stupidity at face value just to try to get to the point. "Which is what you're afraid she'll do to me."

"Listen. I love you, Alisia. She does not love you. She does not love. She is not human, and cannot love. She will try to consume you, and kill you from the inside. Good lord, we must warn Parker!"

With that, Regan ran out the door. Alisia, weary and confused, flopped down on Regan's nearby bed. Regan was insane, of course. It was becoming increasingly clear. If the General only knew, she'd be gone, yesterday. Into some funny farm.

Moments passed, and a shadow darkened the doorway again.

"Reg-" Alisia started to say, sitting up. She gasped to see that it was Kris. "Oh, hi." Was Kris's blouse unbuttoned that low before?

"I was looking for Regan, but... hmmm, whatever." Kris said. "Are.. you two an item? If you don't mind me asking?" There was a distinct predatory tone in her voice. "I mean... Sir?"

"Huh? No! Good lord no." Alisia was jumpy.

"Oh... good." Kris stepped forward a step before Alisia blurted out "Ah, that is, I'm straight and... yeah. So.."

"...hmm. Interesting." Kris leaned back, her midriff showing. Oh good lord, that was Regan's move. It just got worse and worse. Regan didn't need to go to a funny farm, they were already in one.

Then, a timely mixed blessing. The situation was disrupted by a comm call. Zombies had been spotted outside the city of Hatre. It was time to go.

Chapter 31: Something Different

Alisia stood by the airlimb bay door, watching the urban sprawl pass below. How many lives met her eyes as she flew past? Thousands. Each with their own stories, their own lives. Each one the center of a grand story, that was the sum of their experiences on this earth.

Each one was a vulnerable target.

It hadn't taken long. Even if it seemed inevitable that zombies would pop up somewhere again, Alisia hoped that the world would at least give her a little time off. Alisia closed the door and headed toward the airlimb's little mess, where Regan was found doing nothing in particular, sitting at the table.

"Hey Regan." Alisia said, nearly in a sigh. Regan smiled softly, feeling encouraged that Alisia had greeted her first. Sometimes Regan had a bit of difficulty starting conversation with Alisia. Regan found herself doubting herself, wondering what she could say that would be the appropriate balance of affection and respect. These were not the kind of cautious thoughts Regan was used to.

After a moment she decided that it was too late to say anything, and just maintained her smile as Alisia sat down across from her.

"So," Alisia said, tapping a finger twice on the table, "Records show your birthday quickly approaching." Regan silently continued her soft smile and obsessed over the green in Alisia's eyes, and the light spread of freckles found just below.

"What would you like for your birthday?" Alisia asked. Regan smirked and raised an eyebrow.

"*Besides* that." Alisia couldn't help but crack a bit of a smile herself. Regan was nothing if not persistent. And not that Alisia would ever admit it, but it was still just as flattering. Regan thought for a moment. Coming up with nothing else she wanted, she gave a casual shrug, never breaking her gaze into Alisia's eyes. Alisia looked back. "You're being awfully quiet. Something up?"

Regan leaned forward and took Alisia's gloved hand, now affixing her gaze there. She took the glove off of her and touched her skin. "Alisia," she said in a dream-like voice, "You don't know what you put me through."

Alisia cocked back, reclaiming her hand. "What I put *you* through?" She knew very well. Regan wore her heart on her sleeve. And everywhere else for that matter. It made Alisia feel very guilty. No, not guilty. Responsible. Maybe both. Maybe something else.

Their comms popped to life and Captain Kris Taylor's voice reached them. "Major? Everyone? We're about five minutes out from the target area. Local police are on scene and they only see one zombie. Two civilians down, but the area is contained." Regan ground her teeth at the sound of Kris's voice.

Alisia spoke to the comm nestled in her ear. "Check, Captain. Parker, you ready?"

Sergeant Robert Parker's voice manifested. "Roger, Major."

Alisia stood, preparing to go arm herself. Regan slowly followed. "You'd think the cops could handle one freakin' zombie. We could be somewhere getting a tan or something."

The 'or something' carried extra suggestion in her voice, but such subtleties now just rolled off Alisia's back. "Well, they don't have all the information. We'd rather handle it ourselves rather than risk further infection. They're just following the procedure that I myself wrote."

The actual information bored Regan to tears, but the way Alisia spoke about it was entertainment enough. When the job was on, Alisia got very... 'professional' sounding. Commanding. It was something Regan marveled at. Regan was well versed at being bossy, but Alisia was by contrast, a leader.

As Alisia opened an arms locker, Regan latched onto her arm affectionately. Alisia froze, and turned her head to Regan. "Not now." She said dryly.

Regan gave a last little squeeze, then let go. "Later?" Hope springs eternal, after all. "No." Alisia responded as coldly as she could muster.

The airlimb slowed as it approached an industrial and warehouse complex. Police cars were seen surrounding the back and front of one of the bays, a typical two floor warehouse/office facility. "Kris," Alisia spoke into her comm, opening the bay door again, "What do you think about landing?"

"Eh..." Kris mulled, "Yeah, alright. But I'm going to have to drop you almost half a block out if we don't wanna cook the cops with the jetwash."

"I think we can manage a walk."

"Roger."

Alisia and Regan hopped out as soon as they neared the ground. Regan followed Alisia's example and jogged with her towards the target building.

"Kris," Alisia comm'ed up, "Get up and put Parker in position to fire onto the back of the building. Be ready to bring him out front if I say so. Parker? You know your job."

Parker aimed his bulky zipper gun down, and brought up the VTags on Alisia and Regan in its scope so he could track their locations.

"Tag ladies, you're it." Parker's playfulness earned him a playful middle finger from Regan.

Alisia walked over to the police line. "Who's head of this mess?"

The police chief stepped forward. "You are now, ma'am."

"Alright. You're sure no one's come out?"

"Not since we got here. Not unless they dug a tunnel."

"Checked the blueprints?"

"No sewer access or anything like that."

"Good. Tell your people to keep on their toes. If a zombie does come out, feel free to shred it, but keep your distance even after it's down." Alisia changed to a yelling voice as she stepped back, looking to all the other officers. "*Be damned sure to check your targets first! Zombies don't move fast, so it's not like they're going to run up to you before you can get a good look! Neither of us need an ass full of lead! Got it?*"

The police chief replied, "Of course, ma'am."

"I'm not talking to you, chief," Alisia said with a smile, then going back to yelling. "*I was talking to all you holding the guns! Did you GET that?*"

Shouts came out in the affirmative. Alisia turned back to the building and saw Regan chomping on the bit. They readied their P90s and approached opposite corners. They peeked into the widows from all angles as they met by the doors.

"All clear?" "Yeah." They opened the front doors and headed in. To the police, this was a little strange. Their training would indicate a much more aggressive entrance, but zombies don't carry guns, so going in with a careful eye was more important than going in with quick aim. The front office was as wide as the bay, and about seven meters long. A smattering of blood was seen on the back wall behind a desk. The door in the back corner hung open lazily, also showing traces of blood at hand height.

Regan approached the desk by way of the side wall while Alisia kept an eye on her, and the door.

Regan made it behind the desk to find a young woman on the floor. Most of her skull was caved in, and her long blonde hair was matted with it. There were a few ragged gashes in her side as well. The blood on the floor and wall mimicked the patterns one might expect a child to leave around a mud puddle.

"Yeah, she's good and dead." Regan said with revulsion and pity. This was the first fresh zombie kill she had seen in a long time, and it hadn't gotten any prettier.

"Burn the wounds." Alisia said. "We'll pull her out after." Regan pulled out a flask, doused the wounds, lit it, and let them burn out. "Did I do it right?" Regan asked. "Looked OK. Let's go."

They entered the back door and found a narrow stairway up, another door, and an open path to the large back area. Small traces of blood were seen on the stairs.

"Keep an eye on the stairs," Alisia said, "I'm just going to secure the bottom. You see anything, yell."

"You too." Regan's voice betrayed her worry for Alisia wandering alone.

Alisia quickly opened the door to find a dingy little washroom. Nothing unusual for a poorly kept bathroom. She walked slowly into the back area. There were cardboard boxes everywhere, stacked neatly. No blood or damage was to be seen. Alisia made it through to the back door and yelled out to the cops in the back parking area. "Lower floor secure. Goin' up."

Alisia met back with Regan and took point as they edged up the stairs. They were narrow, steep and creaky. Stable enough for use, but surely not up to code. The side walls made of press-wood seemed to consciously surround them, but holding out her hand for support quickly made Regan reconsider. They seemed to be fastened with all the strength of thumb tacks.

They emerged into the upper office, roughly the same size as the one below. It was the only room on the second floor and was a clutter of office paraphernalia. In the middle of the floor was a fresh body. The chest cavity had been opened and the contents were arranged 'neatly' around it. There was enough damage to the rest of the body that they could not even tell the gender.

Across the room, someone was sitting at a computer facing away from them. The hair and clothing were messy, but this was secondary to the soaking of blood.

"Hey asshole!" Regan called out to him. He turned around in his chair. He moved like a human but the sagging and colour of the skin made it clear that this was a zombie. It was a rather fresh zombie. It still looked mostly human. One like this hadn't been seen in a long time.

It looked at them with a spark of intelligence, and then turned back to the computer to make a few quick keystrokes.

"What the hell is going on?" Alisia growled. The zombie turned back towards them, as the spark of intelligence faded. It lunged at them sluggishly, moaning. "That's, uh.. that's better." Regan commented, "Stupid thing."

It stumbled on the body as it came towards them. Alisia opened fire and cut out its knees. If fell to the ground but continued to claw towards them slowly. The girls walked around it as it floundered helplessly to get at them. Alisia looked at the computer screen it was working on. "It's a nanite server. Running solo though, not like the networked ones in Autar." Feeling experimental, Alisia reached for the back of the computer, and finding the power cord, yanked it out.

The computer fizzled out, and simultaneously the wounded zombie fell limp and unmoving.

Chapter 32: Poor Parker

Three hours later, after taking a lot of photos and collecting evidence, the scene was turned over to the disease control people, and all were back aboard the airlimb. The main bay was now host to three sealed body canisters. Two human victims, one ex-human. The salvaged computer was there as well.

After setting course and doing all the little things that needed doing, Kris put the airlimb on auto and turned her chair towards Parker, who had idly watched her work the airlimb's systems. Having decided to hold off discussing the day's action until the meeting, conversation had somehow gravitated towards social affairs.

"So, you're saying you're persecuted as a straight male. Poor baby."

"I'm serious!" Parker snapped, "Here I am, assigned to this tin can with Alisa and Regan, and their little tension war, and then here *you* come along, perfectly happy with the title of an 'evil slut', all of you *friggin hot*, I might add. If I happen to get a little distracted I get labeled a pervert!"

"Boo. Hoo." Kris said, grinning. It was fun to egg him on. He was an open book. And he considered her hot. Useful data, but in Kris's mind... who in their right mind wouldn't? "You *are* a pervert, so?"

"Shut up! *You* are a pervert. *Regan* is a pervert. Alisia and I are the only normal people in this unit!"

Kris raised her eyebrow. Her coy smile disappeared. "What, because you're straight?" She hadn't encountered gay discrimination for a long time, and if she had to tear this little boy a new one in the cause of re-educating him, she was well prepared to do so.

"No, it's because me and Alisia don't throw it all around! We wear *clothes! Properly!*" He pointed at the garter belt showing beneath Kris's skirt, and the open buttons on her blouse showing bits of her black bra.

Well, that was different. Kris was quite happy to hear that she was rattling this poor boy. "Well, nothing says *you* can't dress more revealing." She said, grinning with bedroom eyes.

"What? Ha. Yes there is, we have a *dress code* in this army, and they give us *uniforms* for a reason! Besides, a guy dressing revealing is like a nice paintjob on a toaster."

Kris was broken abruptly from the 'tease mode' she was sliding into. "What the fuck?! A toaster?"

"Yeah!" Parker staggered, coming out of his indignant rant. "Look, a guy's body at best, is dull as hell. We have one part that's a bit of fun, but overall it just does the job needed of a body and that's about it."

"This poor stupid straight guy," Kris thought, "Someone should teach him the proper use of a male body."

Parker continued. "But the female body..." he paused, glancing Kris up and down, "At its best... it's... art, it's sacred, best stuff on earth."

"That's just because you're straight. If you were a straight girl, or gay, you might say the opposite."

Parked scuffed his boot. "Maybe. But I doubt it." He got a little quieter. "Girls have all the fun stuff."

This was too damn easy. Kris stepped forward, formulating a plan to torture the poor lad.

Their comms sparked to life. "Guys", Alisia said, "Meeting time. Someone bring that computer. We're gonna crack the sucker open."

The four of them congregated in the airlimb's small mess hall, and Kris began fiddling carefully with the screws on the back of the confiscated computer case.

"So, what was with that zombie? It was acting almost normal for a few moments." Regan looked to Alisia, even though she didn't expect a solid answer.

"I thought for a moment it was just in the middle of being taken over, but that makes no sense. If he was in his right mind before we got there, why kill the other two?"

"Well maybe it drove him mad before taking full control..?" Kris offered.

"Eh, I don't know. He was the freshest zombie I've seen in a hell of a long time," Regan said, momentarily forgetting her hatred for Kris, "But it wasn't *that* fresh. I'd guess a week or two."

Alisia leaned back. "Parker? Thoughts?"

Parker perked up. He hadn't been paying extremely close attention and didn't expect the teacher to call on him. "No thoughts here, Major. I just shoot things."

Alisia smiled a bit. He could be such a brat sometimes. Kris finally popped the case of the computer. "Damn proprietary screws. Okay. Let's see. Wireless network card of course, to transmit to the nanites and control the zombie.. no mana receiver, good to know."

"I should hope not." Alisia said, "So, nothing unusual in terms of hardware then?"

"No, not really. But..."

"But what?"

"Well, there's a standard network card in here too. It was hooked up. Why a wireless network card too? It could have just been part of the original machine.... I don't know. The wireless card's a pretty new model. Newer than the computer..."

"So it was added recently?"

"Probably."

"Would it be reasonable to guess that a non-zombie may have installed that to control the zombie? Would that mean there's a normal person out there who's responsible for *all* the zombies?"

"Holy shit." Regan said quietly. "We're having that place dusted for prints right? *Oh shit, Kris!* Stop touching the computer! You could be wiping off prints of this guy!"

"Relax, hon," Kris said, "I've been handling it minimally. I doubt I've done any harm."

"Hope not..." Regan scowled.

"Anyway, the lab guys at Yute might know better. I wanna get a look at the software. Can I boot it up?"

"I guess so. Regan, Parker, cover the zombie before we do this. It's legless, but just to be safe..."

Parker and Regan stood guard over the zombie's canister while Kris hooked up an extension cord. It booted up right into the nanite server program.

"Huh." Kris mused, "Replaces the OS. Right from the POST to the server. Tight code. Very specialized." The others had only half an understanding of what she meant.

The zombie stirred. Through the frosted plastic lid, Parker and Regan could see it moving. It pressed its face against the top and tried to look around, making mumbling moans. It left thin smears of blood against the lid.

"Cute." Alisia said, "Okay, shut it down."

Chapter 33: Friendly Fire

The airlimb powered down, nestled in its docking bay on the roof of Yute base. Base crew soon unloaded all the collected evidence.

Regan snagged Alisia by the arm as they were leaving the airlimb. "Hey leesh, got a minute?"

"Well, not really. I have to go report to the General. Can it wait?"

"I just wanted to know if you have any vacation time stored up." Regan asked.

"Yeah, tons, why?"

"I decided what I want for my birthday. I picked out a little tropical spot, and I wanna go on vacation there. Like a weekend or something."

"Well, I guess we could survive without you for a couple days. If something popped up though, we might have to come grab you."

"No no..." Regan's face went a little pale. "I asked about *your* vacation time. Please come with me? Please?"

Red flags popped up in Alisia's mind. Regan wanted to take her away for the weekend? She must be mad. But then she looked at the uncharacteristically innocent, pleading look on Regan's face. It reminded Alisia about the time they tried to go into town. Regan had something akin to a panic attack that day, overwhelmed by all the people. If she was brave enough to go to a resort after that, then it would be cruel to send her alone.

"Fine. I'll see what I can do. But again, if anything pops up, vacation's over."

Regan's face radiated relief and joy. She mouthed the words 'thank you', then quietly returned to the airlimb. There were preparations to be made. She walked briskly towards her room, but was confronted by Kris.

"Get out of my way, demon!" Regan stood as if ready for combat if necessary. Kris put a 'wounded' expression on.

"Come now hon, I know we've had our rough spots, but isn't there any way I can make it up to you?"

"Yes. Die." Regan stormed past and opened her door. "Oh, and don't call me hon." She slammed the door shut, closing out the evil, evil Kris in the hall. Regan sat down at her terminal, trying to force Kris out of her head. She had to get to work if she had any hope of doing the vacation this weekend.

The other day she had converted all her looted cash into online accounts. The Yute base's office had minor banking capabilities, so that was convenient. Now it was just a matter of doing some online shopping. No having to deal with the public at large. Noisy chaotic public. It reminded her of the first fall of Autar. The yelling and screaming, the trampling of other people, wild shots fired by frightened troops, and of course the ever-pressing mob of zombies.

No, no need to think of that any more than need be. Shopping time.

Kris considered going in after Regan. No, she needed to cool down. It had only been what, two years and change? Give her another couple days. In the mean time, maybe she could find that Parker fellow. He seemed susceptible.

Kris sauntered over to his door and prepared herself. Blouse unbuttoned enough to reveal a bit of bra? Check. Skirt high enough to show some garter and skin? Check. What else does a girl need? She opened the door in one smooth, confident motion.

Parker was startled. He had been lying on his bed watching a movie on his terminal. In his fatigue pants and tank top, he leapt to his bare feet and saluted. "Captain, Sir!"

Kris eyed him slowly. Yeah, he was a bit on the naive side for her tastes, but that had its appeal too. He was built well enough. She slithered closer.

"No need to stand so erect, Sergeant. I only require that from Privates."

Parker either failed to get, or chose to ignore the innuendo, and stood easy. "Uh, what can I do for you, Captain?"

"Mmmm, no need to be so formal off duty, Parker. Call me Kris."

"Ah, alright." He said hesitantly.

"Say it." Kris's tone had a hint of demand.

"Uh, alright... 'Kris'."

"Better." She wondered what other tones of voice she could get him to say it in. "Have a seat, Parker. Or may I call you Robert?" She moved in such a way that he had little choice but to sit on the bed, and not the chair.

"Uh, no one calls me that, Si- Er, Kris. Everyone just calls me Parker."

"Yes, I noticed," She said, sitting next to him, and leaning in just a tiny bit. "But that's not what I asked. I asked if.... I... could call you Robert."

Parker blinked. "Uh, whatever turns you- ! I mean, Whatever you want, Sir. Kris."

This was great fun. She leaned back onto the bed, and in a swift motion flung one leg around behind Parker. She now sat behind him with her legs around him and her hands joining over his abdomen. "So, Robert," she whispered. "Would you like to play?"

".....play?"

"Oh, don't be silly. You know what I mean."

"Sir, I-"

"I told you. It's 'Kris'. And don't turn this into a rank thing. I won't tell if you don't."

"Kris… it's just that I really don't know you all that well, and-"

"And rumor has it that I'm an evil, evil slut, right?" She said it with such pleasure, almost purring.

"Well, true, but..."

"Oh, Robert," her voice melted into a sigh-like, innocent tone, "Do you really care that I'm a *bad* girl? I know you're a good little boy but you need to relax *some* time."

Parker was quiet. Kris's soft warmth pressed against him. He could feel his body reacting to her. It was difficult to breathe, his heart was pounding, and all the other physical effects one might expect.

"Robert..." Kris cooed, "It's alright. Alisia won't know. You and her have something, don't you?"

"The Major? No! Absolutely not!"

Interesting. "Mmm, then come on. Don't make me try to get convincing."

Some time later, Regan confirmed the last of her hefty orders. Delivery rushed for overnight. Hungry now, she began to step into the hall. She saw Kris's back sticking out of Parker's door. Kris was giggling. What a fake little giggle from a fake little slut. So... she got Parker. Regan ducked back into her room and waited. Soon she heard Kris wander off. She waited an extra minute and then went over to Parker's. She knocked quietly.

Parker took a minute, but answered, fully dressed. Regan pushed him in and closed the door behind them. Parker was shocked to say the least, and half expected Regan to come on to him despite knowing her orientation.

"She fucked you, didn't she!?" Her words came out almost in a hiss. Regan knew that when Kris was involved, she dominated. Always.

"I- I- "

"Ugh." Regan calmed down a bit. "Look, I don't want you in trouble. Don't you know she's an evil, e-"

"*Yes*, I know..."

"Then what were you thinking?" Bah. Regan knew what he was thinking. Kris had a way of blurring rational thought in others. "Ah, forget it. Look, what do you think is going to happen between you and her?"

"I- I don't know, I haven't really had time to think of it!"

"Hm. Well, don't get too attached. As soon as you're not convenient, or she's grown tired of you, *bam*, it's over."

Parker sobered up a little. "She's really like that?"

"Tip of the iceberg." Regan stared into Parker with ferocity, trying to drive home her point. "I'm not kidding when I say she's evil. Do you understand?"

Parker was quiet for a moment. "So.. what would you have me do?"

"Ideally? Make her fall in love and then dump her ass. But that won't happen. She can't feel love, and you're too nice. I can understand if you want to 'see' her again. I just advise against it." Regan left Parker to think. She stepped into the hall and made sure the coast was clear before she went back to her room and tried to sleep.

Alisia was having such a nice dream. Of what did she dream? Nothing. No zombies, no nanites, no Regan and Kris making nasty faces at each other in the hall. Nothing. Then, a sound. Wait, was that part of the dream?

She felt a weight press down on the mattress near by. No, the dream was over. A weight came down gently on her hips and as she opened her eyes she saw Regan's hand about to brush her cheek. Regan was straddling her, gazing into her eyes.

"Hey, Alisia, you asleep?"

"No, I always snore while I inspect my eyelids. Get out!" Alisia's voice came cranky, but soft.

"We need to talk." Regan sounded upset and serious.

"Ugh. Do I have a choice?"

"No."

"In that case, what's on your mind?"

"Get rid of Kris, please?" Regan's voice teetered like that of a little girl who'd been crying.

"Is it really that bad?" Alisia slowly had to face the idea that she was now wide awake.

"....please" Regan pleaded, barely audible.

"You can defend yourself from her just fine."

"It's not me I'm worried about- it's you. She'll steal you from me." Regan's eyes focused down where she was tracing little circles on Alisia's night shirt her finger.

"You don't *have* me, I'm *not* a lesbian!"

"Yeah...." Regan said concerned, "We need to discuss that, too."

Alisia rolled her eyes. "By the way, I'm much relieved to have woken up with your hand on my *face* this time." She looked down at Regan's finger wiggling on her abdomen, and moved it aside. "Hey, do you wear those nylons to bed or something?"

"Just when I plan to come visit you in the middle of the night."

"So.. always then."

"Yeah. So.. can you get rid of Kris?"

".... She's doing a good job so far. I have no concrete reason to get rid of her."

Regan considered telling Alisia about Kris and Parker's little encounter. No, it might damage Parker's standing with Alisia, and that wasn't fair. "Fine. I'll.... just promise me.. if you have a change of heart about girls in general... you'll come to me, not her...?"

Alisia rolled her eyes again. "Yeah, whatever. Fine."

"No. Not whatever. I'm serious. If..." Regan's eyes were wide, and welling. She grabbed Alisia's hand.

"Fine." Alisia said, grabbing Regan's hand with both hands, patronizing her in an exaggerated manner. "I will. IF."

Regan seemed very relieved.

"Now can I get to sleep?" Alisia asked bluntly.

"Okay!" Regan flumped down on top of Alisia and began to get cozy. *"Get out!"*

Chapter 34: Steeve

Meet Steeve.

Steeve was having a pretty good day, but in the mid morning he began to feel odd. Maybe there was a bug in the air, maybe it was something he ate, or maybe it was the fleet of new and improved nanites *in* the thing he ate. Who can tell with these things?

The uneasy feeling passed soon enough. In fact, Steeve barely noticed that he had died. Neither did anyone else for that matter, since he kept on walking.

Of course, Steeve was no longer home in his body. Something else controlled his body as he returned to the mall where he bought his breakfast. He went back to the food court and found a free seat among dozens of others who had enjoyed a similar breakfast. They were all resting with their heads down on their tables.

A few of the shoppers passing by noticed these fifty-odd folks who were seemingly taking a nap in the middle of the food court. By contrast, *all* the people noticed when all of the napping zombies suddenly sat bolt upright. It was not then long before people began to die.

Alisia's comm barked for attention. She reached out from under the blanket and grabbed it. Silencing its alarm, she placed the little device in her ear.

"Ung... Major Terone here."

"Major?" It was the General. "Another outbreak. A lot more than one this time. We've got a mall going to hell. Local police and SWAT have arrived on scene and are working to contain to the mall, and direct escaped wounded. I'll dump co-ordinates to the airlimb. Any questions?"

"No, Sir. We're gone."

"Good hunting Major."

Alisia disconnected then buzzed the others' comms. "Good morning people. We have a job. Let's hustle. Kris, we should have the co-ords by now, get us in the air."

"Meh?" came Kris' sleepy voice.

Alisia simplified it. "Wake up! Fly big thing now!"

"Meh."

While Kris 'rushed' to the control room, the rest put themselves together. The airlimb jolted to life and rose to the sky.

"Kris?" Alisia asked for a report, walking into the darkly lit control room minutes later. "How are we doing?"

Kris swiveled in her chair to face Alisia, still dressed in what she was sleeping in; panties and a baby T. "We're fifteen minutes out. We're good to auto until we approach the target." Kris leaned back into what Alisia had come to call 'the Regan maneuver', stretching upwards, trying like hell to 'accidentally' expose herself under her top.

"Then go get dressed, Captain." Alisia muttered.

"Captain, huh? You were calling me 'Kris' a moment ago." Kris tried to make eye contact as she stood, but Alisia stared at the forward monitor intently, trying not to look at Kris.

"Go put yourself together. We're on duty as of five minutes ago."

Kris got up and walked past Alisia close and slow. "Roger." Kris purred. She stopped for a moment and looked close at Alisia, who still denied her stare. Kris puffed a hot little sigh her way before slinking off.

The airlimb was soon encircling the target zone, a small shopping mall. A press helicopter was already on the scene. Below, SWAT had contained a tight perimeter around all of the entrances, much like at the warehouse. Several ambulances were on the scene, and paramedics were scrambling over a handful of wounded.

Alisia stood with Regan, looking out the side bay door. "Kris. Make sure those paramedics have the protocols for handling zombie-wounded and drop us off by the nearest entrance. Parker, get talking to the SWAT and co-ordinate with them. When Regan and I are down, you two get into the air and stay sharp."

The airlimb touched down momentarily. Alisia and Regan hopped off, walking through the SWAT lines to the entrance. By now the airlimb was already up again. After a quick check in with the SWAT commander, Alisia caught up to Regan who was standing in the doorway and looking in.

A grouping of zombies had already turned their attention towards them. They looked nearly human except for the seemingly random wounds, the staggered movements, and deathly stare.

These were even fresher than the one they encountered in the warehouse mission. Fresh baked today. Alisia's stomach turned a bit. She knew they'd be fighting a lot of these, but the idea of shooting things that looked so *human*, all suddenly hit her. She had to force herself through the logic. "They're already dead. Shooting them is just disarming a threat to the living." Still... they looked so human. And their families didn't even know yet.

Regan looked into the mob and saw Autar. Memories of screaming pounded into the back of her head. Blood, blood, blood. On the walls, in the streets, on her. And her brother. She lingered in that memory for a while, lost.

The sound of Alisia's P90 snapped Regan back to the real world. In front of her the fresh zombies were beginning to collapse, blood erupting from their newest wounds. Regan collapsed to her knees, eyes transfixed on the newest horror.

"*Regan!*" Parker's voice came over the comm. He'd seen her collapse from the airlimb. Alisia looked to Regan in a minor panic. Seeing no wound, Alisia quickly tried to immobilize the few zombies still approaching.

"Regan?!" Alisia, keeping one eye to the mall's interior, got down beside Regan and grabbed her by the shoulders. "Regan, are you hurt?!"

Regan silently leaned into Alisia and held her.

"She's OK." Alisia called back to Parker. "Gimmie a sec."

Alisia felt Regan's breathing. It was slow and deep, but it trembled. "Regan. Do you want to go back? I can finish this."

"Don't be stupid." Regan said, "There's gotta be a couple hundred running around in here."

"Then we can delay. The situation's contained, no one new's gonna be hurt. Maybe I can get Parker to take a mission, maybe we could..."

"No." Regan's voice became firm and confident. She would not allow herself to be weak like this... not when it was important. She could not fail Alisia. "We're proceeding. Kris, do we have a reading on a nanite server transmission yet?"

After examining the captured server, Kris was now equipped and able to identify the distinct but illegibly encrypted signals used to control the zombies. "Yeah," Kris responded, "About two blocks inside the mall, to your general left."

"Alright." Regan shook off the remaining bits of her weak moment and started ahead.

They found themselves using a lot of ammo, and the tile floor in some areas of the mall came to look like a red sea peppered with shell casings. Between bursts of conflict, the girls walked quietly through a dim path of deathly evidence. The place had become a profound obscenity to life, complete with a choir of pained moans which came from the nearest group of ex-humans which they would have to butcher to proceed.

Alisia kept having to remind herself that they were already dead, but it didn't make the sound of blood under her boot any easier to hear.

A yell was heard from ahead. "Over here! Hey!" The girls popped up from their gloom to see a live, healthy human waving at them from a store with its metal security grating down. Several other terrified faces could be seen poking out from the clothing racks inside. Unfortunately, the survivor's yell also attracted eight or so zombies, and they were closer. When he saw them, the yelling man was smart enough to get back from the grate.

The girls took aim and mowed down the zombies one by one. The last one to fall had already started bending the bars, and one of his arms still gripped it.

Alisia stepped over the fresh kills, kicking aside one that was still putting up a fight with one leg operational.

"Sir?" She said, calling for the civilian. He stepped forward and the other faces reappeared, some of them standing now, a bit less afraid. Several of them were children.

"You're that Captain Terone chick, right?" he said, eyes still looking about the main mall for zombies, but pausing on Regan a few times. "And Regan Grier. You're here to save us!"

"Major Terone, yes. We hadn't expected to encounter survivors, actually. We're here to clean out the zombies." Alisia pondered the options while Regan made friends with a curious little girl, touching fingers through the grate. There was a decent possibility that the path to the exit behind them was still clear, but it was a risk. And these kids didn't need to see any more corpses than they already had today. Alisia called up to Kris.

"Captain, we have survivors here." Alisia put a VTags on the floor of the shop so Kris could view their location. "Does this store have a back entrance?"

The man replied before Kris. "no.."

"No," started Kris, "But the one next door does. I'm routing some SWAT there now."

Alisia looked to the store next door. It had been attacked and there was blood around, but there were no zombies in it. Alisia got the survivors to open the grate and sent them into the other store. Just as they were half way through, a loud crash was heard from the back and a few SWAT members hustled in.

"Ok folks, follow these guys out, get checked out by the paramedics, and hopefully we can get you home quick." Alisia tried to suppress a smile from this small victory, and watched Regan say goodbye to her little friend. Soon they were alone in the mall again.

"Well," Alisia said, "That felt good." But then she turned around and saw the mess of blood again. The joy of saving a handful of people felt suddenly very small. But they continued.

They closed in on the server signal and found it to be surrounded by a great crowd of zombies clogging up the entire width of the mall. With some help from Kris they managed to put a VTag on the approximate location of the server. Sure enough, it was right in the middle of the crowd.

Alisia looked at the crowd and considered the amount of P90 ammo they had. "This is ridiculous. I'm going to soften them up."

Alisia slung back the P90 and drew forward the Bad Mojo. Regan hopped in anticipation as it hummed to life. Alisia aimed the bulky rifle at the right side of the crowd, but clear of the estimated location of the server.

"Here's to property damage!" Alisia pulled the trigger. The dull but sharp sound echoed against the hard walls as a mass of walking dead were thrown back, and apart. Windows broke and bits of wall flew. Regan loved the destructive aspect, but her enthusiasm was cut short by the red spray that these fresh zombies created in their wake. Alisia was sickened by the sight as well, but took aim again, this time at the left segment of the crowd. This time, Regan turned away.

The sound rang out, and when Regan turned back, she saw devastation. Her knees felt weak. Alisia stood motionless, stunned by the horror she'd caused. "They were already dead, they were already dead." she chanted in her mind. She could feel her arms tremble a bit. Focus. *Focus.*

About two dozen zombies remained in the middle, spared from the terrible onslaught. The carnage on either side was littered with squirming parts. Blood dripped from the ceiling. Regan stared at the surviving zombies, who looked confused but unconcerned. But one of them was different. One was not so new.

A decayed hand rose from the older zombie's side, holding a revolver. Regan screamed, and tackled Alisia down. A shot rang out as Regan scrambled them behind a large potted plant.

"What the fuck?!" Alisia said.

"One of the zombies! Has a gun! He shot at us!" As if by cue another shot rang out, and a chunk of their concrete cover broke away.

"It can't be a zombie! Are you sure it's not some human defending himself or something?"

"No! He was rotting! Definite zombie!"

Alisia was still skeptical. "*You! With the gun! We're human! Cease fire!*"

"*Kiss my zombie ass!*" came the response with another shot.

The girls looked at each other, puzzled. A talking zombie who knew how to use a gun? Regan carefully stuck her head out the side to peek. Sure enough, the older zombie was slowly walking towards them, holding his gun. He walked smoothly like a human and his expression showed intelligence. He spotted Regan, and as he corrected his aim she ducked back in. A bullet ricocheted where her head had been, but by now, Alisia's P90 was aimed and a short volley of bullets shattered his arm. The arm and the gun fell to the floor.

The zombie stopped.

He looked at his arm.

He looked at Alisia.

"Bitch!"

He stooped down and used his remaining arm to pry the gun loose. Alisia wasn't about to have that, so she shot off his other arm. He stood and looked at both arms laying on the ground.

"Ack! You've disarmed me!"

"What the hell?" Regan said, "We're talking with a zombie! What's going on here?"

The zombie looked at Regan. "Well, what do you expect, *this?*" The light of intelligence suddenly left him and he moaned, staggering forward.

"Well.... yeah!"

The zombie didn't respond, but kept advancing.

"Screw that." Regan opened fire and took it down.

"Missed me!" Came the same voice, but this time from the ambling crowd of zombies who were only now cluing in to Regan and Alisia. One of them jumped forward, breaking into a run, moving like a human. It dashed for the fallen handgun which was closer to it than Regan or Alisia. They dropped him in mid stride before he got far. The newly fallen zombie called out from the floor.

"Uh... that didn't hurt!" Then his face went dim and stupid like a normal zombie. The voice came from within the group again. "Didn't hurt at all!"

Yet another zombie broke apart from the crowd, this one diving for nearby cover. The girls didn't manage to hit the new one, but deciding to narrow their opponent's options and remove variables from the battlefield, they shot down the remaining handful of mindless zombies.

"Ooooh, my toys!" the last zombie bemoaned from behind his potted plant.

"What the hell are you?" Regan said as Alisia walked over to its first body, the older zombie.

"I'm a zombie! *Duh!*" he called out.

"Yeah, fine, but why are you talking?" Regan said.

"I get so lonely!"

Alisia glanced at Regan. "A.I.?" She asked softly.

Regan opened her mouth, but was interrupted by the zombie. "Haha, I am not an A.I."

"Good ears." Alisia commented.

"The Autar A.I. was a magnificent piece of code, if I must say so myself," the zombie said, "But it's not capable of holding conversations, and it still had a pretty feeble understanding of bodily kinetics. And no appreciation of firearms."

"So you're either a much better A.I., or a human controlling zombies through the server." Alisia said, prodding the body of the older zombie with her boot.

"Duh." The zombie taunted.

"I'm guessing human. I assume you caused this?" Alisia's boot found something big and hard lodged in the older zombie's chest cavity.

"Ya, that's me." The zombie replied. Regan's head spun at the thought of a human causing this on purpose. At least Autar's fall was an accident, right? It was a faint hope she'd clung to for the sake of faith in humanity.

Alisia reached down getting a hold of the twenty centimeter wide metal canister she had found. It was caked in dried blood. She held it up for Regan to see, then looked towards the zombie. "So, this would be your handiwork then. What is it?"

"Well..." The zombie hesitated. "You're going to find out anyway, I guess it doesn't make a difference." He took the opportunity to brag a bit. "It's a mobile server. Good long battery, can carry a shitload of nanites, and a half decent transmission radius. Keep it, I have lots."

Alisia found a clasp and opened it up. As promised, a battery, and a lot of circuitry.

"It could have been a bomb." The zombie said. "You're pretty brave.. or dumb."

"It didn't seem to fit your M.O. to use a bomb." she said, fingering a power switch inside. "So, what's your name?"

"Ha! Nice try. But I guess you have to call me something.. how about... uh.. what's Autar backwards...? Ratua? No, that sucks. Uh.... ooh, this is cool, how about Samhain?"

"Samhain?" Regan asked.

"Hmm.. you're right. A bit dorky still, and fact is, he wasn't actually the Celtic god of the dead. *Ooh!* Egyptian! Anubis! No, no, that's been done. Charon? I'm not into boats." The zombie looked off into nowhere while he thought and rambled. "Namtar? Rudra? Dorky, no. Thanatos has been *so* done. Tartarus? Tartar sauce. No. Hm. Erebus! Yes! Call me Erebus! Son of Chaos, brother of Nyx!"

"What the hell ever! Why are you doing this?" Alisia asked.

"Did you know that Erebus has a volcano named after him? Some people used to think of Erebus and Hades as the same guy, but I think the-"

"Shut the fuck up." Alisia pressed the switch in the mobile server, and he fell limp. The scattering of writhing parts they had made stopped moving, and the rest of the zombies in other areas of the mall fell to the ground.

Marking notable things with VTags on the way, the girls carried the mobile server out, trudging through the cooling gore. They came to the entrance as decontamination teams were arriving.

Alisia's head spun with worries and tried to grapple the implications of this 'Erebus'. She looked to Regan. She just looked tired. That sort of deep-soul tired. Regan looked to Alisia. Under the warming sun and the press helicopters, she held onto Alisia and pushed back weary tears.

Chapter 35: Unwind

While Alisia took care of the paperwork and other post-mission business on base, Regan and her rattled nerves wandered towards the base bar. Parker spotted her on the way and tagged along. At first Regan resented the unexpected company, but Parker's easy demeanor soon chipped away her resistance. Before she realized it she was thankful for the company. It wasn't long before they were seated in a booth, lagers in hand.

"So, what's up?" Parker asked.

"Up? We just came back from a successful mission and I thought I would come down and pollute myself a bit."

"Regan, come on. Me and anyone tuned into the news today saw how rattled you were."

"*The news?!*"

"Yeah, there was a press chopper sharing the air with us when you guys came out."

Fuck. Just what she needed. The entire world watching her have a breakdown. "Lovely." She took a deep drink of her beer. "Don't tell me... ugh, I don't *wanna* know what they said about me." Weak, they would say. Weak, damaged, fragile survivor of Autar. No wonder Alisia was repulsed by her.

"No.. nothing overdone. Something like 'here we see Major Terone and Regan Grier, obviously this has been a trying day,' blah blah blah."

"Well.. that's survivable. Nothing like 'Look at the lesbian crybaby curling up to her unrequited love for a little cry'?"

Parker smiled softly with sympathy in his eyes. "No, your secret's safe from the world for now. It was pretty rough though, huh?"

"I've seen worse, it just reminded me of a lot of stuff."

"The first fall."

"Yeah. What a mess that was. Seeing all those people.. well..." Regan slid into her own little world and her eyes began to glaze, staring into her drink.

Parker tapped his finger abruptly on the table. "Topic change!"

"Meh?" Regan looked at him, still a little removed from the world.

"Let's talk about something else."

Three body canisters containing samples from the mall mob were wheeled into the Yute base lab on trolleys. Alisia was now a passing acquaintance to the aged lab head, 'Doc Brock' who looked like he was in desperate need of some sun. She handed him the mobile server she had recovered and told him what she knew.

"So, if you can figure anything more, or if you notice anything different about these zombies, it might help track this guy down."

"Why would these zombies be different?" the wiry scientist asked, already prodding the canister.

"Whatever or whoever was controlling them, and taking possession of them.. well, these ones might have something extra on them or in them to make it possible. I don't know. Also compare them to the one we brought in from the warehouse office job. I'm pretty sure our new friend 'Erebus' was in there too, for a bit."

Alisia thanked him, and waved towards the back of the lab where she spotted a few faces eyeing her. She headed back to the airlimb and arrived just in time to see a civilian delivery man with a forklift style dolly loading a palette of miscellaneous goods onto the airlimb under Regan's supervision.

"Just leave it in here," she said, gesturing to the floor of the main bay. "I'll worry about it from there."

"What the heck is this?" Alisia asked, a little annoyed.

"Heeeheee... I went and did some net shopping the other day. It's here!" Regan peeked into the plastic-wrapped bundle of products as the delivery man set the hand cart's forks down. Regan thanked him with a chipper smile, and dismissed him. He walked past Alisia who was still a little stunned.

"What the fuck did you buy?"

"Oh, all kinds of things. Hey, 'leesh, do we have a new mission?"

"No. Until the lab boys tell us something or another attack breaks out, we're on easy standby."

Regan dug her nails into the plastic package and smiled like a little girl who'd had too much sugar. "*Ha!* Then it's time to go!"

"Go? Where are y-" Then Alisia suddenly remembered about Regan's birthday. "Oh, Regan, I haven't had a chance to get you anything...!"

"Bah! I don't need your presents; I just need your presence! Remember? My tropical spot! Get Kris to drop us off!"

Alisia regretted agreeing to come with her on her little vacation, but it was too late to back out. With any luck she could park herself by the hotel pool and Regan wouldn't pester her too badly, being surrounded by the public. Ack. The public. Regan might react badly. She would need support. This was going to be an interesting and difficult trip.

Chapter 36: Evil Exposed

Kris settled down and curled up to her new favorite victim, Parker. The heat and sweat would be unpleasant in a while, but for the moment they just soaked each other in, nested into Parker's bed.

"So, you have *no* interest in Alisia?"

"No," Parker said, "What an odd thing to bring up now.. got a jealous streak or something?"

Kris sneered to herself. So the nice little puppy had a *bit* of ego. "Mmmmm, no," she purred, "I just wondered..." She paused, and touched Parker in a way that got his attention. "I was just wondering what she's doing right now..." Kris sighed, "She's got to be feeling... lonely, in that big room, all alone."

Parker smirked. "It sounds like *I'm* the one who should be feeling jealous."

"Mmmmm, no...." Kris made a fake little giggle, the type that men seemed to like to hearing. "She doesn't like girls. I think I know what she needs..." Her touch became a bit more suggestive.

"What the hell?"

It wasn't quite the reaction Kris was hoping for. "Come on... she's hot, isn't she? She could probably use the attention of a man..."

Parker's stomach turned at Kris's implied vulgarity. "She's my commander!"

"She's a wommmmmmannnn...." Kris gasped.

"What? No! Why do you want me with her? I thought we were doing ok right here, you and me."

Oh great, he's grown attached or something. Press on.. "Yeah, we're doin' ok, but you and Alisia... think of it.. she's so strong on the job, so commanding.. then off duty, she's so... demure.. so... mmmm.... wouldn't you like to get deep into her- head,... and see what makes her... makes her... tick?"

Parker leaned back and widened his eyes. "You're after Regan..!"

"*What?!*" Fuck, that was an unexpected and unwelcome jump of logic.

"You want Regan but you need to get Alisia away from her, and you want me to do it! Well too bad." Parker was now rather insulted. Feeling regret and disgust crawling up on him, he sat up and started looking for his clothes.

Kris gave up on the seductive bit. "If I wanted a girl, there's billions of em out there. Regan's not special!" Kris spoke with notable spite.

Parker fumbled into his shirt. "She is so! You and her were an item right? You wouldn't want to get back with her at all?"

Kris's eyes narrowed behind her glasses, and they flashed of hate for just a moment. "No." She started getting dressed, intending to leave.

Parker was a little startled. Then it hit him, and he spoke before considering it. "You just want to hurt her."

Motion and sound stopped.

Kris turned, half dressed, to look at Parker. Her eyes told no tales, but her jaw trembled. "Shut the fuck up. Where the hell's my bra?" Her voice was quiet and eerily calm.

"You didn't bring one." Parker replied. His flat tone demanded a response to his prior accusation, but Kris ignored him. "She rejected you, didn't she? You didn't dump her, it was the other way around." Parker's tone was softened now, but only a little. Kris stared into him with an expression which refused to reveal anything. Parker pushed his luck. "Don't tell me *you loved her*.. you, the evil, evil slut?"

"I thought I told you to shut up. Love is a crutch."

Parker tried to read her tone, or her voice, but she had practiced them too well. "Yes, love is support. It was meant that way. It keeps people together."

"I'm going to be sick." Kris snapped away and left, stumbling on the doorframe. Parker considered giving chase... but no, not now.

Kris was still putting herself together after she got to her room, still angry, when her comm popped on.

"Kris?" It was Alisia. "I supplied some co-ordinates to the 'limb. I could use a drop-off, then we're on leave for a couple days."

"Fine." Kris snapped. What she was feeling was "Fine, what the fuck ever." Fucking Parker. She could feel him just down the hall. She could feel him judging her. For the first time in a long time, the phrase 'evil slut' hurt her. She stepped out of her door, doing her damnedest to rip the door off its tracks as she opened it. She stormed around the corner and almost ran over Alisia.

"Woah, Captain, slow down." Alisia seemed to be in 'non-business' mode, although she was still in full uniform.

". sorry Sir. If you'll excuse me, I'll get us airborne. Where the heck are we going?"

"I don't know the details. Some resort Regan picked out."

"Regan?" Kris bitterly applauded Regan in her mind. Sneaky little bitch. "I see." Kris walked off towards the operations room. She walked with such a spiteful stride that Alisia was surprised that her heels didn't leave dents in the plate metal floor. Alisia had never seen her so mad before... Kris was always so smooth and aloof. The aloof side was unnerving, but this one was outright frightening. A part of Alisia hoped that Kris would do something stupid and give her an excuse to transfer her out as Regan wanted.

Chapter 37: Trapped

Alisia opened the bay door and felt tropical warmth flood in. The shore of an island could be seen ahead. It grew closer. At least Regan had taste. The airlimb slowed to a stop thirty meters from shore, three meters above the sea. The engines revved down to a quiet hover. Alisia could now hear the sea, gently singing its ancient song.

Regan approached. She was rolling her giant palette of cargo along. It dwarfed Alisia's overnight bag. Regan was already in the spirit of things. Her usual skimpy outfit had been replaced with a different skimpy outfit. A racy swimsuit under her usual leather jacket.

"You're taking that whole thing?" Alisia asked, pointing at Regan's cargo.

"Yeah, I bought most of it just for this trip!" She gazed out to the island shore. "It's amazing. The satellite photos don't do it justice."

"Sate....? What? Where are we?"

Regan smirked. "It's unnamed. There's no tourist trade here. I found it by pouring over satellite photos and this looked ideal."

Alisia had to admit, it looked amazing. Soft white sand, cerulean water, and seemingly untouched jungle farther up the beach. "Uh.. wait a sec. Are you telling me there's *no* civilization on this island?"

"Correct! A private little spot to spend a weekend! That's why all the luggage! This is also a camping weekend!" Regan spread her arms as if to embrace her little island. Previously unnoticed, Kris chose that moment to shove Regan out the door. Alisia gasped and reached out to Regan in vain. Regan formed a fist for Kris in reflex just before hitting the water.

Kris laughed in delight.

Alisia watched Regan flounder amidst various curses. "... You realize she's just gonna kick your ass."

Kris kept watching Regan, and quietly responded ".......yeah."

"Was it worth it?"

"..... yeah."

Regan finally stabilized, and shouted up at Kris. "*What the hell?!*"

Kris waved coyly. "That's your fee. I fly you out here and pick you up, and I get to make you wet!"

Regan muttered something. Alisia guessed that it was something about 'evil slut'.

"Alright smartass!" Regan yelled up, "Get onto the beach and unload the gear!" Regan turned and started swimming to shore. Kris headed back for the operations room.

Alisia looked at Regan and thought. "Aw hell, that's not nice." She stripped her boots and fatigues and tossed them on the luggage heap, revealing her own swimsuit. Looking at it now, she wished she had something a little more frumpy, but what the hell. The airlimb started to float towards shore accelerating, but Alisia jumped out landing a few meters in front of Regan.

She righted herself and found Regan looking at her with curiosity.

"I couldn't let you swim to shore all alone and sad," Alisia said cheerfully, "It's your freakin' birthday. We're here to have fun, right?"

Regan smiled the most carefree, innocent smile Alisia had ever seen on her. Regan swam over and hugged Alisia. "That's the spirit, 'leesha!"

Alisia knew there was nothing sexual about the hug, but she couldn't help being very aware at how scantily clad they both were and how much skin contact was being made. "Let go, stupid, I need to swim!"

They met the airlimb on shore. Parker had already unloaded the gear, and he was trying to not look like he was watching as Alisia and Regan came out of the water. After some goodbyes, the airlimb lifted off.

Alisia watched it as the engines grew quieter in the distance. That's when it all sunk in.

She was alone.

With Regan.

On an uninhabited tropical island.

For the whole weekend.

Nowhere to run.

She turned around slowly, expecting to see Regan with an evil, evil grin, possibly in some suggestive pose. Thankfully, Regan was simply digging through the luggage for a towel. She tossed one at Alisia, too.

"Thanks." She did a quick job of drying off and noticed Regan watching her a bit. A whole weekend of this. What were they going to do? She dreaded to think what Regan was planning. As if Regan read her mind, she spoke up.

"So, I brought a lot of stuff. There's an inflatable raft if we wanted to do that, I have a portable terminal in here somewhere, a tent, all kinds of food, you name it." She grabbed a couple beach blankets and laid them out. Alisia spotted a large beach umbrella in the heap and set it up.

Soon, they were both sitting, enjoying the sun, the sounds of the surf, and a couple sweet, colourful drinks.

"Not a bad birthday party you've thrown yourself here, Regan. I feel a bit silly."

"Why?"

"Because this kind of thing is supposed to be set up by your friends, not yourself."

"Would you have done *this*?"

True. Alisia was planning a cake, and maybe a short pub visit. That would have probably been preferable, but she did promise. Why was that, again?

Regan rolled over and wiggled like an anxious little kid. She let out a giggle then rolled off onto the sand, and kept going.

Alisia watched, waiting for it to make sense, but Regan just kept rolling around, throwing up sand. "Alright you toddler, what the hell are you doing?"

Regan halted and faced Alisia with a big grin. She looked like a puppy who'd just heard its name called. "Our own beach! No tourists! No fat, sweaty men in speedos! It's all ours!"

Alisia smiled a softly amused giggle.

Regan ran over to the terminal and started up some music. "Let's go for another swim!" She whipped out a couple meter and a half foam pole pool toys from the luggage and tossed one at Alisia. "Come on!" Regan started running for the water.

Alisia stood, holding the foam pole like a quarterstaff. It was amazing how alive Regan seemed here. It was nice to see for a change. Alisia started running after Regan after being coaxed some more. Alisia loved the water. The feel of it, the weightlessness. She was soon in up to her shoulders. Regan was nearby doing underwater flips, rotating around her pool toy. Oh god. Toys. Did Regan have any other 'toys' in the luggage? Fear spread through Alisia. What the hell was she doing here?! At that moment, Regan's foam pole descended on Alisia's head. *Fap!*

"*Pow!*" Regan yelled. No, this was not the same Regan that made sexual innuendos and brash attempts at seduction. She did, however, deserve retaliation. Alisia started to lift her foam pole out of the water, but not in time to block the next strike. Alisia used the pole to send a large wave at Regan, which made her recoil for a bit. Alisia chose her actions very carefully.

Playful, fine, but she wasn't going to be dragged into some wet, tropical 'pillow fight'.

While Regan was in a minor retreat, Alisia flipped back and floated onto her back, gently kicking away. It served to end the little fight before it got too physical. Alisia felt very proud of the flexibility of her heavily trained tactical mind, but there was one effect she hadn't thought about.

Regan stood there, half-floating, water lapping just below her nose. In the sudden quiet with only the sea, and distant music, she watched in awe as Alisia swam slowly away.

It was art. No, it was something greater than that. Alisia lifted her arm slowly and reached back, to stroke the water again. Regan just watched silently as her goddess floated along. Time was meaningless.

Alisia was suddenly aware that it was too quiet. Worried that Regan might not be okay, or worse, that she was sneaking up on her, Alisia rose to an upright position and looked at Regan. She was now several meters away. Regan's eyes were wide, but the expression told little.

"You okay?" Alisia said quietly.

Regan took a moment to realize that her goddess was addressing her. ".... uh, hi." She said, momentarily rising her mouth above the water.

Alisia suddenly looked very worried. "Hi. Are you okay, Regan?"

Regan sighed and closed her eyes, unable to endure the goddess's gaze any further. "Yeah, I'm fine." She said, wondering if her voice was convincing. She felt the water move her around, and listened to its sounds. Regan imagined the vision right in front of her that she could not bear to actually look at.

Alisia treaded over to Regan. The sound it made became all Regan could think of. She listened to Alisia's body getting closer and closer. Less than a meter now? Close enough to touch, for sure. Alisia let out a tiny sigh, a music beyond beauty to Regan's ears.

Regan opened her eyes, surprised that no tear escaped. Alisia was looking right into her eyes. My god, those green eyes. Regan felt like trash in front of this perfection, which looked at her like this, with compassion.

Alisia clued in a bit. "Maybe this wasn't such a good idea." she said, turning her eyes to shore. "Maybe we should go back."

"I'm okay." Regan sighed, closing here eyes and floating back like Alisia had before.

For some time, the two enjoyed the sea, floating peacefully, but keeping a distance from each other. Alisia worried while Regan cried salty tears into the salty water.

Some hours later, Regan realized that the sky she'd been staring up at was turning dark. She righted herself and looked around. She had floated farther from the shore than she thought. She looked around for Alisia, finally spotting her up on the beach, sitting back on the blankets. She swam back to the beach, but when she got closer to Alisia, Regan found she was already asleep. Regan thought about setting up the tent, but with the weather as it was, it seemed like the tent would not be needed on this trip. She made herself a 'nest' out of blankets near Alisia and watched TV on the terminal for a little bit. It was still a bit early.

She turned her attention to Alisia, sleeping peacefully and oblivious. She was on her back, leaning up a bit on a couple of blankets under her head and torso, just lazily spread out. It was far better a thing to watch than the terminal, so Regan turned it off. Alisia had a surprising number of empty cooler bottles near by. Three was a lot for Alisia. Maybe it was a sign that Alisia was relaxing a bit, finally. Was it because Regan wasn't around at the time?

It was all so awkward. Regan curled up close, but not too close, moving a couple bottles out of the way. She watched Alisia breathing. Her chest rose and fell, and Regan found her own breathing becoming faster. She reached out for Alisia's nearby hand but decided not to touch.

It felt like forever, but even with her greatest temptation laying nearly naked just an arm's reach away, Regan finally found sleep.

The next day found Alisia awake first. Although Regan had packed mostly junk-food and pre-fab meals, Alisia did her best to arrange what she felt was a presentable breakfast, which she laid in front of Regan for when she awoke.

When they were both ready for the day they made some use of the inflatable raft, and later explored the jungle a bit. There were no awkward moments, Regan put extra effort into not causing them, but it was very difficult.

When the evening came, they settled into their nests and watched some TV on the terminal over a snack-ish supper, and more drinks than Regan had ever seen Alisia pack away. The movie broke to commercial, and Regan turned down the volume.

"Leesha?" She asked in a shy voice, "Have I been good today?"

Alisia was a bit surprised. "Good? Oh. You mean... well... yes, you've been really good, actually... When you brought this whole thing up, I was expecting some tourist trap resort. To be honest, I had all these plans to.. well.. not avoid you.. but escape the kinds of situations where.. well..."

"Where I would hit on you..." Regan said shamefully.

"Well, yeah. But here, I can't rely on any of the distractions I was counting on. I wanted separate rooms, but that didn't work out because there are no rooms!"

Regan giggled under her breath. "I could have used this time to be really bad."

"Yeah," Alisia said, getting a bit nervous, "I... heh. Have no where to run."

"Since I've been so good, can I.. do something?"

Alisia's eyes widened with fear. She didn't speak, not knowing how to say "Oh god, please no, just leave me alone!" without sounding hurtful. Regan got closer and put an arm across Alisia's middle, snuggling up close.

Alisia's body was rigid with tension. Was that it? Could be worse. Regan felt the tension and was already ashamed. No, not ashamed. It was just painful to think that her touch would bring such displeasure.

The movie came back on and Regan turned the volume back to normal. She felt the humidity between her arm and Alisia's abdomen. The movie was not important in the slightest.

Alisia tried to ignore this woman, latched on to her side. If it was just a friend, it would be awkward, but this woman loved her. Stupid lesbian. She tried to relax. Better to watch the movie than give herself an ulcer over this. Just imagine it was a big teddy bear. In a bikini, who's smelling your hair. "Oh my god," Alisia thought, "She's smelling my hair."

Regan was in heaven. Holding Alisia wasn't quite as nice as she'd hoped, since she was so tense, but Regan was thrilled with having her face buried in Alisia's fiery mane. The gentle scent seemed to fill her heart, when suddenly, magic happened.

Alisia relaxed.

Suddenly, this tense bundle Regan was holding just melted. Regan felt them fit just a little bit better together. A tiny bit more body contact. It was incredible. Regan felt her heart speed up again. Her body filled with adrenaline. The relaxing moment was over for Regan, just as Alisia had found it. Regan began to tense up, fighting her passion. She closed her eyes but found only irrepressible, erotic urges. Alisia was right in her arms! Regan imagined all the things she might be able to do before Alisia could squirm away. No, no. That wouldn't do. That would ruin everything. But she had to do something.

"Alisia," Regan whispered nearly in a rasp. Alisia's body tensed again, but this time it only served to fuel Regan's lust. "I want my birthday present now." She almost sounded as if she were in pain, and in a way, she was.

Alisia backed her head up so she could look at Regan. "Uh... I told you, I didn't get a chance." She knew that's not what Regan meant, but she could hope. Regan tightened her grip on Alisia. "I... may I kiss you?"

Alisia tossed back her head. "I came with you to your little trap, you've been cuddled up to me for half an hour, isn't that-"

Alisia felt a kiss on her neck, followed by hot, heavy breath, and another kiss closer to the chin. Alisia was shocked. The next kiss was bound to be aimed at her mouth. She felt Regan's breath draw near, her hair, everywhere, her near-closed eyes looking up at her own. She was almost on top of her.

"No" Alisia whispered, pushing Regan away gently. "That's more than enough." Despite her objections there was pleasure in the kisses on her neck. The tingle of them still remained, and she was terrified of it. She faced Regan who was sitting with her eyes closed, and breathing heavily, still awash in the moment past.

"Alisia... " Regan swept her hair out of her face and looked at her. "I'm so sorry. I didn't mean to. Not like that."

Alisia curled up with a nearby blanket. She'd never been so close to Regan's .... Regan's heat. They looked at each other silently for a while, hoping the other would say something.

Eventually, Alisia lay back down, covered by the blanket. She looked back at Regan and held out an arm. "Come back here, friend." She was inviting Regan to cuddle up again through the protection of the blanket.

Regan was speechless. Slowly, as if afraid of a trap, she returned to the original position, and they continued watching the movie. Alisia felt the need to break some tension. "Now see, silly? You made us miss part of it."

Regan giggled, tightening her hold, happy to again have a face full of red hair. Her giggle silenced and slowly turned into a meek little cry.

"Shh." Alisia soothed. This only made Regan cry harder. Regan didn't know if she was crying because she couldn't have Alisia, or because Alisia called her 'friend' with such a compassionate tone, or that she allowed her to cuddle back up. Whatever it was, it hurt somehow. The more she tried not to think of it, the harder it was, and she was soon sobbing uncontrolled. Alisia clutched Regan hard.

"Hush, Regan. Nothing's wrong. I'm doing my best not to hurt you, but this is only going to get harder."

Regan struggled to get words out, "I know!"

Alisia turned off the terminal and held her sobbing friend tight, with all the love she could dare to give. Regan's crying and the soothing sea were all there was to be heard, until mercifully, sleep came to take away their problems until the next day.

Chapter 38: Bitter Reunion

Parker stood silently at the entrance of the dark operations cockpit, leaning against the bulkhead. He'd been there for some time. Kris sat facing away, watching various displays, none of which were important. She could feel Parker's eyes drilling into the back of her chair. She couldn't stand it anymore.

She removed all emotion from her face, and turned around. "What do you want?" Her voice was calm, but accusing.

Parker scuffed his boot onto the floor and looked down grimly.

"Sex?" Kris asked, "If that's it, go away. I'm not in the mood."

Parker stood silent for a moment more, then replied. "No." Then a long silent pause before he elaborated. "I'm not sure what I want."

"Then bugger off." Kris turned around, back to her meaningless displays.

Parker stayed. He struggled to find the right thing to say. "I'm sorry." It always seemed like a safe thing to say.

"What? What the hell for?"

"Accusing you of using me to hurt Regan."

Kris turned back around, looked at him, and hunkered down on her elbows. "Why?" she shrugged carelessly. "I did."

Parker had hoped he was wrong. "So... that's it?"

Kris's expression turned bitter. "What the hell do you want? You want me to run into your arms and profess my undying love or some shit?"

Parker was silent. No, he didn't expect that, but he was hoping she'd say that there was *something* between them. Parker stood straight. "I'm sorry to have inconvenienced you, Sir." He turned and left for his quarters.

Kris stared spitefully in his direction for what felt like a long time. She'd show him. A small sound came from her terminal. They were approaching the island.

Regan and Alisia spotted the airlimb and were ready for pickup. They didn't talk much that morning, but the usual tension was sprinkled with a small, temporary confection of peace. Regan walked over to Alisia, who was leaning on the big luggage heap.

"Hey, 'leesh, wanna mess with their heads a bit?"

Alisia raised an eyebrow with a small smile.

"Hehe, good. Then just play along a bit when we see them. Let me handle it. Subtlety is the key." Regan lowered her own shoulder strap and let it fall into a lazy position. The airlimb was soon parked on the beach. The bay door opened, revealing Parker.

"Hey ladies, how was your weekend?" Alisia noted that he seemed to lack a bit of his usual enthusiasm.

Regan gave her most seductive smile and glanced her hand across the small of Alisia's back as she walked past her. "Mmm, no complaints." She then 'noticed' that her strap was down, and pulled it back up with an exaggerated motion which caused her assets to bounce a bit. If Parker took the hint, he wasn't showing it. He stepped forward to help with the cargo. "Good, good."

Regan's tease did hit one target though. Unnoticed in the relative dark in the far end of the main bay, Kris walked off, back towards the ops cockpit. "Great," she thought. "Look at the happy couple." She considered flying the airlimb into the nearest rock. Of course, between the limb's safety systems and remote HQ piloting assistance, that would be impossible... but it was still an attractive thought.

Chapter 39: Poor Parker 2

Officially, AZU-1's leave was over, but there was still nothing new to do. Zombies had kept quiet, and Doc Brock's crew were still fussing over the samples taken.

Alisia noticed that Kris and Parker were both acting odd. She wasn't too concerned with Kris, but she was worried about Parker. Alisia kept an eye out for an opportunity to corner him, and finally she noticed him going into his room. She followed a little after, and knocked.

"What?" His voice came a bit sharply.

"Parker? Can I come in?"

Through the door, she heard him jump up and approach. The door opened, to reveal Parker's surprised face. "Major! Sorry, ah, what can I do for you?"

"You OK? You seem ... off."

"Oh, no Major. Nothing to be concerned about. I'm perfectly fit for duty."

"That's not what I asked."

"Major?"

"Look, Parker. I've worked with you a long time, right? I requested you for this post and you're just kinda...my responsibility." As she said that, it reminded her of parts of her feelings for Regan.

Parker, on the other hand, took it differently. "Oh, Major, don't worry. I'm not going to do anything to endanger the unit or anything!"

"No, no, no. I'm not worried about that. Stupid, I'm worried about you. Are you..." she pointed at him and jabbed his chest with her index finger, "alright?"

At that moment there was the sound of a door opening down the hall. Parker was immediately alarmed that he would have to face Kris, and forgot the obvious; that Kris's door was right across from him and still closed. He yanked Alisia by the jacket and pulled her in, closing the door. He rested his back against the door with an expression of fear. He then realized what he'd just done, and looked over to Alisia.

She looked furious, but somehow calm. "Parker. Robert. What the fuck is going on?"

"Oh shit.. sorry Sir!... ah...."

"Sit down, stupid."

Parker obeyed, and sat on the corner of his bed, head in his hands. "It's Kris."

"What, she's hunting you through the ship with a harpoon?"

"Damn, for all I know, she is." He took a breath and began to spill his guts. "We... uh.. slept together a couple times, and she wants to hurt Regan, and she thinks I wanna marry her or something, and she's kinda scary when she talks to me now, and Regan warned me, and-"

"Hold the hell on." Alisia needed to absorb a bit. "Ok, first, she wants to hurt Regan?"

"Yeah. She wanted me to seduce you and take you away from Regan, just to hurt her."

"You? Seduce me?" Granted, Parker was attractive enough, but even ignoring the whole rank thing, she and he had a very smoothly running platonic working relationship, which neither of them would want to change.

"Yeah, that was her plan. She tried to trick me into it, but I called her on it, and now she's mad or something, and things are ugly."

"So... now you're avoiding her. I noticed she was acting funny too. It explains a lot... I can't believe all this happened under my nose...!" She just now began to absorb the part about the Captain and the Sergeant sleeping together.

"Er.... sorry...?"

"Ugh. You've gotten yourself into a mess, Parker. So, what happens now?"

"You court marshal me and have me shot?" Parker joked, but he *was* worried about official ramifications.

"Relax. I'm not a stickler for those kinds of rules. What are you going to do about Kris?"

"I don't know...."

"Are you in love or anything?"

".....I don't know. She's not very nice, you know... but..."

"But she's hot? Is that it?"

"Well, yes, she is, but..."

"How am I supposed to give you good leader-like advice when you don't even know what you want?"

"Major?" The General's voice popped into her comm, interrupting the conversation.

"Yes General?"

"I've just been talking with the lab boys. Put the unit on active standby. We have some interesting news. Can I see you in my office?"

"On my way."

Chapter 40: A Rat in a Hole

The airlimb quickly approached an abandoned-looking complex of warehouses, once used to process and store fish. Brock's lab traced many of the parts of the mobile nanite server, and other departments ran down recent shipment records.

The various components had all been shipped in proportional quantities to this remote, seaside facility. Whoever made the mobile server was a whiz at electronics, but no criminal mastermind. Kris brought their attention to a modern communications array which looked very out of place among the rest of the older, weathered structures.

As the airlimb made a slow circle around the shoddy complex, Alisia spotted some damage while watching out the bay door.

"Hey guys, look at this." She placed a VTag marker on a large hole in one wall. "Looks like it was bombed or something."

"Nah." Kris said, "The debris pattern suggests some kind of missile. From the air, probably."

Regan looked on quietly while Alisia closed the bay door half way. "Zombies using missiles and aircraft?" Regan said with cynicism.

"Well, if this Erebus guy controlled a zombie into doing it, it would be possible I suppose, but that doesn't make sense. For one thing, it doesn't seem to be his style. And if this is *his* base of operations... why attack it?"

"Maybe he left," Parker reasoned. "Used it to build what he needed, left, and blew it up to cover his tracks."

"Hmm. But the wall... it's part of a large warehouse, but the damage isn't near anything important looking." Alisia observed.

"It's an entry point for a ground based attack?"

"Yeah."

"So he forcibly invaded an abandoned fish warehouse?"

"Nope" Kris said, "This is fresh. Not more than a few days."

"Someone else got here before us." Alisia mumbled to herself. "Well, now I'm curious. Kris, bring us in."

The airlimb set down near the damaged wall in such a way as to provide the most cover from all sides when Alisia and Regan got out. Silently, they crept to the edge of the hole, and Alisia peered in. The warehouse looked a lot bigger from the ground. Three stories high, and about two blocks in area. Thin metal support pillars broke the expanse of the interior, as well as the occasional pile of abandoned forklift palettes and crates.

The smell of death was in the air, but was it zombie flesh or merely the legacy of billions of fish who passed through? They stepped through the hole and hugged the wall inside. They were both a little confused what to be more worried about; zombies busting through walls and grabbing them, or Erebus controlling a zombie with a gun and spotting them if they walked in the open.

The charred ground was still dry and powdery, confirming Kris's opinion about the damage being fresh, but more telling were the clean areas.

"Looks like someone swept up here." Alisia said.

"Janitorial zombie?" Regan joked. Then she spotted a glint of metal, just to the side of the swept area. "There was a gunfight here." It was a fragment of a hollow point bullet. "I can't tell what kind of round it was, or the cal, but it's not a P90 round."

"That confirms it. Someone else got here first. Hey Kris-"

"Yeah." Kris said through the comm, "I had the same thought. I called around though, no one we know has been here. The General was quite firm in that notion."

"Great. Terrorists or something? That's not my department." Alisia sighed.

"We're not leaving, are we?" Regan said, scanning her surroundings.

"No. Not yet. Kris, take the limb up and keep Parker in a good support fire position. We're gonna take a walk."

"Roger."

Alisia and Regan stepped farther into the warehouse, following the wall to the left. The sound of the airlimb faded as it rose and its shadow passed across the floor. They headed slowly towards a door that led towards the newer communications array. They stood to either side of the door and Alisia tried the doorknob. It was unlocked. She pushed the door in and peeked in quickly before backing off around the doorway again.

"Looked clear. Dark, but clear."

"Not too dark, we can adjust." Regan said, looking in from the side. They burst in and checked all the corners. Nothing moving. Alisia found a light switch by the door and flipped it on. The fluorescent lights flickered hesitantly to life, some of them burnt out. They saw an empty desk, a chair, and a pull-out sofa. Empty boxes of various non-perishable foods were stacked sloppily in the corner. It was a big room, but largely empty.

Alisia looked closer at the floor beside the desk. Dust and grime revealed that there was once something on it with round pads. "Another desk here." she assumed. "Wow. I guess whoever came, they took Erebus, and all his toys."

Regan found another bullet fragment under the sofa. "Yeah, with force."

A 'thump' sound came from across the room. Instantly, the two girls had their P90's aimed at it. A roughly square ring of dust was rising from the floor. The girls made eye contact with each other, and nodded.

With the dust now freshly disturbed, a hatch in the floor planks could now be clearly seen. Alisia walked up to it carefully. She knocked three times with the front grip of her P90, and hopped back.

"Who's there?" A familiar voice came from below the hatch.

"Erebus?" Alisia called out, "Get the hell up here, and keep your hands where I can see them!"

The hatch raised, eight fingers grasping onto the edge of the floor. In the darkness under the semi-opened hatch, two frantic eyes darted back and forth. "Hmm, it *is* you."

Regan stepped up to the hatch, and brutally kicked the hatch cover across the room. The wiry, grungy man inside cringed down in his dirty little hiding hole. His messy hair was white, but he couldn't have been older than thirty.

He hissed, squinting against the light. "Blah! Light! Who is it? *One!* One gun-toting bimbo! Ah, ha ha ha ha. *Two!* Two gun-toting bimbos! Ah, ha ha ha ha!" He tried poorly to contain his self-amused snickering.

Regan imagined what would happen to his stupid little grin with a few good solid kicks from her boot.

"Kris?" Alisia spoke into her comm, "Feed me the procedure for making an arrest or something. I've never had to read a zombie its rights."

Chapter 41: Dangerous Civilians

When they arrived back at Yute base, 'Erebus' was escorted by soldiers from the airlimb to a holding cell. Alisia left the others on the airlimb, and went to deal with the reports and talk with the General.

After some time, Alisia returned to the airlimb and called a meeting for the unit. They met in the airlimb mess as usual.

Alisia stood up once the others had settled. "Well, 'Erebus' was less than forthcoming, as expected, but his prints, DNA and dental records confirm him to be one 'Jonathan Coll'. Interestingly, he used to work at AutarLabs."

Regan made a sour face. "Ugh. He might have even worked alongside my brother." Regan had actually seen Coll before, but the encounter wasn't memorable enough for Regan to remember from before Autar went to hell.

"Possibly. But shortly after arriving there, he started his own projects on the side. It seems no one at AutarLabs gave it much thought. Rumor implies he was being paid for these projects by an outside organization." Alisia said, thumbing through various printouts.

Parker spoke up. "Fuck, you're kidding. Does this mean the fall of Autar...?"

"Oh, hold on, there's more," Alisia said, "There's hints about this organization, who somehow got Coll extra freedoms in AutarLabs, but this group is not named in any records, and no one seems to know what it is."

"So what does that all mean?" Regan asked.

"Well... it means it's almost certain that this mystery group and Erebus were responsible for the fall of Autar. Conventional weapons development divisions *may* have had a hand in it, whether they intended to or not. Same goes for AutarLabs."

"What the hell? So the fall was what... a field test of a bio-weapon made by some black-ops research unit?" Parker asked.

"I asked the General about this mystery group. He was as surprised as I was, and seemed determined to question the weapons dev. people about it, and their own sealed files."

"You trust him?" Regan asked grimly.

The others suddenly felt a little shaken by the thought that their General could have had something to do with Autar's fall. Alisia thought about it objectively for a moment before responding. "Yeah, I do."

"Alright."

"There's something else I haven't figured out though." Alisia pondered, "If Autar *was* a weapons field test... well... why Autar? There was a lot of money and expectations poured into Autar.. wouldn't it make more sense to attack a less important city... or even one in a non-friendly country or something?"

Everyone was quiet for a moment, considering everything.

"Maybe it was an accident after all.. " Parker suggested, "Maybe this mystery unit just slipped up and it got loose. Or maybe they were working on it with Erebus, but it was AutarLabs' fault anyway, as we thought..."

Kris popped in. "That doesn't totally explain it all. The Autar A.I. was pretty advanced. That kind of behavior doesn't just evolve on its own, by accident. There had to be some intentional influence.. And if we assume that Autar wasn't a logical test site for the zombie-nanites...."

"Then whoever triggered it did it as just a plain old attack. It was on purpose." Parker said.

"Which would mean a hostile country, or terrorists.. the mystery group could be working for... it doesn't make a lot of sense..."

"They didn't do it. They maybe developed it, but Erebus was the one who triggered it." Regan said, staring a hole into the table, grinding her teeth.

Alisia looked at Regan. "But why? What motive?"

Regan looked up at Alisia. "Motive? You saw the mall.. what he did to that person in the warehouse office, controlling that first zombie.. He's a fucking madman, that's his motive."

Erebus sat in his cell, pondering recent events. Somehow, despite his own genius, both Lancer and AZU-1 had found his hideout. He could have stayed hidden from AZU-1 probably, but since Lancer had taken all his toys, boat included, he needed a ride back to mainland. What else was he expected to do, swim?

Fucking Lancer. Sure, he took advantage of the position they put him in, and he essentially ignored the projects *they* wanted, in favor of his own fun, but they were taking things way too personal. They wouldn't have hesitated in the slightest to kill him on sight. At least AZU-1 was squeaky clean enough to play by the rules. Still, they could have put him in a nicer room.

Enough of this shit. He groped the inner side of his upper arm gently with his fingers. Where the hell is it? Finally he found the lump he was looking for. He held the lump between finger and thumb, and squeezed. It hurt. He should have put it under tougher skin. The lump popped inside his skin, dumping its payload. The skin still hurt, it was sure to bruise.

"Fly, my pretties, fly!" he whispered to the spot where the lump had been.

"So, you killed my brother." Regan's voice came out.

Erebus looked up to see Regan standing on the other side of the bars.

"Hello Miss Grier. I killed a lot of people, so there's a good chance."

"Harold Grier. He was in Autar. He worked with nanites in AutarLabs"

"Doesn't ring a bell."

"So, he didn't work with you?"

"I wasn't there very lo- Oh.. I see.. you want to know if *he* had anything to do with the fall, right?"

"Well?"

"Not that I know of."

It was a minor relief to Regan, even if Erebus didn't seem positive about it. "But the fact still remains," Regan said, aiming her P90 at him, "You still killed my brother."

Erebus hadn't accounted for this. These military folks are trained to follow rules, but Regan was a civilian. "You mean you don't want to see me go to trial, and all that?"

"Why? So you can become a celebrity on the news? Buy a year or two of time, maybe get acquitted? Maybe thrown in a looney farm and eat free on tax dollars?"

This was not good. Come on, think, Jonathan, think. Leverage. He needed leverage. "News celebrity, hm? Like you?"

Regan narrowed her eyes a bit.

"I caught you on the news just the other day, " Erebus said, "Coming out of the mall incident. Big hero. It looks like I hurt your feelings." He paused, but Regan did nothing. "You rely on the Major sometimes, don't you?" He watched as Regan's breathing betrayed her. Aha. That hug outside the mall... "You're.... close to her, aren't you?"

Regan tensed. "You shut up about her." Her grip on the P90 tightened, and she adjusted her aim.

Oops, maybe that was the wrong nerve to hit. "Ah, if you blow my head off now, you go to jail instead of me. Murdering a murderer is still murder, hm?"

Regan considered giving him a flesh wound instead, just to make a point. "It's a small price to pay to see you dead."

"Really? You're so impatient for an execution that you'd go to jail and be separated from your .... little friend?"

Regan began to hate the manipulative little bastard on a whole new level. In some ways, it just gave her more reason to pull the trigger. So she did. Bits of cement rained down on Erebus' head from where Regan had fired a single round near the barred window. A guard ran up from around the corner, rifle ready.

"At ease, soldier," Regan said, "Seems I had a little accidental discharge." The guard sized up the situation and gave Regan a little nod before leaving. Regan was expecting a little bit of satisfaction, but after she left, it was Erebus who was smiling.

Chapter 42: Stupid Lesbian

Alisia walked out of the Airlmb onto the base's top deck. It was a warm evening, and the sun was just reaching that part of the sunset which did its best to mimic her hair.

Regan was not far off, sitting on one of the knee-height walls near the edge of the roof. She was facing away, towards the sunset, just enjoying the evening and trying to get Erebus out of her head for a while. A six pack sat nestled in her jacket on the ground, the first of which was now in Regan's hand.

Alisia felt social, so she wandered over. Before she spoke, Regan picked another can off the pack and held it out for Alisia.

"Hey love. Brew?" Regan's face was relaxed and happy. It was nice to see.

"Love, huh?" Alisia gave Regan an odd look as she accepted the can and sat down. She matched the softness Regan spoke with, but not the happiness. "You actually love me, don't you?"

"Yup." Regan confirmed with gentle cheer.

Alisia looked at Regan with a bit of surprise. "That.. doesn't bother you?"

"Nope. Why should it? You're great."

Alisia chuckled a little "Uh, because I don't love *you*?"

"You love me." Regan said with quiet confidence.

"I do?"

"Yup. You're just straight is all."

Alisia sighed. "And *that* doesn't bother you?"

"Hmm," Regan paused, sounding less happy, but still relaxed. "Nothin' to be done about that..." She leaned back and looked into the sunset, trying not to look at Alisia.

Alisia felt Regan's serenity slowly cracking, and felt guilty. "You... you still think I'm gonna give in, dontcha?" She smiled at Regan, who looked up with a little smile. Her eyes were glistening, and it made Alisia think. She looked down into her lap, and the open beer that sat there. "It... " Alisia took a deep breath. "It hurts me when you cry."

Regan's eyes widened a little, and as if by cue, a built up tear escaped. It rolled down the side of Regan's face away from Alisia's view. "Cry...?"

Alisia gripped the edge of the wall, and stared hard into the beer can. "I've heard you. I... I've seen you. And on the beach, I felt you. It feels like hell. I don't know what to do about it. It just hurts."

They were quiet for a moment that went on forever, when a footstep was heard from the airlimb. They both knew Parker wasn't around; it had to be Kris.

"No..." Regan whispered. "I can't deal with her now. Make her go away, do something." The whisper trembled. She was terrified.

Alisia did the only and first thing that came to her mind. She leaned over, and kissed Regan.

Regan's eyes widened again, and as Alisia's hand touched her cheek. Regan closed her eyes and kissed back. Alisia felt the wetness of the tear on Regan's cheek. And the warmth and softness of her lips.

Regan's mind was instantly numb. She was enslaved by blinding bliss. It could have been a second, or an hour, but eventually Alisia's lips drew away. The cold of the air touching where Alisia's lips had been felt cruel by comparison.

"She's gone." Alisia said quietly.

Regan was still leaned in, eyes closed. "Huh?"

"Kris. She's gone."

Regan began to slide back into reality. "Oh....? Oh..." She opened her eyes and was transfixed on Alisia's lips. Did that really happen? Alisia read Regan's face and looked away, concentrating very hard on taking a drink of her beer. But that wouldn't save her for long. She had to think of something to say. Regan was still staring at her, stunned. She put down her beer and stared hard into it.

"It... it didn't mean anything. It.... it got Kris to leave us alone, didn't it?"

Regan was silent.

"Don't go thinking I'm gonna go lez on you." Alisia said it with defensive spite, still denying Regan's stare.

Regan was silent.

"*Say* something, dammit!"

".....wow..."

"Aren't you listening? It didn't mean anything!"

Regan spoke softer than the breeze "You all but admitted you love me.... and then you kissed me.."

Alisia exploded. "*It's not like that, and you know it!*"

Regan maintained her gentle voice. "Don't care right now..!" She got up, and slowly ambled back to the airlimb.

Alisia watched Regan disappear into the airlimb, and stared for a moment. Alisia stood, quietly.

.....

"*Stupid fucking lesbian!*" Alisia threw her half empty beer off the building with all her might. A trail of flying, foaming beer streaked across the sunset behind it.

She watched it land in the grass far below with a snarl on her face, and was disappointed that the very earth didn't shatter by the impact. A glint of light could be seen as the can's remaining payload ensured a headache in the morning for a handful of grass.

"Stupid, stupid stupid." Alisia muttered. '*Kiss her*'? Was that the only way to keep Kris away from Regan? She could have walked over and talked to Kris, even ordered her away, but *no*, the first thing that had to pop into her head was a god damned kiss. Since when was it her job to protect Regan from Kris anyway? None of her business. Fucking stupid.

Alisia looked at her hand. It was cold where she had touched Regan's tear. Maybe it was her job to protect her. She looked down. Regan had forgotten her jacket and the four remaining beers. Alisia picked them up. The jacket kind of smelt like her.

Alisia wandered back in, kicking herself all the while. She stopped by Regan's door and dropped the jacket. She was going to take the beer to the fridge in the mess, but Alisia decided she wanted a couple. She knocked on Regan's door.

It was a short moment before the door slid open. Regan still had that stupid, blissful look on her face, which lit up at the sight of Alisia.

Alisia kicked the jacket on the floor into Regan's room.

"I'm taking two beers." She handed the other two to Regan. "Drink these, get buzzed, and go to sleep."

Alisia walked away for a couple steps. "And don't come into my room in the middle of the night."

Alisia walked away for a couple steps. "And would it kill you to actually *wear* your clothes?" She said, glaring at the jacket.

Alisia walked away for a couple steps. "And you'd better have something decent to wear for when we have to talk to press. I'm getting you some goddam pants at least. Fatigues."

Alisia walked away for a couple steps. "*And stop thinking about kissing me!*"

Regan beamed a smile that would burn the sun. Alisia grunted in disgust and stormed to her own room. Regan went back to her bed, now with two fresh beers, and held Alisia's old dog tags tight.

Kris slithered into the base club booth across from Parker, surprising him. "Well, I failed. Happy?"

"Huh?"

At that moment, the waitress came by to take an order from Kris.

"Oh," Parker said, "What do you want, Kris? I'll buy."

Kris reflexed to her usual teasing attitude. "Oh, I don't know, something hard."

The waitress did her best to ignore it, and Parker rolled his eyes.

"Fine," Kris said, "uh, house white, I guess."

Parker touched his finger to his stein and looked at the waitress. "May as well bring another of these, too." The waitress left.

"Hey, it could have been worse. I could have ordered a 'screaming orgasm', 'sex on the beach', or a 'long hard screw against the wall'."

Parker shook his head slowly with a smirk. "So, what am I supposed to be happy about you failing at?"

"Ugh." Kris leaned back. "Regan. I just saw her and the Major making out. Not to mention whatever they did on that beach."

Parker looked a little stunned. "Really? The Major gave in? No...."

"Looks like it. By now I bet they're... hmm."

The both of them slipped into their imaginations for a moment, when the waitress arrived with the order. She left, and Parker took up a new topic. "So.. what about us?"

"What, wanna fuck?" Kris said dispassionately.

Parker coughed a little. "That's not what I meant."

"Aw geez. Look, Robert. You're kinda fun and stuff, but this whole drama queen side of you really isn't my thing, alright?"

Parker just kinda looked into his beer, and drank down a mouthful.

Kris looked at him. "Christ, if you cry, I'll punch you."

"Would it be so bad if we were...?"

Kris downed her wine quickly, and put the glass down firmly. "Grow up, Parker." She stood, and began to turn. "Thanks for the drink. Come see me later if you find your balls." And with that, she started back to the airlimb.

Stupid baby. Next thing, he'd be asking her to the prom or some shit. She passed by where she'd seen Alisia and Regan kiss, and trouble brewed in her mind. She was soon standing between Regan's and Alisia's doors. Which were they in? Were these damn doors soundproof? Oh well, try one, then the other.

She whipped open Alisia's door, and pointed. "*Aha!*"

Alisia turned her head away from the terminal and looked at Kris. Regan wasn't here. "Is there something I can help you with?" Alisia asked sardonically.

"Eh?" Kris was shocked not to find the two of them at the very least, lip-locked on the bed. "Er.. never mind." She left and closed the door. She then turned around and opened Regan's door just wide enough to stick her head in.

Regan was in bed, half asleep. Her peaceful face soured at the sight of Kris. "What do *you* want?"

Kris looked around. Aside from the few beer cans on the floor, there were no signs of any particular fun. She looked Regan in the eye. "Wuss." then backed out, closing the door. What was wrong with these people?

Captain Harringer sat in the ops room of the unmarked Lancer airlimb. He stared at the communications terminal, waiting for Mr. Book to answer the call.

Finally Mr. Book's remarkably joyless face appeared. "Ah. Harringer. My apologies for making you wait so long. To keep things quiet,-"

"No apologies needed Sir, I understand entirely. The regular military, unit A Zed U one, has captured Coll. He's taken up the alias 'Erebus'."

"Really?" Mr. Book leaned back in his office chair, loosening his tie a little. "That's good I suppose. Someone should have him. Where Did they find him?"

"Right where we were looking. We must have missed him somehow. Either he was out at the time, or very well hidden."

"Damn it. Slippery bugger. Well, what's done is done. Can they link him to us?"

"Unlikely. Should we move to reclaim Coll? He might start talking about the wrong things."

".....no, I'm not willing to make a move directly against the regular military over this. We'd lose more than we'd gain. Keep an 'eye' on him though."

"Of course, Sir."

Chapter 43: A Brisk Walk

Jonathan lay in his jail cell, waiting. The little toys he released into his bloodstream should almost be done their work. He could have taken advantage of the effect already, but he saw no reason not to let them finish their task before exerting himself.

The guard came around about once an hour, and when the toys were done, he had just passed.

It was time to move. Jonathan was ready; *Erebus* was ready.

He got up to his window and gripped the bars. He strained hard and his newly nanite-reinforced muscles helped him pull the bar out of the wall. Chunks and bits of cement crumbled down. Erebus looked back around to see if anyone heard, or cared. Well, too late to go back now.

He yanked another bar, making a gap he could get through. First he did a sloppy job of making his bed look full. There was only one pillow but it might be enough to fool someone at a quick glance. Enough to buy some time. He squirmed out, and dangling three stories up, put the bars back as best as the damage would allow. Yeah, *that's* really gonna fool them for a long time.

He looked down and let go, sliding three stories down the wall. *Thump.* Hmm. That didn't hurt too bad. He looked at his hands. They were sore. They had already bruised badly from pulling the bars out. Hopefully the nanites would take care of that quickly. Alright. Now to run to the nearest electronics shop. And run he did. Not as fast as a car, but much faster than human. By the time he was noticed to be missing he'd be halfway to Meston.

Alisia pawed her nightstand for her buzzing comm and put it in her ear. "Hello? Major Terone here."

"Major?" It was the General. "I thought you'd like to know that Erebus has escaped."

"*What?*"

"We have people looking for him, but we're not having any luck. He's been loose up to an hour, so he couldn't have gone far. There are no vehicles missing."

"We're on it, General."

"Major, I really only wanted to keep you informed. There's not much else you can do right now that we're not already doing."

"Maybe not, but I'm not going to just sit here."

"Very well. Good luck, Major."

Alisia disconnected, and woke the others. "People, Erebus is loose. Let's go."

Shortly, Kris had them airborne. Alisia went over some logistics while Parker and Regan scanned the terrain out either side of the airlimb, through the scopes of zipper turrets. Regan had next to no experience with the zippers, but she had Parker give her a quick lesson one day.

"Parker," Regan said, "if you spot him first, let me take him down."

"Don't you think we should capture him?"

"Fuck it. He had his chance for a nice little trial and he decided to run. I wanna smear the fucker all over the ground."

"Yow. A little angsty, aren't we?" Parker hadn't seen Regan like this.

"You've seen what he's done. You tellin' me he doesn't deserve worse?"

"This wouldn't have anything to do with your brother would it?"

Regan paused. She'd always blamed her brother's death on the whole Autar incident.. some programming accident. It only recently sunk in for her that if Erebus caused it, he effectively killed Harold. "My bro worked with nanites for medical purposes. He and I were close. I can tell you for a fact that he had nothing but good intentions. This guy.. why the hell... but yeah, I guess this has a bit to do with my brother. Is that a problem?"

Parker smirked to himself. "Nope, just as long as we're clear."

Erebus staggered and collapsed against a tree. He'd been running for the better part of an hour. The Meston lights were an attractive pale hue over the horizon now. How far had he gotten in that time? Eighty clicks? He'd stayed within sight of the highway, and from what he could see, he'd been holding his own in terms of speed compared to the cars. His body burned though. Nothing the nanites couldn't take care of, of course. And the sooner he made it to Meston, the sooner he'd be safe- or at least safer- from search parties. He dragged himself up again, and shot off towards Meston.

"All this ground's been covered." Alisia mumbled to Kris as they both looked over different luminescent displays in the airlimb's darkened ops room. "He's either gotten some kind of ride, or he's underground."

Kris tapped around a map overlaid on the main navigation screen. "Well, there's no major underground infrastructure in the area that would get him anywhere useful, but there is the highway. Pretty easy to hitch-hike, I guess."

"There's already a checkpoint in place. They're stopping every vehicle to check for hitch-hikers. Presumably no one's going to hide a hitch-hiker from us. I hope so anyway. They're not about to strip search every vehicle.."

Regan's voice came to Alisia through the comm. "Hey, leesha, can you come here a sec?"

"Alright, hang on." Alisia left the ops room and headed back through the dim halls to where Regan was manning a gun. "What's up?"

Regan answered warmly. "I just wanted to see you."

"Yeah, here I am, what's up?"

Regan kept her eye on the scope, but reached out and took Alisia's hand. "I told ya, I just wanted to see you. Didn't wanna leave here, in case I missed him."

Alisia smiled a bit to herself. "I really should get back up there."

"Kris can handle that on her own." Regan said assuredly, "You wanna discuss tactics with her, you can use the comm."

"Aw, how cute," Alisia thought, "She's jealous."

"Well, that's not quite as effective. I need to see the maps and such. Don't worry, Regan." Alisia gave Regan's hand a little squeeze before leaving for the front again.

Erebus pushed through the pain. He was used to it. You have to be if you're going to experiment on your own body. Just think of the pain as a blinking light reporting bodily status, and then ignore it. The bruises on his hands from opening the barred window were almost entirely healed, but now it was his feet doing the complaining.

He had passed by the area of the checkpoint long before it was even set up- and even if he hadn't, he wasn't directly taking the highway anyway.

A gas station was coming up. He slowed down and came to a stop behind it as to not attract attention. He was a bit hungry. Certainly the nanites were getting a little low on juice by now, but they would have to wait just a little longer.

He walked in the front doors and greeted the clerk with a casual wave and easy smile. He stuck a chocolate bar in his pocket and opened a bag of chips, and started eating them right away. The clerk assumed that no thief would be quite so brazen, but he was cautious none the less. He rang up the two items as a subtle hint that he did indeed notice the chocolate bar.

Erebus looked around. "Oh, hey," he said, walking back for a pop out of the cooler, "Got any kind of pain killers?"

"Aspirin, Tylenol, Bayer..." The clerk said, adding the pop to the bill.

"Yeah, " Erebus said, walking back towards the counter, "Lemmie see those."

The clerk put them all on the counter for examination. Erebus immediately started opening one, and after picking out the cotton, he started swallowing them, washing them down with mouthfuls of pop.

"What the fuck?" The clerk said, now not so worried about shoplifting, "You tying to kill yourself?"

Erebus started opening the second bottle. "Nah. I have a unique metabolism." He sniffed the opened bottle. "No, this one's no good." He threw it aside, the pills scattering on the floor. He started on the last bottle.

The clerk looked at him with eyes wide. "I'll call the cops...!"

Erebus looked up at him wryly, and then looked down at the phone just behind the counter. He reached over and pulled it up. "With this?" He considered putting the phone though this poor idiot's head, but reconsidered. He ripped the phone upwards, snapping the cord. A panicky clerk whining to the next customer would attract him attention much slower than the next customer finding a corpse.

He stuffed down the rest of the pills and picked up the chips again. He thanked the clerk and headed out, passing a gas pump.

"Freeze!" Erebus turned around to see the clerk holding a gun at him. Erebus smirked, and kept walking.

Krak! Pain in his right shoulder. The little twerp actually shot him! Alright, now this is personal.

"Mr. Book, Sir. Coll has escaped custody." Captain Harringer talked with the image of Mr. Book while consulting various displays. "Our 'eye' tells us he ripped the bars out of his window and jumped out three stories before taking off. He's assumed headed for Meston."

"Damn it." Mr. Book sighed with all the weight you'd expect from an aging, heavyset man. "Well, that confirms the data we confiscated from his bunker. He's been 'playing' with himself."

"Ah, yes Sir. What should we do?"

"Well, if he's running around loose, we might be able to grab him without too much exposure. That airlimb you're in now is the one with the nanite-tight chamber?"

"Yes Sir. I thought the nanite lab onboard would be more applicable to this mission than the dedicated gunship. So we're to take him alive?"

"I'm really not worried about it, but if you do kill him, scoop his body and anything he bleeds on, and get it into the chamber. The less of him left sitting around, the better."

"As you know Sir, that chamber isn't able to hold out forever against a dedicated nanite colony. I'm sure the ones Coll is using are-"

"As long as it holds long enough, Captain."

Chapter 44: Look Here

"What the hell?" Parker placed a 'look here' VTag by the horizon, but he didn't really need to. Soon, everyone saw the fiery plume rising and heard the explosion faintly. Kris simultaneously turned the airlimb towards it and started looking through zoning records and such, to find out what was there. By the time they were close enough to see what it was, Kris had the blueprints in front of her.

Several cars were parked around it, and people were standing around watching. It seemed AZU-1 was the first unit there. Kris turned on the airlimb's external loudspeaker.

"People! Please get back from the fire. There could yet be further explosions. If anyone saw what caused this, please stick around. Anyone who has *no* information is please asked to continue on your trip, and get out of the way for emergency vehicles."

Kris turned to Alisia. "I lied. It's pretty obvious that whatever could blow, has already blown. Aside from the fire itself, it should be relatively safe."

Alisia and Regan were soon on the ground. They walked over to the three cars that still remained, to talk to the drivers. Other helicopters were now circling the area, and a report came in that fire crews were seven minutes away. Alisia spoke to the nearest civilian. "So. What happened here?"

"I don't know. I just saw this explosion and pulled over, an-"

"Didn't we say that if you had no info, that you should leave?" Alisia yelled so that everyone could hear. The near guy muttered "sorry" and got into his car, as did the others.

When Alisia turned, Regan was looking into the building with her scope. "It was him." She passed Alisia the scope. Through the flames she could see blood smeared all over the walls inside.

"Sick bastard."

Chapter 45: Everything You Need

The sun was not yet up, but its light was already filtering out to this strip mall in a suburb of Meston. Erebus raised his fist at the plate glass window of a small electronics store.

"No, no, stupid." he said to himself. Why damage your hand when you can throw a mailbox through it?

He looked at the little sensor attached to the inside of the window. No, no... then we would still have the alarm going off. He looked through the window and examined the wall. Just a few layers of drywall separated the electronic shop and the hair dresser's next door.

The hairdresser's window didn't have an alarm attached to it, so he threw the mailbox through the hairdresser's window, and then used it to bash open a respectable hole in the wall. Voila. No alarms. He looked at the wall clock. Five thirty or so. Looking at the store hours, he saw this gave him ample time to shop before any staff showed up. He reached out to grab a laptop and noticed that his hands were still bloody from the gas station clerk. Ick. After cleaning up with some paper towels he found behind the counter, he collected the laptop and a few dozen electronic parts and components. "Oh fuck," he said to himself just before he left, "Tools! Duh!" He went back and collected some of the essentials. For good measure, he opened the cash register and took an extra laptop, mainly to make it look like a basic robbery. Maybe they wouldn't connect it to him right away.

Now the trick was to find a nice little hole to hide in; to work in. He looked back at the mess he'd made. He'd have to be a little more subtle for a while if he was going to get any work done. After doing some back-alley running to get some distance from the latest crime scene, he then went shopping for some office space. After a little cruising of commercial and industrial areas he found a four story building with an 'office for rent' sign on the top floor.

He was soon standing in the hall of the top floor. No one was around. He placed his hand over the lock of his target door and gave a short, strong push. The inner doorframe snapped out of the way, and the door gently opened. It didn't make so much noise that it would attract anyone from any of the other office suites, so he went in and closed the door. It wouldn't stay perfectly shut, so he stuffed his cap against the bottom of the door to keep it in place.

The office wasn't furnished but it had lights, power, communication outlets, and a kitchenette. First, he used his new laptop and the office communication port to access his own FTP and download his collection of software and specs. He used the specs to customize the RF transmitter he grabbed, and hook it up to the laptop. Then he ran a certain bit of his own homebrew software, and cut his finger. He held a nine volt battery up to the cut, as a signal.

A few commands later, and half the nanites in his bloodstream began racing towards the signal, out the cut. After a while, a slight, grey, metallic crust was forming around the contacts of the battery, eventually growing into a mass a bit smaller than a billiard ball.

"Yay! Now I just need about a zillion more! If each of *them* builds two friends, and *they* build two friends...." Erebus ran a few commands on the laptop. All it would take now was some time and some raw materials for the nanite farm.

"I'm seeing burst transmissions, Captain." The pilot of the Lancer airlimb squinted at a display while Captain Harringer leaned over to look. "It's very faint, but it seems to fit the parameters of a nanite server."

"Can you read it?"

"Fraid not, Sir. They've got it encrypted."

Harringer grumbled. "It's him."

Chapter 46: Giddyup

"Major?" Kris's voice popped on the unit's comms. "There's an unidentified airlimb headed for Meston."

"What do you mean, 'Unidentified'?"

"It refuses to answer, it carries no transponder signal, and base says the satellites can't even see any markings on it."

Alisia groaned. "Well what the fuck is *this* now?"

"I've plotted an approximate course for it, and looked at things in its path, and you'll never guess what I found."

"Don't keep me in suspense, Captain. I'm not in the mood." Alisia said tiredly.

Regan piped up. "Damn."

Kris replied. "There's a signal that could only be a nanite server. It's very weak though."

"Fuck. Erebus is setting up shop. So this unknown airlimb is probably the same guys that trashed his other base."

"Shall we?"

"Giddyup."

Chapter 47: Christmas

Erebus heard a little whisper in the corner of his head. It told him Lancer was coming, but Erebus expected this. Presently he stood on the roof of the building he had been working in. The new coat of metal he gently 'installed' on the roof using his latest fleet of nanites shimmered almost like water in the morning sun.

Erebus stared into the sky, straining his eyes on the tiny, approaching dot. It grew closer and closer.

Aboard the Lancer airlimb, Captain Harriger looked at the display, showing Jonathan 'Erebus' Coll, standing on a rooftop, facing them.

"I'll be damned if he's not staring right at us." Harringer grumbled.

"Sir, there's no way he can see us at this distance without binoculars or something."

"Hmm." Harringer knew better, or at least suspected. Short range nanite transmissions, and then Coll's there, smiling away without a care in the world. Harringer spoke through his comm to his troops.

"Alright men. When we land, our objective is to capture the target, Coll. It is *not* necessary that we take him alive, but I would like to avoid injuring him if possible. We must assume he's carrying some variety of nanites in his body. Splattering him all over could cause infection to us. Keep your distance from him. We'll surround him and herd him into the airlimb, where we'll seal him in the chamber. Do we understand?"

Affirmative replies flooded the comm channel.

"We can almost guarantee an ambush by zombies on first landing but we've handled that type before. You all know the rules."

Erebus tried hard not to smile as the dot in the sky got closer, and grew, finally descending over the roof. Lancer's airlimb hovered about fifteen centimeters over the surface. Harriger poured out with ten other soldiers. They checked all directions as they moved in a wide circle to surround Erebus, keeping a minimum of four meters away from him.

"Coll." Harriger greeted.

"Hey. Kept me waiting." Erebus said.

"That mean you're coming along peacefully?"

"Sure, why not?"

"Picked up some nanite signals. Kinda thought we'd be seeing some zombies here today."

"Oh, no, haven't made any of those lately." He raised his hands slowly to the sky, in a motion of surrender. A terrible wrenching cry seemed to come from everywhere. The floor shifted below them, forcing the soldiers to adjust their footing.

"Fuck, the floor! *Drop him now*" Harriger yelled.

Erebus closed his fists as torrents of bullets tore into his body. The metal floor screamed with rage, and buckled into two meter high razor-like spikes of folded metal.

Most of the soldiers were killed instantly.

Some had a moment to wonder what happened before they died.

An unfortunate few were treated to up to half a minute of unimaginable pain. Among these were Harriger, who stared at Erebus in the stunned, horrified realization of what had happened, and what would happen soon.

Erebus stood, buckled over a bit in pain and bleeding profusely. But he did stand; easily over a hundred bullets in his body. He composed himself and smiled peacefully as the last of the moans around him faded into oblivion.

"I won."

He walked up to Harriger, who was stuck on a few of the spikes, taking the comm from his ear and his handgun. He put the comm into his own ear.

"Helloooooo? Bookie?"

No reply came. While Erebus waited, he commanded the nantie infested metal floor to release and flatten out. The dead soldiers fell to the smooth surface like puppets with their strings cut. Nanites quietly invaded their bodies, installing strings for a new puppeteer.

"Bookie-poo, would you like to speak to Harriger?"

"He's alive?" Mr. Book asked in a flat tone.

Erebus put the comm back into Harriger's ear. He closed his eyes, and took control of him. Erebus spoke through Harriger, using Harriger's voice. Harriger's eyes moved around while the nanites worked to enslave more of the freshly dead body.

"Hi Mr. Bookie-poo, I'm Harriger!" Erebus forced Harriger's corpse to say, "I'm such a freakin doofus. Not only did I get killed, but really, I didn't stand a chance! At least I managed to *see* Coll. After all, he designed half the augmentations in this airlimb and actually could have taken it over from a mile away, and simply ran my entire squad into the ground. *Jeesus fuck*, why didn't we even consider that, Mr. Bookie-poo? We're so fucking dense!"

175

Mr. Book signed off. Yelling and commotion was heard just before the signal disappeared. Erebus returned to his own body.

"Oops," Erebus said, watching his own nanites seal his 'trivial' wounds, "Was that in bad taste?"

He looked around at the soldiers, slowly coming to their feet. He looked at the empty Lancer airlimb, and made a mental inventory of the resources that were probably inside it. "Merry fucking Christmas!"

Chapter 48: A Fall

All of AZU-1 had watched the 'battle' through a satellite, sending its pictures to their airlimb's monitors. They didn't know who these soldiers were, but their deaths were still startling and disturbing. At first, it was hard to tell what happened. From the high angle the spikes didn't show up so well, except the shadows they caused. Then the blood. Then... then only one person was moving.

"He has got to die. Today, now." Regan said.

"I think that would be appropriate." Alisia said in a somber tone. Despite Erebus' deeds, it was still difficult to decide to kill a human. A person.

Erebus didn't 'sense' the AZU-1 airlimb the way he sensed the Lancer airlimb, brimming with his own little microscopic spies, but he heard them. Heard the engine. He searched the sky and saw it. Soon it was above him. He prepared his witty repartee with which to tease his favorite pursuers.

But no conversation was offered.

The air splintered with the sounds of hate as Parker systematically shredded Erebus, and every one of the newly created zombies. The sound of the zipper gun seemed to go on endlessly. If the blood Erebus had spilled from the soldiers was a horrible sight, then this was just stomach turning. Only after Parker ceased fire did he really see what he had done.

The sounds of the engines seemed deafening against the silence of those on board.

"Well... I guess we should go down and confirm." Alisia said. They assumed a hovering position, much like the Lancer airlimb, but on the other side, and not above the nanite-trap floor. Regan and Alisia stood on the edge of the airlimb bay floor while Parker looked at the mess through his scope. The girls didn't dare go near the trapped roof of the building. Alisia used a scope to look at Erebus close up. Enough of his face was still visible. Most of the rest of his head had been torn to shreds.

Regan looked for the last time into the face of the man who had killed her brother, and most of the residents of Autar. She wished she could make him deader.

"Yeah," Alisia sighed, "He's dead. Kris, contact local authorities. We're going to evacuate the building and try to do a controlled burn of the roof."

With a sudden growing hum, the Lancer airlimb bucked back to life and began to rise.

"Kris! Talk to whoever's flying that thing!!" Alisia yelled into her comm.

"AZU-1 to unidentified airlimb. Respond." Kris said.

"Hello AZU-1", came Erebus' voice, "This is 'unidentified airlimb', here. What's your sign? Over."

Kris didn't recognize the voice at first, but Regan and Alisia both closed their eyes in a frustrated moment of exasperation. Jonathan Coll's body was certainly dead, but 'Erebus' was alive in the systems of the Lancer airlimb.

"Unidentified airlimb," Kris started, "Please identify yourself and prepare to be escorted to Yute base."

"Ah, negative AZU-1, chew my knob. I have things to do." The Lancer airlimb began to rise again.

"*Parker!*" Alisia yelled, "*Take him down!*"

Parker opened fire again. Shots dented the exterior and fragments bounced around in the exposed bay, but it wasn't stopped. It began to get some distance.

"*Kris*, keep us in optimal firing range. Parker, keep the heat on! Regan, get to the other zipper gun, just in case."

"Damn" Erebus thought, "I should have jumped my mind into some heavy machinery long ago!" Sure, it was a bit disconcerting to look down at your own mutilated corpse, but hey, it's a new era. Why cling to old bodies when you have a new shiny ass-kicking one? Granted an airlimb isn't the fiercest thing in the sky by a long shot, but it has its uses. Especially this one, which Lancer conveniently delivered. It had been outfitted as a mobile nanite lab, which he had filled to the gills with little techy toys, almost all of which were now at his disposal.

Mechanisms had already begun moving about, putting this into that, and pouring those into there, and soon the onboard lab had assembled and loaded fifty large canisters.

Now AZU-1 was shooting at him. How rude. He thought of the zipper gun, and cursed that it needed a person manning it. He should have moved a couple zombies onboard before the slaughter. Bullets pounded against Erebus' hull, making a resonating sound that irritated him through nearly all the sensors at his disposal.

Oh wait.. what was that noise? That ominous hummmmmmmm....... He'd heard that before, and he did *not* like it. He had to launch the canisters *now*. Damn, three had been damaged by enemy fire. It looked like forty seven would have to be the lucky number.

Alisia kept the Lancer airlimb in her sights as the Bad Mojo fragmenting rail launcher charged up. Suddenly, a stream of objects poured out of the top of the Lancer airlimb. Alisia paused- was this damage? No.. this was bad. She snapped a decision, and squeezed the mojo's trigger. The air split and the Lancer airlimb's bay was wrenched nearly in half, bits flying out on the far side. Like a snake hit by a shotgun. A minor explosion erupted out of it as it began to fall.

"Shit, it's gonna fall into the city!" Parker gasped.

Alisia had hoped it would explode, and maybe take out the canisters, but they'd been tossed clear already. Then her fear and suspicions were confirmed.

"Major," Kris reported, "Those canisters. They're transmitting. They're nanite servers."

As this sank in, the canisters were falling over a wide, wide area, and they streamed out a wispy smoke of nanites.

"Shoot them down!" Alisia ordered. Parker and Regan opened fire, many of the canisters now visible from Regan's side.

They fell, and soon were crossing the horizon. "Don't..... don't be afraid to fire into the city. Hitting a civilian is better than them being infected." Alisia collapsed to her knees, hearing her last order resonating in her head. She knew it was the right call, but .... this was worse than killing a fresh zombie, one that looked and bled like a human... this... this was just horrible. She looked over her shoulder and saw Regan, as her grip on the zipper's controls loosened and she slumped down.

Parker heard Regan's zipper stop firing, and let go as well.

"I.... think I might have gotten one. They're fast, and small. I...."

Jonathan "Erebus" Coll descended across the city, a mind with forty seven bodies, and billions of children. And he planned the fall of Meston.

Chapter 49: An Ascent

While strategists and officials fussed and planned, and tried to think of what to do, AZU-1 was ordered to fly back to Yute base and rest. "When we have a plan, you can bet you'll be spearheading it. When that time comes, I want you ready." The General's orders were clear. Alisia's muscles and eyelids didn't argue.

Despite this, Alisia found herself staring at the ceiling of her room aboard the airlimb, unable to sleep. She saw in her mind the zipper rounds flying towards the city. They'd stopped firing before much damage or injury could have been done, but it still agonized her. She imagined a handful of zipper rounds flying into someone's kitchen window and fragmenting, and the bloody screaming of a worst case scenario.

Regan emerged from her room, intent on going to Alisia's. As she took the few steps across the hall, she peered around the corner towards the mess area. She saw Parker and Kris sitting quietly in the dim light, staring at their coffee mugs. So, even the mighty Kris was affected. Unimportant. On to Alisia.

She slid Alisia's door open and closed it behind her. She shuffled over to Alisia on her bed. Alisia quietly composed herself, and spoke in a steady, deliberate tone.

"I'm not in the mood for your non-"

Regan grabbed Alisia's teddy bear angrily, flopped down onto Alisia and held her tight. Alisia felt Regan's body tremble softly, on the edge of crying. Alisia held her as platonically as possible.

"Regan, what's wrong?" As it left her lips, Alisia realized what a stupid question it was. What's right?

"He's not dead, is he?" Regan's voice was in that 'defenseless little girl' tone that Alisia had heard once or twice before.

Alisia strained for a way to answer that sounded positive. "His body is.. we just.. we just have to deal with what's left."

"Those people.. in Meston...."

"I know. We'll do what we can."

"No, you don't know. If you'd been in Autar back then....and it's going on right now.." Regan squeezed her love tightly.

Alisia had no reply, and just squeezed the terrified little girl. Those eggheads had better come up with something good. Something better than nuking Meston.

While officials in Meston tried desperately to hunt down the nanite servers, they inhaled the microscopic invaders, and slowly became the enemy.

Two thirds of the population became zombies. Fresh and unwounded zombies. Erebus willed them to rot unnaturally quick so that they would look the part. Many calmly attacked each other, ripping redundant flesh and spilling unneeded blood. Proper zombies can't go walking around looking like yuppies, can they?

These zombies were notably organized and under Erebus' direct control. Wordlessly they herded the 'untouched' third of the population. Hostages.

When Erebus was convinced he had everyone in the city where he wanted them, his voice came from every zombie at once.

"Greetings, people of Meston. I am the one who took Autar. I have now taken you. You may call me God."

Chapter 50: Erika

Erika awoke. What had happened to her city? It was so fast. She had been taken to a school gymnasium with a few hundred others, guided by a few thousand corpses.

She didn't have a gun. No one did. Even if she did, would shooting at the zombies do any good? They weren't hurting anyone but each other at this point anyway. This situation wasn't quite like Autar. Anyone who'd tuned into the news in the last two years would be able to tell that much.

She knew she had to get out of there. She had a purpose. Someone would come. Someone would. They had to. It was inevitable. She had to find them. She had a purpose. She had a purpose.

Chapter 51: As a Sledgehammer

Alisia awoke, blissfully forgetful for a split second about what had happened to Meston.

The hum of the airlimb engines eased her to back to reality. Peeking at the clock, she assessed they must be close to Yute base. There would be a lot of important people, very upset and worried. People barking orders around, half of them probably trying to figure out if they might be blamed for the whole mess.

The moments of waking blessed her with momentary forgetfulness about such things. She yawned and noticed Regan's hand dangling around her side. Just sort of flopped there. She was getting ready to yell at Regan when memory returned.

She had after all, given Regan permission to crash with her. (*Above* the covers, thank you very much.) She just wanted to stop Regan's crying. It didn't work so well. But she was quiet right now. Alisia sat up and looked down at Regan. She looked so peaceful, but they'd be at Yute soon.

"Regan, get up." Her voice was heavy with sleep. "Regan."

Regan stirred, and her hand moved innocently into Alisia's lap. That tore it. She tossed Regan's hand back at her. "*Hey*! Wake up!"

Regan's head rose and she wiped her face of the drool on one corner of her mouth, trying to not look like a total dork in front of her beloved.

Soon, they emerged into the hall, to run into Kris.

"Ha!" Kris scoffed, "Did you girls have a nice 'nap'? Is this really the time for that?"

"We're *not*-" Alisia sighed. "What do you have to report, Kris?"

Regan excused herself. "Gonna go for a shower. I'm just all... ooh, sweaty."

Alisia rolled her eyes. "So, Kris?"

"Nothing much. We'll be at Yute any minute. You must have gotten her into a *good* mood, if she didn't spit at me on sight."

"Nothing happened, *Captain,*" Major Alisia Terone told her subordinate scornfully. But despite her authority, Alisia felt the need so add further explanation, almost under her breath. "I'm not a lesbian, remember?" Alisia hoped it would end the discussion.

"Me neither," Kris agreed, "I'm bi. Flat out lesbianism.. so... *Limiting!*" She tossed her hands in the air to emphasize her point.

"Look, I'm not bi either. I'm just straight."

"Got a problem with being gay?"

Alisia regretted ever bringing it up at all. "Kris, I'm fine with people who are gay, I just want it known that *I* am not."

"No no, Major, What I *asked* was, do *you* have a problem with being gay?"

Alisia snapped back- "What? *Yes!* Because I'm *not.*"

Kris smirked. "Ah, I know where you're at. You grew up assuming you're straight. Now if you begin to question that, ya feel like you're questioning who you are. It's not who you are, just who you do!" Kris giggled her practiced giggle, and walked off.

Alisia shook her head at headed towards the showers. She stopped as she got close. Damn. Regan was in the women's shower.

She stood for a little while and the crossroads between the two shower rooms, staring at the lettering on the wall. Two words, each with an arrow pointing opposite directions. "Men" "Women"

Maybe she could grab a quick shower in the men's. She stepped a bit closer, and heard water running in both directions. Parker must be in the men's. Ok, fine. She'd have a shower later, no biggie. She turned around and started walking away. She paused and looked back.

The two words still stared at her. "Men" "Women"

She looked up as if speaking to the fates. "Laying it on pretty thick today, huh?"

Chapter 52: Brewing Storms

The AZU-1 airlimb set down into the Yute base dock. The eleven other docks were filled as well, and swarming with soldiers sporting a distinct emblem.

"Storms." Alisia informed Regan. Storms were fairly elite units. Almost all 'stromfronts' operated out of airlimbs, having first dibs on new military hardware.

When she first learned AZU-1 would be getting an airlimb, Alisia was a little in awe. Now among the stormfronts, she felt humbled. Her little unit must seem like unworthy ants.

Alisia headed inside with her crew in tow, and struggled past busy, hurrying people, some with folders in hand, some with weapons, until they made it to General Westmore's conference room. It looked a bit more like a war room now.

Alisia stood quiet for a while, trying to get an idea of what was going on. There was too much happening at once. The room had a dozen or more people in it at any one time, many of them coming and going with reports or orders.

Alisia's three subordinates lingered behind her with varying degrees of patience. After a bit, the General spotted Alisia.

"Terone" He called, waving her over. He didn't seem pleased, but right now there were very few reasons to be.

"Sir." Alisia said. "What's the plan?"

"We're sending in the storms. Standard hostage extraction operation with adjustments made for zombie resistance."

"Yes Sir. Keep in mind they may be using small arms now. When do we leave?"

"Terone, AZU-1 is ordered to get some sleep and rest up. The storms can handle this. One more unit in an operation this size won't make a lot of difference. Get some rest and be ready when we *do* need you."

Alisia slumped her shoulders a bit. "Oh, uhm, yes Sir. Is this because-"

The General interrupted, and looked up from his papers. "Major, I've seen the report you sent in, and the recordings. I'm fairly certain there was nothing else you could have done. Just get some rest."

Alisia nodded. Her little nap earlier didn't last all that long, and how long had she been awake before that? It couldn't have been long, but it felt like it. "Permission to be excused?"

"Dismissed, Major. Let us take care of it."

Alisia saluted, and turned to herd her group out of the way and down the hall. "You heard the man, people. We're on standby."

Chapter 53: Right

Regan, Parker, and Kris sat in a booth at the base bar. It was quiet. Most of the base personnel were helping to prepare for the upcoming operation.

"So, what was that all about?" Parker asked, "With the General...?"

"I think our Major expected to be in trouble." Kris said.

"What? We did everything we could.. as soon as those nanites got spewed out and the servers dropped out of sight, all we could do is get out of the way! It's not like there was any other thing we could have done."

Regan spoke up softly. "It doesn't always feel that simple." She got up and excused herself quietly, heading back to the airlimb.

Parker mumbled to himself. "If anyone dropped the ball, it was the goons that let him escape."

Regan remembered the moment she had her gun aimed squarely at Erebus' head, and decided to play honourably. Her honour just cost the people of Meston their lives. Her footsteps faded down the hallway.

A silence was brought to the table in Regan's wake. Kris was grimly running circles in her head, when Parker's hand covered hers. She looked back at him with spite in her eye, and her voice. "Horny? Now?"

Parker withdrew his hand and let out an exasperated sigh. "Ever think maybe I wanted more than sex?" he mumbled. Part of him wanted to yell it at her, but the modest part won.

Kris stared at him and sneered a little. "Idiot." She stood, and began to leave. She turned back to look at Parker. "Are you coming, or aren't you?"

They stared at each other for what seemed like a long time, perhaps trying to figure each other out, perhaps waiting for the other to clue in. Parker finally answered. "Not with that attitude."

"Idiot." She mumbled to herself. She kept an eye out on her way back to the airlimb for someone else she could play with. She spotted a few likely candidates that caught her eye, but she passed them all by. No, she wasn't in the mood anymore. Parker's stubborn clingy wussiness had sapped all the playfulness out of her. She took the long way back to the airlimb, just sort of wandering. When she finally got back and approached her room, she saw Regan across the hall, sitting in a nightie by Alisia's door, holding some scruffy looking teddy bear.

"What the fuck are you doing, Regan?" It came out a bit more bitter than she intended, but it's not like she cared at the moment.

Regan looked up, a little shocked. "Just waiting for Alisia."

"In the hall? Dressed like that? And what's with the bear?"

Regan looked down at the bear, then back at Kris. "It's hers. I borrow it sometimes. I think she knows. I'm waiting here so I catch her when she comes back. If I wait in my room, I might miss her. And the battery on the visor I've been using as a hallway camera died. Do you know where she is?"

Kris stared a little at the pathetic orphan that sat there in the hall. "She's talking with the nerds, I think."

"That Doc Brock guy? Still? Must be planning something. I can wait."

"Wait in her room, doofus, the hall is cold."

"She might not like that."

"Frig you're whipped, Regan. You two haven't...... have you?"

Regan looked a little down. "I still have hope."

Kris opened the door to her own room, and stepped in. "Idiot." The door slid closed behind her.

Regan decided Kris was right about one thing. The hall was indeed cold. She grabbed a blanket from her own room and cuddled up back down by Alisia's door. She didn't remember falling asleep, but she awoke to the sound of Alisia's voice. "Regan."

Regan looked up at Alisia with a sleepy smile. "Leesha... can I sleepover?"

Alisia remembered the nap before. "You stay on top of the blanket and keep your hands to yourself."

Regan smiled and stood, taking her own blanket into one arm, the bear in the other. With the blanket down, sloppily folded, her nightie was revealed. Alisia looked at her with a grim expression. "Lose the nightie."

"*I thought you'd never ask!*" Regan slipped the shoulder strap down a bit, teasing Alisia, and stopped, seeing that Alisia wasn't amused.

"Cammo pants and a normal T-shirt, minimum. And *gimmie my damned bear!*" Alisia grabbed her bear and stormed into her room. Regan went and got changed. When they finally settled in, Alisia was curled up facing the wall, clutching her bear tight. Regan rolled towards Alisia and flopped her arm over her. Alisia took her bear and shoved it in Regan's face. "Hug that."

Regan obeyed, and watched Alisia settle back down. She held the bear and gazed into the hues of orange and gold in Alisia's hair.

Alisia muttered, her voice becoming sleepy. "You know there's never gonna be anything romantic between us, right?"

"Right." Ragan answered.

"I'm just letting you sleep here cuz you're my friend, and I realize this is a very stressful time for you, right?"

"right."

"You're just answering the way you think I want you to, aren't you?"

"Right."

"Go to sleep Regan."

"Right."

"Shut up Regan."

"Right."

Chapter 54: Plan A

Morning light found eleven airlimbs cruising towards Meston, each with a compliment of two airlimb operators and a six member stormfront. Aboard the lead airlimb, Captain Greg Jackson briefed his five subordinates.

"OK, boys and girls, we can expect *massive* amounts of these 'zombies' running around. Luckily, most of what we know about them and their combat methods indicate that we will be able to manage them fairly easily. We've all seen the footage from Autar's first fall. It was a bloody mess, but keep in mind that no one really knew what they were dealing with then, and they were taken by surprise. The one thing we may have to watch for is the occasional zombie using a firearm. This means we'll want to walk a narrow line between keeping under enough cover to evade bullets if need be, and staying far enough away from places where zombies might break out from. I know your ability, this shouldn't be too tough."

The others murmured with cautious confidence.

"The operators will locate a probable location of hostages and bring us as close as we can get. Our job will be to pile as many as we can onto the airlimb, and get em back to Yute. If we can't take on all the ones we find, we'll call another stormfront that can take the rest. We're expecting reinforcements from all over to help in this operation, but in a best case scenario we're still talking about evacuating about a third of Meston's original population. I hope you all had a good night's sleep, it's gonna be a long day."

A Corporal spoke up. "Sir, what if the zombies threaten to kill hostages?"

"We'll just have to kill the zombies first." His reply didn't ease them much. "I know it stinks, and there's a good chance that as soon as this Erebus guy figures out what we're doing, he'll kill every hostage he can get his hands on, but it's still more of a chance than we had in Autar."

A few minutes passed, when the operators began talking a bit louder, in urgent tones. Captain Jackson walked forward to the ops room to ask what was wrong.

"Just go sit down, Sir! We need to work!"

Jackson looked around at the monitors. One showed a trail of smoke across the sky.. no, two... now three... Another monitor showed a strange structure in Meston, on a rooftop. "What the hell is going on here?"

The one operator fumbled with the controls. "I *told* you to sit down." The airlimb heaved up, preparing to turn around. Jackson fell on his back, just in time to evade an iron construction girder ripping up through the floor at an angle, and puncturing the ceiling behind him.

The impact shook the whole craft, and caused ripples of panic through the highly trained passengers. Jackson scrambled to his feet to check on his team. "Everyone OK back there?"

"Sir?? What the fuck?" Another hard jolt rolled the airlimb onto its side. Jackson was the only one not strapped in, and fell into the laps of some of his crew.

From the front, the operators' panicked voices told him what he could already guess "Engines are... fuck! We're down to one!"

Jackson realized that their airlimb was now one of those streams of smoke across the sky. He climbed over to a locker and started tossing parachutes at people. That was when they hit the ground.

General Westmore watched the situation on multiple monitors at Yute. Only three arilimbs made it out, and one of those had a girder sticking though it. Satellite video showed that several of the downed airlimbs had as many as five beams of iron stuck in them, in the middle of a mangled mess.

The General growled at the monitors. "What the hell just happened?"

Chapter 55: Plan B

Alisia awoke again to find Regan's arm flopped over her side, hand dangling in front of her. She could feel her teddy bear pushed into her back a bit. This implied to her that Regan didn't cuddle up on purpose.. otherwise, she would have gotten the bear out of the way, right? Unless she was half-asleep at the time, maybe.

Alisia grabbed Regan's hand, ready to toss it back, but she was surprised to feel how warm it was. Her own fingers felt cold, and without thinking, she paused to feel Regan's warmth for a bit. Time slowed as Alisia's mind glazed over a little, holding Regan's hand.

Suddenly Regan's hand moved. Her fingers wrapped around Alisia's, to hold her hand in return. To Alisia it was as if she spotted the movement of a spider out of the corner of her eye. She yelped a little and threw Regan's hand away. It landed on Alisia's hip, causing her to leap out of bed.

Alisia stared down at Regan, who was only waking up. "Leesha, what's going on?"

"Nothing!" she said, "Nothing, I, we.. it's late, we slept late, we should get up! I'm getting up! Just because we're not on assignment, doesn't mean we can sleep together all day. I mean- fuck! No, I don't mean 'fuck'! I mean.. shut up! Stop looking at me! I'm gonna take a shower." She walked out briskly, closing the door decisively behind her.

Regan relaxed back down into the bed with a smile, and giggled softly to herself while she ran her hand across the spot on the bed Alisia had left warm.

"It's a home-made rail cannon!" Doc Brock said, pointing at the close-up of the satellite image. "The design is crude, but to construct a dozen or more of these things in the amount of time Erebus had is amazing! There must be quite a fleet of nanites at work by now."

Alisia had come to Brock's lab after getting caught up to speed by the General. The rest of AZU-1 was along for the ride.

"Rail cannon?" Regan said, looking over to Alisia, "Is that like your bad mojo thingie?"

"Yes! Yes!" Doc Brock interrupted, "The principle is very similar. Both use a set of electromagnets to hurl a projectile, but these cannons are much larger. They'd have to be in order to use construction girders as ammo and throw them as far as we've seen them go! They also have to consume a lot of power to fire."

"Where's he getting this power?" Alisia asked, "Meston's supply has been cut off, and we *know* there's no mana drive or nuke generator in there."

"We can only assume he's depleting backups or a stored supply." Brock suggested.

"But they'll run out sooner or later, and then we just have to watch all the zombies fall down..." Parker said.

"Erebus isn't stupid. He knows he needs power, especially now that he doesn't have a human body. He'll try to pull *some*thing off before he runs out. Hopefully that 'something' doesn't involve killing the hostages."

Doc Brock looked over to the image being fed by the satellite. "Remember when the Autar A.I. transmitted out of Autar at the last minute? I think I should have someone check on the status of any satellites in range of Meston....."

The thought of Erebus potentially floating around the planet as data in satellites was not a comforting one for anyone to absorb.

"Anyway!" Brock broke the grim silence, "Sergeant Parker, Erebus' new toys have inspired me to requisition some gear from a few other departments, and with some modification, I'll be making you a new toy soon!"

"I... I'm getting a rail cannon?"

"Well.... no... a rail propelled sniper rifle. I expect amazing range."

"Cooooool."

Alisia stepped in. "Boys, how is a new fancy sniper rifle going to help us here?"

"Fear not!" Doc Brock chirped, "I have a cunning plan!" He rolled a small bullet-like object towards Parker across the table. Parker stopped it with his index finger, and picked it up. It had none of the components of a normal bullet. No firing cap or anything, just a tight seam. "What the heck is this?"

"A nanite server." Brock explained, "Built to function like the ones we've managed to confiscate. Of course, this small size is thanks to the additional resources we had available to build them."

"But can't Erebus just... build things on a molecular level with nanites?" Kris asked.

"Yes, but I suppose that method wasn't available... or maybe just not necessary when he made his. Which is lucky.. I doubt we could have reverse-engineered such a thing in any timely manner. This one also doesn't need to carry a payload of nanites, saving space. Once I have the rifle assembled, we can fire it from out of his cannon range, and assume control of a nanite colony."

Parker smirked with a shrug. "Remember, I'm just here to shoot things."

Kris matched his smirk, and shook her head. "Shoot it into a zombie, and we can control it- Boom, an instant spy in Meston."

Brock nodded. "Yes. Exactly. I'll be bringing the control deck aboard your airlimb soon. The control deck can have two operators."

"Well, that will be Regan and I," Alisia said, "Obviously we need Kris running the airlimb, and Parker manning a zipper just in case. "

"Can't Erebus jam it?" Regan asked.

"Doubt it." Kris said. "Even if he *does* detect it in the mess of signals flying around Meston, he needs the airwaves clear about as much as we do."

Parker was still smirking at the server bullet. "And I have to bury this in a zombie from... almost a kilometer away?"

"To avoid the heavy guns, yes, and the airlimb will have to keep moving." Brock said. "Can't use anything as slow as a rocket, or anything with guidance, as it'll be detected on its way in. The server bullet goes in 'dead' and undetectable. The rail rifle I'm building compensates for the range needed."

Parker rolled his eyes, thinking about wind conditions over the distance. "Greaaat. Any other things to make this shot easier?"

Kris answered. "You have to get it to hit the spinal nerve between the fourth and third vertebrae."

Parker's eyes became wide as saucers. "*What*?!"

Brock burst out laughing, quickly containing himself. "Easy, sergeant, just get it in anywhere."

Nearly twenty four hours later, Parker strolled into the airlimb's ops room. They were still docked at Yute, and Kris was passing time, checking up on the status of various operations revolving around the Meston infection.

"Hey, Kris. Whatcha watching?" Parker tried to be diplomatic.

At the sound of Parker's voice, Kris's mind teetered between a sneer and a smile. "Did you know he's been trying to take control of satellites?"

Parker looked at the various displays arranged around Kris and considered what it all meant. "Oh my god.. the bastard.. it was his plan all along... he's trying to get free satellite porn!"

Kris turned around in her chair to face Parker, still divided between annoyance and appreciation. None the less, her voice came forward with a degree of amusement. "That's right, Robert. You've uncovered his evil, evil plan. He did it all for porn." Unconsciously, her body language flirted with a submissive lean back, and a little 'accidental' ride up of her skirt.

"I knew it! Even after having his fleshy body destroyed, all he needs is some lovin'. Awww."

Kris rolled her eyes. "Aaaanyway, since he used a satellite to get data out of Autar before it was bombed, everyone's rather nervous that he'll jump out the same way again if he manages to hack a satellite. Either way, sooner or later he's going to figure out a way to do something very very bad."

"Well, hopefully Doc Brock's little experiment will get us some info to help us get the hostages out, or something... I suppose they'll have to bomb Meston eventually to stop him from taking another city, hostages or not."

They let the notion settle in for a bit. Kris spoke up. "So why aren't we going in with that railgun thing right now?"

"Brock's still setting stuff up. It's gonna be a while. I just saw some of it being dragged in."

Kris looked up at Parker and raised an eyebrow. She tapped a button on one of the consoles, and all the monitors around her flickered out, leaving the room dimly lit by light from the hall. "So. You're saying we have some time to burn."

Chapter 56: A Lively Stroll

Parker continued the examination of his new toy, which sat pointing out the open bay door on the side of the airlimb. The frenzied air of flight rushed around him, and the ground blurred by below. The front end of the gun looked just like a normal zipper gun, and for a very good reason. At the range they'd be at, a normal zipper would not be able to reach Meston, and if Erebus saw them, he would hopefully only think that they were trying to take a peek. Parker looked at the three little magic 'bullets' on a neat little rack beside the handle, like a miniature, modern quiver.

Behind him in the bay, Doc Brock was strapping Alisia and Regan down to a large table with bulky headsets looming overhead. "So, when we have control of a zombie, the sensor I'm going to tape onto the back of your neck will pick up impulses in your nerves and translate it into motions for the controlled zombie. In return it will send images and sound back to the headset. Since this isn't a true cyber VR, (I didn't think you ladies would want to be implanted for that, nor do we have the time...) your actual body will be moving too. This system doesn't stop that, so the strapping is there to prevent you from.. well... flailing around here and hurting yourselves."

The girls nodded in rough understanding, and Brock skittered over to the console attached nearby to run calibration tests. Kris chose this moment to wander in from the front of the airlimb.

She sauntered up to the table and smirked down at Alisia and Regan, half strapped down. "And here I am without a stick of butter."

Regan rolled her eyes and looked up at Kris. "You're enjoying this, aren't you?"

Alisia looked over to Regan with wide eyes. "*Her*? What about *you?!*"

Regan pondered. "Well... I've had worse Saturday nights."

Alisia closed her eyes in mild exasperation. "Kris, how long till we're in range?"

Kris 'innocently' rested her hand on Alisia's knee, and watched Regan's face for reaction. "Any minute. That's what I came back to tell you."

Regan glared at Kris's hand, then up to her calm, smiling face. "You couldn't have used the comm?"

"What, and miss the bondage party?" She strolled back out with her smirk, to take her station.

Soon, the airlimb had attained an 'orbit' around Meston, with Parker's new toy pointed at it. He used the scope to look around exposed streets and such for viable targets, looking for single zombies who once controlled, could slip away unnoticed.

"Kris," he spoke into his comm after a while, "Hold it here. I see a few." The airlimb lurched to a stop, hovering in place. Through the sight, he looked at three zombies milling around by the opening to an alley. "Three zombies, three magic bullets." Parker commented.

"And two people who can use them." Alisia said from the table.

"Yeah, well, that's not my fault." Parker readied his first shot. The capacitors warmed up, and a soft hissing sound came from the base of the gunnery. Alisia mentally noted that it sounded much different than her bad mojo, and wondered if it was time she got Brock to build her an upgrade.

With no detectable recoil, the gun fired, and Parker watched silently for a moment that felt like forever. "Got one." He said with calm satisfaction.

Brock made himself busy at his console. "Ah, yes. It's good. Lets get another set up, then the ladies can 'go in'."

Parker lined up his shot for the next nearest zombie.... and fired. "Damn."

"What happened?" Alisia asked.

"I hit the same one. It stumbled in the way at the last second."

"Oh," Brock said, looking at his console as if It might try to bite. "I hope that wasn't my fault."

"No matter. I guess that's why we have a third bullet."

Alisia looked out under her head set at Regan. Her eyes looked nervous. "If we only get one in, you'll be saved the trouble. I'll have to go in without you." Her words suggested she wanted to spare Regan, but her *voice* suggested she didn't want to do this alone.

Parker fired. "*Fuck fuck fuck!*"

Alisia closed her eyes and sighed.

"It went clean through. Yeah, I can see bits of the bullet in the wall. Some chunks below." Parker mumbled curses at himself.

"Alright Brock. Put me in." Alisia said.

"Hm. Yes."

Parker watched through the scope as the struck zombie jiggled into a controlled state. The monitors inside Alisia's headset came to life. "Kay. I'm seeing through its eyes, I guess. *Whoops!*" The zombie fell down onto its side. "Hey, I got a drunk one."

"Ah, it will take a bit of practice, I should think." Brock suggested.

Alisia moved her restrained arm, and saw the zombie's hand come up in front of the display. "Yick. Anyone got any moisturizer? Say, Parker, where'd you land the second bullet?"

"Left shoulder, front."

Controlling the zombie was tricky. It was difficult to ignore what she felt-the table and its straps, and her actual motions, and instead focus only on the visual feedback she was receiving. After some fumbling, Alisia managed to make the zombie dig the bullet out. "This still working, Brock?"

"Yes, wh- Oh, I see!"

Alisia looked over to Regan again.

"Do it." Regan said.

Alisia's zombie lunged forward, and stuck the spare bullet into the calf of the next nearest zombie. It moaned in surprise, which startled the third zombie enough to make it wander away. Brock pushed a few buttons on his console. "It... it's good, you can go in any time, Ms. Grier."

"OK," Regan said, "I'm ready."

Regan and Alisia took some time to get used to their remote control zombie-bodies, practicing a little with a short zombie slap-fight.

"Silly bitch!" Alisia said, slapping Regan's zombie with a cheerful tone.

"*Aha*! The claws come out at last, huh, leesha?" Regan retaliated with another slap of her own.

"I am not Alisia! This is a male zombie.. I am....AL!" Another slap punctuated her statement.

"Hey, dipsticks." Kris' voice came over the com. "Don't slap those things apart. We need them, don't we?"

"Yeah.. well.. one more thing." Regan staggered back and came forward with an attempted roundhouse kick which resulted in her zombie falling flat on its back. "*Ow!*"

"Ow?" Brock asked, looking rather concerned for a moment that somehow the system had fed back pain to Regan, even though he knew full well it couldn't.

"Well... it sounded painful." Regan said.

"Yeah." Alisia agreed, putting Al's hand out for Regan's toppled zombie. "Come on. Get up, uh... Reggie."

'Reggie' took Al's hand, and started to pull himself up. "You should have heard it from here." Regan said.

"Let's get moving." Alisia said, looking around with Al's eyes. "Parker, we're looking for hostages, so um... can you see maybe a gymnasium or something where they might be held... and hopefully a route that keeps us away from other zombies as much as possible?"

"Yeah... um... I picked zombies more or less as far in as I could, so.. er... I don't really see a whole lot past you..."

"Captain Taylor to the rescue." Kris chimed in dryly, "I already have Meston's map loaded up, and if Brock will allow I'll stick a VTag in your display for you to follow."

"Of course." Brock said, having spent an extra hour putting the Vtag feature in. A "go here" VTag icon appeared on their displays, seemingly pointing out a building obscured by several others.

"Ok, Kris, where is this we're headed?" Alisia said, starting Al walking down the street. "And how far?" Slap fights had gotten easy enough, but walking with any useful speed without falling over, proved a bit more difficult. "Well, now I understand zombies a bit better."

"It's a pharmacy." Kris said, referring to the VTag, "Alisia said she wanted some moisturizer." Regan rolled her eyes, but was cut off before she could come up with a comeback. "Eh, really though," Kris continued, "It's a high school. It's got a big gym. Seems like a good place to keep a lot of people. It was one of the first places the Storms had intended to check out."

And so, Al and Reggie staggered down the street in the general direction of the VTag. "Frig, I could get out of the airlimb, actually *walk* there myself, and get there before the zombie." Regan complained.

"Yeah, and get skewered by a rail-propelled iron girder or zombified y-"

Alisia was cut off by the sound of a little scream from behind a garbage bin they were passing. Al and Reggie turned to look and saw a young lady with long dark hair, perhaps a bit younger than Regan and Alisia. Alisia held out Al's hands in a calming gesture and said "It's ok, we're not ... uh.. not bad zombies...."

"She can't hear you Major." Brock said, "We couldn't pull that trick off in the time we had."

"Bah." Alisia looked around and made Al grab a rock from the ground, and walk over to the wall. The lady flinched as Al got close, but was blocked from escape by the garbage bin and Reggie's presence. Alisia started scraping a message into the wall with the rock. "HUMAN CONTROLLED ZOMBIES. HERE TO PLAN RESCUE. CAN'T TALK. CAN LISTEN."

Al stood back, and pointed at the message. The young lady read it, and looked back and forth between Al, Reggie, and the message. "You're kidding..."

Al shook his head no.

"You're.... ew, that's messed up."

Reggie nodded.

"Well... um... I'm Erika. Um.. nice to meet you?" She motioned to shake hands out of habit, then changed her mind.

Alisia took Al back to the wall, and wrote more. "WHERE HOSTAGES?"

"Oh! Oh, yeah, I can help! Follow me!" Erika said, a little excited. Al nodded, and Erika started a brisk walk down the sidewalk. After a bit, she looked back to see the two zombies trying desperately to keep up. "Wow, you guys got cruddy ones, huh?"

Reggie stopped walking for a moment to nod, (doing both at once would almost certainly result in falling down,) while Al maintained its pace.

"This is tiring!" Alisia called out aboard the airlimb. Convincing the dead flesh to move required a lot of strain against the restraints.

"Yeah. Hey leesh, this Erika... a brunette running around in a city of zombies... remind you of anyone?" Regan said. Reggie caught up to Al, and grabbed Al's butt.

Erika stared. "Um.. gay zombies, huh?"

Regan nodded while Alisia tried to figure out what Erika was talking about. She turned Al around, and slapped away Reggie's hand. "Uh... supposed to be working here, Regan." Alisia said.

"Aw, come on, leesh, when do I get the chance?"

"Like you haven't before!"

"Yeah... well... this time, I can't feel it when you slap me."

Alisia reached her hand to the side straining against the strap, and poked Regan's hand with her nail.

"*Ow!*"

"Can we get going now?"

The three of them walked along for some time, eventually nearing the gymnasium and its VTag.

As Al passed some wreckage, Alisia made him pick up a pair of utility goggles, a lot like the kind Regan had once used like security cameras in Autar. It wasn't on, but it was operational. Being in a 'borrowed' body, Alisia didn't have the option of bringing her usual equipment, so she took it along and familiarized herself with the settings and buttons as they continued on.

Erika opened the door of the gym to show Al and Reggie the crowd of people inside. It looked similar to a scene you might expect after a natural disaster like flooding, when evacuated people can't stay in their homes. Well, except for the patrolling zombies wandering around. The people looked at Erika, Reggie and Al.

"They must think we're zombies that found Erika wandering around." Regan said.

"Fine," Alisia said, putting on the goggles. "Kris, walk me through this. Let's see if I can find any nanite servers here. It we find one, maybe we can disable all the zombies in this area, and get these..."

As she put the goggles on Al's face, they were in infra red mode. "Oh shit."

"What, what now?" Regan asked.

Alisia made Al look around the room with the goggles. The people, Erika, and of course the zombie guards, and themselves. "Regan... no one here's giving off any heat."

"What?!"

"They're *all dead.*"

Although this conversation was unheard in the gym, Erika turned around to see Al with goggles up to his face.

"Aw darn." Erika said. At that moment, her eyes grew lifeless, and every body in the room started walking towards Al and Reggie. Erika, the guards and the 'hostages'. All dead, and approaching for attack.

Regan turned her head away from the Reggie monitor, and looked to Brock. "Hey Doc, the jig is up, may as well un-strap us."

As Brock walked over, Regan looked back into the monitor and over at Al. Alisia had chosen to fight. Al's arms flailed wildly at the crowd. Alisia yelled out, forgetting that her voice wasn't coming out Al's mouth. "*I came to save you, you bastards!*" Tears erupted from Alisia. Regan looked back into her monitor to see that Reggie had already been ripped to shreds by the mob.

Al was doing a bit better until the crowd got a hold of one of the wild swings and ripped Al's arm off. Alisia saw it come loose and screamed. "*My arm!!*"

Regan was half freed from the table, and snapped at Brock. "Go shut this thing off! Now! Alisia! Forget it! Ignore it!" Brock ran to power down the terminal, and Regan strained over to loosen a couple of Alisia's straps. As soon as she could, Alisia grabbed onto Regan and trembled. "There's no one left to save in there. Everyone in Meston, all dead."

While Brock undid their ankles, Regan held Alisia and tried to comfort her. "You're alright, leesha. Just a video game." Regan was a bit rattled too, but she was becoming increasingly glad that she had the opportunity to be a support to Alisia for a change, instead of the other way around.

"Erika..." Alisia mumbled. "It was Erebus. The hostages never survived the initial attack. They were just kept better preserved... they're decoys. The zombies weren't meant to be an attacking force this time. They're just by-products. Like fallout."

"Then... there's nothing protecting him. Let's go see about getting him nuked."

Chapter 57: Got Wood?

Aside from Parker, who kept watch on Meston through his scope, everyone on board met in the ops room. The General was on the screen.

"Well that does make things simple then. I've already recommended a slow-burn carpet bombing. The planes are on the runway now."

"Sir?" Alisia said, "How do we know there aren't other *living* hostages in Meston?"

"There's been no attempts at communications, and no sign of resistance since the initial invasion. We didn't know why till now. We just assumed that the zombies were just that effective at occupying the city. Still, it explains a lot. If he still had live hostages, he'd be parading them to us right now. Do you see any real possibility of there being anyone alive there?"

Alisia paused. There was doubt in her mind, but the slim chance that there was a living human left in Meston seemed so small, especially next to the threat of Erebus expanding to other places. "No, Sir. The slow burn is the best solution."

"Come on home people, it's over."

Regan and Alisia wandered out while Kris and Brock compared some notes.

"Leesha..? What's a slow burn?" Regan asked timidly.

"It means.. the bombs will leave behind napalm. It'll probably burn for days. The same thing was used at Autar. It makes sure no nanites will survive."

"And if there is a human?" Regan regretted asking it as soon as she finished. Alisia stopped, and looked at her feet. "The initial explosion would easily kill a normal human instantly. They wouldn't suffer. Not any more than they already have."

Regan stared at Alisia for a few moments. "You're still blaming yourself for Meston's fall, aren't you?" Regan leaned in for a soft hug, and to kiss Alisia on the cheek. Alisia just sort of stood there, eyes a little glazed, staring forward. Regan let go, and pointed a finger at Alisia. "Stop it. You know you did all you could."

Alisia slid back a bit out of her trance and forced a little smile for Regan. "Alright."

The comm sparked to life. "Folks?" It was Parker. "Meston's aiming something at us. It's uh... it's a big log."

"What the hell?" Kris matched her view to the location Parker had just marked with a VTag. "It's a big log!"

"That's what I said. A big log! In one of those rail cannon things!" Parker sounded almost bemused with disbelief.

"That's stupid, a log can't be fired with magnetics!"

At that moment, the log shot forward towards the airlimb.

"Ohhhhhkay, I'll just stop talking now." Kris said. "How about I move us out of its way?"

"Sounds good." Parker said. The airlimb did indeed move out of the way of the log's trajectory in plenty of time. It was moving a lot slower than the iron girders Erebus had been launching before. But it was arching. An arched trajectory is nothing new for improving range, but Erebus had not used it before, instead relying on sheer velocity to attain the range he had been getting. It occurred to Kris that this was a tactic to lure targets in closer until he found a target he really wanted to hit. *But a log?!*

As the log began to come down near them, the front end of it exploded. It was a log with a warhead. The wood splintered out in almost every direction, and six beams of metal were revealed as the log unraveled. The beams spread out a bit like a shotgun blast, and all were relieved to see that they had not spread wide enough to hit the airlimb.

The wood on the other hand, spread much wider. The airlimb resounded with a pangs and bangs as a few chunks of wood and a hail of splinters struck the hull, and bounced around inside where the open bay door allowed them in.

"*Ow* damn." Parker pulled an inch long piece of wood out of his shoulder, it being one of the few parts of him exposed from behind his gun and scope.

"You okay Parker?" Kris said.

"Yeah, it's nothing. Gonna need a bandaid though."

Another explosive noise struck at that moment.

"What the?"

In the confusion of dodging flying logs, they'd momentarily forgotten about the incoming airstrike. The sound was that of the bombing planes streaking by above the speed of sound.

The bombers were already gone before anyone realized they were there. The sonic boom hit at the same time a flourish of genius-missiles appeared over the city. They idled for a split second, then locked onto their assigned co-ordinates and began descent.

They watched, breathlessly anticipating the same display of destruction they saw at Autar, when something odd happened. All the missiles died at once in the sky over Meston. Most fell, landing in the outskirts without exploding. A few detonated in the air.

"What the hell?" At the same time, the lights on the airlimb flickered, and Kris nearly had a mild heart attack. The airlimb's computers recovered from a hiccup. "Geezusfuck! That was an EMP!"

Alisia looked around the Meston cityscape through the smoke and trails of napalm burning away in the sky harmlessly. "An EMP? Like from a nuke? Call me nuts, but I don't see any nukes going off."

Brock attempted to offer an explanation "There has been talk of projects which can create a pulse without-"

"Whatever!" Kris interrupted, "All I know is that we're lucky to still be in the sky after that. Much closer, and I don't think we would be. I'm taking this brick back to base before we drop."

Alisia grunted in the affirmative.

Brock sighed, deep in thought. He blinked, and focused on the present for a moment. "I'm going to go see about Sergeant Parker's wound. Kris, if you can, try to gather all the relevant information for me."

Chapter 58: Closer to Home

After dumping a pile of readings into a database that Brock could wade through, Kris wandered back to check on Parker. He'd left his station, so she went to his room and wandered in without knocking. Brock was on the floor, bleeding and unconscious. Parker was there, about to lean down over Brock. Parker saw Kris and stopped, putting his finger to his smiling lips. "Shhhh."

It was obvious to Kris, about the little wound Parker had gotten. She backed up and yelled into her comm. "*Parker is Ereb--*"

Regan and Alisia started running. Alisia ran to check Parker's Zipper gun, and Regan ran towards his quarters. Alisia found no one at his gun, and soon heard what she feared over the comm.

"Leesha! Found him!" Regan sounded like she was in the middle of a fight. "Got no gun! I've fought zombies hand to hand before, but not one with Erebus' speed! Hurry! Guns! Kris is KO, Brock might be dead!"

By the time Regan finished, Alisia was already almost there with her P90 and the Bad Mojo. She rounded the corner and threw her P90 over Parker/Erebus' head to Regan. Regan didn't fire right away. Partially because it was Parker, and partially because Alisia would be in the way of any bullets that missed. This was all the time Erebus needed to use Parker's hand to knock the P90 out of Regan's grip.

Erebus had to make a quick decision. Kill Regan now or turn around to deal with Alisia, who probably had another gun aimed at him at that very moment. Deciding an unarmed Regan was of little threat, he turned to Alisia.

Regan ducked around the corner, so as not to be in 'kill zone' when Alisia used the Bad Mojo.

Alisia looked at the familiar looking face approaching her, being worn by Erebus. She remembered the carnage she'd seen the Bad Mojo wreak against fresh zombies. And she remembered watching her own puppet zombie being ripped apart. She imagined what it would feel like. She had almost convinced herself to squeeze the trigger when Erebus struck, trying to knock the weapon out of her hand. She held on tight.

Instead of being knocked loose, the Bad Mojo was smashed against the wall, Alisia still holding the handle. The top third of the weapon shattered off along the 'barrel'. The electromagnetic accelerator rails were bare to the air, and the large, fragmenting shell fell loose from the chamber, onto the floor.

Poor Parker's arm didn't do so well either. His forearm was bloody and raw. Erebus raised his other arm to smash Alisia's skull. Not even seeing this, Alisia reached forward and mashed her opened weapon against the bloody arm, and pulled the trigger.

The Bad Mojo's stored electrical charge meant for launching projectiles, instead ran through Parker's arm and body, frying the nanites that had taken him. Parker fell to the ground.

Silence.

Alisia bent down cautiously while Regan's head peeked out, worried she'd see Alisia dead. "You're Ok? And no bloody walls either?"

"He's breathing, he's alive." Alisia said, "We have to get to base decontamination. There might still be more nanties running around."

Chapter 59: If it had been

"*What in blazes was that?*" General Westmore asked the moment Brock came into his office.

"The- the log?" Brock stammered, gripping a file folder.

"Not the log, I already know about the damned log! What caused that EMP blast? There sure as heck was no nuke going off!"

"Oh! Ah, of course." Brock picked a couple printouts from his folder, and rested them on the General's big oak desk. "It's something that's been under development by a sister company of AutarLabs in Meston. It actually uses many similar principles of the mana drive."

"Not another one of those…!"

"No, no. This device, the 'tightpulse EMP' has a much more controlled effect than the hypothetical overload of Autar's Mana drive. The tightpulse affects *only* the electrical reactions of inorganic systems. Just like the EMP from a nuke. Unlike a nuke, it's over a second after it's triggered. No residual."

The General sighed. "Meaning what, tactically?"

"Our people are safe from it, as long as they're not relying on any electronics to keep them in one piece, and communications will only be affected for a second at a time."

"Does that help us?"

"Yessir."

A few splinters of wood were found on and around the airlimb containing active nanites, but all the people were clean, even Parker. However, he and Brock were rushed to the nearest hospital, Yute Base only having a minor aid station.

Brock was already conscious and working hard before they even got back to base. Parker, however, was still knocked out. He was now slated for a battery of tests to see if his mind would recover from the short term nanite infection, and the electrocution.

Kris was released around the same time Alisia finished her preliminary report. Soon Kris, Alisia and Regan were now waiting for Brock's plan, and all loitered around the area of Parker's hospital room.

Alisia quit pacing, and sat next to Regan on the bench across the hall. She watched as Kris laid her head down at Parker's side. Kris had no serious injuries, and practically got into a fight with a nurse to come see Parker.

The music drifting in over the hospital speakers changed to a new song. It was a gentle song Alisia knew well, and although it was almost too quiet to hear, it seemed to drown out everything else. She stared blankly forward at Kris, who held Parker's hand and wished she'd appreciated him more earlier.

The music soaked into the weary Alisia. Without realizing it, she began to silently mouth the words, singing quietly in her mind.

Regan curled up to Alisia, holding her arm and watching her lips move to the music. The verse ended, and Regan squeezed Alisia's arm a little.

Almost in a trance, Alisia turned her head and looked into Regan's eyes, and swallowed hard. Alisia looked tired, but an undercurrent of thought was almost visible on her face.

"Kris always pushed him away, kinda." Alisia said. "Now look at her." Regan looked back over to Kris. She was still holding Parker's hand and resting her head on the edge of the bed.

Alisia swallowed again, and slowly stood, reclaiming her arm gently from Regan. She walked over to Parker and Kris. She put her hand on Kris's shoulder and softly spoke. "I'll be back in a sec. Gonna get some air." Kris nodded.

Alisia looked at Regan as she turned the corner with a strange, steely expression. "If.... if it had been you..." She glanced back at Parker, turned away, then disappeared down the hall. Regan decided to follow.

Outside the emergency doors, an ambulance pulled away into the night. Military people were scattered about. Regan didn't see at first where Alisia went, but soon found her around the corner in a little out of the way alcove only a few paces away. Alisia had her back to the brick wall, and her head was bowed slightly down, staring at the ground.

"Alisia?" Regan asked, stepping forward cautiously. Alisia looked up a bit, strands of her hair grazing across her face. Her eyes were welled up a little, and she stared right through Regan into nothingness.

"What... what's wrong, leesha?"

Alisia's hands formed fists and pressed against the wall firmly. Tiny bits of the brick flittered down to the ground. She turned her head and bit her lower lip as if preparing for an injection. "You... you have to kiss me."

Regan stopped cold. Her stance relaxed, and her breathing stopped. "...what?"

"You're going to have to kiss me. I can't kiss you, I can't. I..." A tear trembled from her eye, and her breathing edged towards sobbing. "I can't, you have to..."

Regan stepped forward more out of concern than her own wants, and held Alisia's face up with both hands. She wiped away Alisia's tear with her thumb. With a soft but concerned expression she looked into Alisia's eyes. "...really?"

Alisia's wide eyes looked around a bit nervously. Panic, fear, self doubt. Regan could feel her jaw trembling in her hands, then a soft little nod. Regan bit her lip softly to wet it, leaned in, and placed the softest, kindest, most perfect kiss she could muster onto Alisia's lips. Alisia kissed back and found her arms were already around Regan, so she squeezed her, and held her closer, moving her head over her shoulder. "Oh my god."

Regan stared forward at the wall, holding Alisia, stunned. "Does this mean..."

"I.. I think it does."

"Oh my god."

"Yeah." Alisia giggled softly though her breathing. "Um... One step at a time, though, kay?"

"Of course, oh, of course...!" Regan sniffled a bit.

They stood together for what seemed forever. Finally Regan broke the silence. "Do I still get to crash in your room tonight?"

Alisia let go and laughed. She was still shaking from the step she'd just taken. She wiped her tears, folded her hands behind her back, sighed, and strolled back into the hospital.

Regan stood there, still absorbing what had just happened. As she drizzled back into reality, she saw a couple of soldiers looking her way. "*Hey!* What're *you* lookin at?" She laughed out loud, and went inside.

Chapter 60: Sparks

Kris looked up as Alisia walked back into the room. Alisia was trembling and smiling, and it looked like she's been crying. "Um... Major?"

Alisia sat down and sighed, wiped her eyes, still with a nervous little smile. "Ahhh, it's alright Captain. It's just been one of those days. Ups and downs."

Kris raised an eyebrow. "And just what the fuck was up about today?"

At that moment Regan sauntered in, looking to be in a similar condition as Alisia. "Oh." Kris said, allowing herself the tiniest bit of a smirk. "I see. Well I take it congratulations are in order."

Regan flopped down on an opposite seat and took a deep breath. "Yup." she said with a sigh. She looked over to Alisia. "Now half my problems are solved."

Alisia rolled her eyes. "Yes yes, fine, gloat. But do it later. We need to worry about the other half of your problems."

The various emotions floating around the room were pushed into the background, and the three of them focused on the topic of Erebus.

"Wanna bet Coll's mind is still in Meston?" Kris said.

"Of course. The program he put in Parker was just a copy. Probably just a partial copy. Or just remote control." Alisia said, "Leaving his safe haven entirely would have been stupid."

"Figures." Regan mulled, "We hack some of his zombies, he hacks one of us. He probably thinks it's hilarious."

Alisia glanced at Parker, then back to both of them. "I'm gonna go out on a limb, and say he was planning that log thing before we got into his zombies. Just coincidence."

Regan peered at Alisia with a smirk. "Out on a limb. Log. Airlimb. Oh, now *you're* the comedian."

"Well, that EMP can't be good for Erebus or the zombies, either. I'm betting he shuts everything down for a moment to fire out a burst, with whatever he's using to do it with." Kris said.

"Well, if we're gonna talk shop, we may as well go do it with Brock. I'm sure he's a few dozen steps ahead of us."

"I'm thinking we need a lot of missiles." Brock said with confidence shortly after the three showed up at his lab.

Alisia paused, stunned by the seemingly over simplistic idea. "What, keep bombing him until the EMP breaks down?"

Brock scoffed, and looked at her like she was an idiot. "......no. *But* while he's deflecting all the incoming attacks he's going to have a heck of a time shooting down an incoming aircraft, thanks to his own tightpulse EMP."

"Alright," Kris said, "So what's keeping the EMP from royally shredding the electronics of the airlimb?"

Brock grinned. "*Screw airlimbs!*" He paused for dramatic effect. "Low tech, all the way!" Brock was slipping from confident scientist to insane nerd.

Alisia nodded. "An older aircraft. Like really old. No electronics. It would be unaffected by the EMP."

A lightbulb went on over Regan's head. "So why don't we just bomb with low-tech bombs?"

Kris let out a frustrated sigh. "Be*cause*, non-guided bombs can't get to the target fast enough without getting shot out of the sky, not to mention the sub-sonic bombers that would get skewered by flying iron girders long before getting in range.

"So," Alisia started from the top, "We start a flurry of brilliant missile bombings, forcing Erebus to use his EMP so much that he can't operate his other defenses. Then we can slip in with some ground forces in a chopper or something, and take out the EMP generator entirely, leaving him open to more missiles."

Brock nodded. "But we're not made of missiles. It would be nice to keep bombing continuously, effectively forcing him to shut all the zombies down while you're looking for the EMP, but as it is, once you're in...."

"The zombies will come back online.. back to 'life'." Regan said.

"Correct." Brock said.

"So once in, the zombies will come out to play. No problem!" Alisia said, switching to a more confident tone, "I'm a professional!"

Regan linked her arm with Alisia. "*We're* professionals!"

"Good lord." Kris said, rolling her eyes. "It's not over yet, rambettes. I need to find us a ride with no electronics, and *someone*'s gotta set up all this bombing."

"The bombing schedule is already being planned by the General I believe," Brock said, "and Kris, I can help you with the aircraft a bit. I have some ideas we should talk about while we're at it."

Alisia made it back to her assigned quarters after stopping by to see the General. Her airlimb quarters were too noisy to rest in, since the airlimb was under considerable maintenance from its EMP exposure.

She opened the door to her new quarters and saw Regan sitting on the bed. The teddy bear was seated comfortably in Regan's lap. Alisia's trained reflex was to kick her out, but instead she smiled softly, remembering earlier events.

"Hi Regan." She sighed, closing the door behind her.

Regan smiled. "So I wasn't hallucinating."

"No." Alisia said, biting her lip and nervously looking at the floor. She sat right next to Regan and put an arm around her. "But ...."

The word but sent terror though Regan. Oh god, she'd changed her mind. No no no NO NO!

Alisia looked down at the innocent little teddy bear in Regan's lap, and sighed with a meek smile. "But this is still... kinda a new idea for me to be considering seriously, y'know. Remember, I think I said something about 'one step at a time'....? If you're here to...."

Regan signed in relief. "Oh, leesh." She wrapped her arms around Alisia and squeezed. "I just... now that things are different, I just wanted to be with you. Be near you. Whenever I can... things... things *are* different now, right?"

Alisia squeezed back and sighed. "Oh boy, are they ever. Then again," she chuckled, "I'm still unexpectedly finding you in my room, so how different is *that*, really?"

Regan looked into her eyes and they stared at each other for a while. "The difference," Regan whispered, "is that you touched me first this time. And that..." she closed her eyes and kissed Alisia softly. "…that's everything."

Chapter 61: Phoenix

The ancient beast of a machine glistened in the afternoon sun as Kris quietly grinned at it. It may as well have had a big red bow around it.

This discarded VTOL prototype, the Harrier AV-8T 'Aytee', had been shipped to Yute from a museum. Its original intended destiny was to replace helicopters as troop carriers, but it was too costly to put into production, and only carried six. Now it was all but forgotten as the vastly superior and more versatile airlimb began to fill the role that was once 'a good idea that didn't work out'.

For anyone versed in aeronautic lore, The Aytee bordered on legend. Despite being decommissioned, it didn't take a lot of work for Brock to give it an OK for flight. With further meddling it was even OK for flight in an EMP.

Still.. it would have been nice to have a craft that could carry as many troops as the airlimb could. As it was, Kris was dismayed when she researched the craft and found it only carried six people and the pilot.

She was *mortified* when Brock sacrificed four seats to install the non-electronic components. Then she realized it would mean just her, Regan, and Alisia were going in. And she laughed.

"What are you cackling about, witch?" Regan's voice echoed across the hanger.

Kris whipped around with a grin to see Regan and Alisia. Her smile melted off her face. "Are you two *holding hands*?!"

Alisia gave a small scoff and pulled her hand out of Regan's. She locked herself into 'professionalism' mode. "Captain Taylor, I certainly was not. This civilian may have been, but not me."

Kris rolled her eyes with a sneer. "Whatever." She turned back to the Aytee. "Well, not only am I going to be dumping you two rambettes deep into zombie-infested territory from which you may never return, and your failure may result in the eventual collapse of human civilization as we know it, with no additional backup whatsoever... but you're gonna be damned cramped on the way!"

"You seem like you're having cramps already." Regan sniped.

"Only because you're a pain in the ass. Are you guys ready or what?"

Alisia nodded. "Let's take a look at our luxury seating."

Kris waved the two to follow her up the scaffolding to check out the cabin of the craft. As Alisia got close to Kris, Alisia touched her arm and softly said, "I just came from the hospital. They say Parker's doing good."

Kris snapped back at the unexpected comment. "Why should I give ... " she sighed. "Thanks."

The interior was worse than Alisia has been led to believe by Brock. There was *barely* room for three thanks to the mechanics that encroached into the cabin. Information that was previously communicated to the different parts of the craft by a few simple wires was now controlled by a nightmarish system of crude metal shafts and levers, all leading to Kris's seat.

To make things even less comfortable, the seats themselves were backless to save space and all lined up in a row, essentially a bench to be straddled by the three of them.

Kris got in the front seat to pilot, leaned forward into the controls, and looked back over her shoulder. "Who's gonna cuddle up behind me? If someone grabs me, I'll try not to make any telling moans."

Regan and Alisia stared at Kris's back and backside and pondered for a moment. "I don't wanna." They both said. They looked at each other and did paper rock scissors. Alisia went for rock, Regan went for paper.

"Alright, fine." Alisia put her P90 and other gear on the Aytee floor, and sat down. Regan filed in behind her.

"Leesh, I'm kinda falling off the back here. I'll end up bonking the machines." Regan said.

Kris burst out laughing. "*Bonking the machines! Ahahahahaha!*"

"Shut up, bitch." Regan growled before magically changing her tone for Alisia. "Leesh, you're gonna hafta scooch up a bit further."

"Yeah, that's it Major," Kris said, "Cuddle up to my tight lil' butt." As Kris taxied them out of the hangar, the engines hummed to life and the control mechanisms churned around them. They couldn't even lean a foot to the side without risking a kiss with moving metal.

Regan scoffed. "If your flabby butt turns Alisia off lesbianism, I'm grabbing the controls and driving us all into the ground." Her voice ended sounding a little hurt and fragile. Dealing with Kris in such close proximity was having its toll on her. Sitting up behind Kris would have been bad, but having Alisia sitting up against Kris was worse. In hindsight, Regan wished she had taken the middle seat.

Alisia leaned back, and pulled Regan's hands around her waist. She whispered to Regan. "You don't have to worry about her, just those little zombies, OK? Just focus."

Regan squeezed Alisia and quietly repeated to herself. "focus.. focus.." her hands traveled up Alisia slowly. "focus.. focus."

214

"Reeeegan.. now is *not* the time to 'focus' on 'pushing my envelope'." Alisia giggled.

"Oh geez. If you two make me vomit in this thing, it's gonna get on all of us. Just so you know."

They were soon ready to take off. "This pig's gonna be rough." Kris said.

Alisia heard Regan inhale to make a comment and stopped her. "Shh. Behave."

"Aha, so *that's* -" Kris started.

"You too, Captain." Alisia's tone was monotone and calm. "Any more fighting, and we'll turn this thing around and go home." Despite the levity of her words, her voice had a tone that said "ok, this is serious now."

Kris chattered back and forth with flight control as the Aytee found its launch mark. The purring turbines tilted to aim the craft down the runway then tilted again to make the launch run. The dull, almost soothing sound of the engines during taxiing turned into an all-encompassing roar.

Regan had never flown in a craft that felt so flimsy compared to the airlimb, and watched out the glass with silent intent, a little nervous, squeezing Alisia. Alisia was more worried about the convoluted control mechanisms all around them; a little worried that one of these exposed moving parts would clip her in the head.

"There's something to be said about old birds like this," Kris said as they felt themselves leave the ground behind. "Ya just feel like there's less machine between you and the sky." Regan and Alisia failed to appreciate the value in that.

Chapter 62: Insertion

Alisia checked her watch. It was less than a minute until they expected to be within detectable range of Meston. Well, more accurately, close enough that Erebus might find them suspicious. There was no way to confirm this however. They had no complex instrumentation, and were under radio silence.

Meston wasn't yet more than a speck on the horizon when the distant sky erupted with a sudden crack of sound that left behind growing contrails from missiles. The cover-bombing had begun. Surely the tightpulse EMP was now hard at work, fouling up the incoming brilliant missiles in all sorts of messy ways. Some could be seen to explode in the air while some simply dropped like rocks. The next wave came shortly after.

The tension in the Aytee rose noticeably. Regan squeezed Alisia's middle again, so Alisia looked back at Regan to check on her. Regan gave a confident nod laced with nervousness, her eyes fixed on the bombings.

As they got closer, the sounds became clearer. Kris dropped to a minimal altitude and put her trust in the brilliant missiles to not pummel them. Of course brilliant or not, it doesn't mean that one wouldn't just drop on their heads after the EMP shredded its guidance system.

"Well, there goes my watch." Alisia said. The little screen was now blank. She brought a cheap little one just for this mission. She would have put extra effort into finding an old mechanical watch, but exact time wasn't that important from this point on.

Now mostly in hover mode, the Aytee passed the outer small buildings. They could see zombies laying in the streets, 'dead'. In the occasional pause between EMP pulses, they would all start to slowly get up only to fall again, shutting down for the next pulse.

"Hey Kris-"

"Shutup, navigating."

Alisia shut up. With only a small crude paper map and memory, Kris was concentrating on getting them to the ideal drop-point, all the while keeping an eye out for random stray missiles dropping on them.

"This looks about good as we can get, " Kris said, pulling a compass out of the dash, and handing it to Alisia. "Get ready to get out."

The Aytee's turbines rotated into full hover mode as they reached the middle of an intersection with only a few zombies lying on the ground. The wheels set down. Regan and Alisia piled out, weapons slung over their shoulders. They climbed down the little fold out ladder, still requiring a bit of a jump down.

"*OK, Kris,*" Alisia yelled to the cockpit from the ground, "*Clear in ten!*"

Alisia led Regan running away from the Aytee. Ten seconds later its engines roared up again. Soon the Aytee disappeared down the street, taking its noise with it.

They looked around, surrounded now only by the sounds of the bombings. Nearby was a crater where one of them had come down uncontrolled. "That makes me feel safe!" Regan said.

"Think of it this way," Alisia said while readying her P90, "Lightning never strikes blah blah blah."

"... *That* makes me feel safe." Regan sneered.

Alisia leaned over and quickly pecked a kiss on Regan's cheek.

"Now *that*... well.. it doesn't make me feel safe exactly, but it's a step in the right direction. Speaking of which..."

"Yeah yeah" Alisia said, pulling forward the compass. The needle had been jerked away from north by the EMP. When the EMP went off, the needle quivered, reaffirming the direction of the source. It pointed down one of the streets, and off by about twenty degrees. "That-a-way!"

They started down the street, and got half a block or so, when silence suddenly surrounded them.

"The bombing is over," Alisia said, "We know Kris is clear now."

"Oh thank god," Regan said, "I know my loathed ones are safe."

Alisia chuckled softly, and started looking around. In view there were a dozen or so zombies on the ground, and they were all starting to get up. "Ok, let's conserve ammo unless they take notice of us," Alisia whispered, "No sense in causing a fuss before we have to."

Regan nodded, but held her P90 close nonetheless.

The small mob didn't seem to care about them, more preoccupied with a nearby crater.. Walking to it, stumbling on the rubble, one falling in.

"I see they're still in total idiot mode," Regan said, "I guess that means we weren't detected....?" Regan was trying hard to not let the city get to her. It looked a lot like the early days in Autar. The blood was everywhere. And fresh. She had seen it through the 'Reggie' zombie before, it was quite a different thing to actually be here.

A few blocks later, a creature about the size of a bull, made of bodies, walked into view. It *did* notice them. Its four legs were each made of several arms, twisted together like pipe cleaners. The rest of its mass was harder to identify, but it was definitely human parts. Upon its massive shoulders, there was no head, but a generic, plastic cartoon mask stuck on the front.

On seeing Alisia and Regan, it split into two parts; front and back. The two sections each formed a third leg out of donations from the other two legs they had. Once they gained their balance the two 'tripods' began running towards the girls.

"Oh, screw this bull." Regan said. Alisia smirked as they both took aim. Alisia took two legs out on the slightly larger one with the mask, and it fell to the ground, rolling a bit.

Meanwhile Regan had only gotten one of the legs of the little one, and it still managed to charge fast. Regan sidestepped around a parking sign then grabbed onto the post to leverage a kick to the side of the beast. It toppled over towards Alisia, and she stepped out of the way easily.

The two halves of the bull squirmed comically, trying to right themselves. "Should we finish them?" Regan asked.

Alisia debated it in her mind. They could just keep going and keep an eye out behind them, but she decided it was an unnecessary risk. "Let's just liberate them from their working limbs." So they shot apart the three remaining legs. Splintered and bloody remains of people's arms twitched beside the revolting masses. "I hate my job."

Chapter 63: 0,0

The 'bull' was not the first 'abomination' either of them had seen, but it wasn't to be the last by a long shot. As they passed block after block, they regularly ran into creations made from bodies. These abominations were all faster and bigger than normal zombies.

The largest was a five meter tall human shape, but the most creative was a meter wide crab. Luckily none of them put up a lot of fight. Slowing them down often took a good deal of ammo however, since some of them had very thickly designed legs. Hollow points work miracles, but sometimes you need a few extra miracles at a time.

The compass was no longer truly useful. After the last EMP pulse went off, it just stayed fixated on the wrong direction relative to north. With a little sense of direction, they managed to stay on course.

Then they saw something unexpected.

A clean street.

Not clean as if the killings had simply not stained it. Not clean as if no bombs had landed here.. but clean. The kind of clean you could eat off of.

The street and the surrounding buildings were all a smooth, shining marble. Except that the marble seemed to be composed of random colours and patterns not typical to marble. The shape of things were different too.

The street itself was perfectly flat with no curb where the sidewalk should be. No lamp posts or parking meters, no fire hydrants, not even seams where you might expect them.

Regan looked around at the buildings. They were similarly lacking geometric detail. "Using nanites to reshape things? From the colours, I'd guess he used whatever was laying around. Geez, I thought Autar looked clean when it was new... That was creepy in its own way... but this..."

"He's..." Alisia squinted, and tried to come up with some reasoning to it. "Making a home for himself?"

"Pfft... I always figured he wanted to remake the world in his vision," Regan said, "But I somehow figured it would involve more... uh.. bodies and blood and stuff..." Was it quieter here, or did it just seem that way?

They kept walking, finding that the 'clean zone' went for farther than they could see. The next intersection revealed that this 'cleanliness' had spread in either direction as well. Ever since entering the clean zone, they hadn't run into any zombies or abominations.

"So.. wait a sec, he's a moron." Alisia said. "If he *is* creating a home... this is a dumb place to do it."

"Why?"

"Well... he's operating on whatever power reserves he found in the city when he took it over. Outside power's been cut, and there's no significant means to generate power in Meston. He's also gotta be sucking up a lot with that EMP."

"Nothing I can't handle. Call this place a rough draft." A familiar, feminine, but unwelcome voice came from behind them. Regan and Alisia swung around to see 'Erika'.

"You're surprised? I can't blame you. This body got pretty badly messed up in my fight with those zombies you guys hijacked.. fun move, by the way... But I fixed her up. I kinda like her. I'm not sure why." Erika held her arm out in front of her, and through Erika's eyes, Erebus studied the frail flesh. "It's not like I knew her, or for that matter, have any sexual desires about her body, since I don't have such human wants anymore. In fact, I'm starting to lose sight of why humans are needed at all, now."

Regan gritted her teeth, and checked her aim. "Leesh'... is there any reason we're not shooting her?"

Before Alisia could reply, Erika interrupted. Her voice now sounded more and more like the voice they knew as Erebus. "*Regan!*" he shouted as if he just noticed her. "Oh, did you know that I *remember* you? From even way back when. I remember your brother now, too. Logs from the Autar A.I. told me he didn't do so well. I.."

Regan hollered "*Shut up!*", and prepared to fire. Before she pulled the trigger, Erika convulsed as if being shot. Blood splattered back, and little bits of flesh went flying, all in relative silence except for Erebus' mocking gasps of pain.

Erika collapsed on the clean ground, nearly in pieces, blood spreading around her. Her face was still in tact, tilted to the side, eyes aglaze.

Regan and Alisia looked around. "I didn't hear any gunfire." Alisia said. "Or even any ricochets... or anything like that... She... he... did it to himself?"

"Oh," Erika's face spoke, only her mouth moving, "Sorry, I skipped ahead I think. But this is more or less what you were gonna do to me, right? I mean, I've seen it happen to enough zombies to know how it goes."

Alisia walked over to Erika and looked down at her face. A face that used to belong to a lovely, innocent young lady. She looked deeper, and saw Erebus staring back at her. "Jonathan.. your lack of a human body is the least of the reasons that you're inhuman." She fired a few rounds and shattered Erika's face, just so Erebus could not use it to speak anymore. At least not for a while.

"We still have a job to do here," Alisia said, patting Regan's shoulder. "Let's get moving."

It only took a minute of walking before the eerie quiet and cleanliness began to gnaw at them again.

"I love you." Alisia said, eyes still on the road ahead.

"What?"

"You heard me. Just thought I'd repeat it."

Regan raised an eyebrow. "Is this some kinda 'I don't expect to live, so I'm getting my feelings off my chest' thing? Cuz I don't plan on let-"

"Nah," Alisia interrupted, "It was just too friggin quiet."

Regan nodded. "Ah. Well then, ditto. In fact, for that matter.. "

Regan stopped short. She spotted something unusual as they entered an intersection. To the left, the next intersection was round instead of square, and much bigger then normal, nearly a block wide itself.

The surrounding buildings looked like they had been pressed back like putty to make room for this space. Centered in this round intersection was the framework of a dome, large enough to encircle several houses. It was seamless, and made of the same material as the streets.

The supports were about a meter wide each, reaching up in a hexagonal pattern, leaving gaps about eight meters wide.

Regan and Alisia approached the outer edge of the dome cautiously while checking to make sure they both had full clips.

When they got about twenty meters from it, they could see a gap in the ground slightly less than a meter wide. This gap ran along the perimeter of the dome like a moat, just inside the supports. It was filled with blood and indistinguishable pieces of gore.

Scattered throughout the dome, there was a variety of debris. Some seemed like random wreckage. A burnt out car, raw pieces of building somehow avoided being used in the strange material, and things of that nature. Towards the middle there was a field of what looked like dead people stuck part way in the ground.

"They're all Erikas." Alisia said. True enough; a magnified view revealed that forty or so Erikas littered the middle area. None of them were moving, and all of them were stuck in the ground to some degree. Most were complete only to about the ribcage area. A couple of them were as far developed as the knees or so. Looking closer, there were some that were merely faces on the ground.

Some had deformities of various kinds, but all were as expressionless as a corpse.

Most importantly, in the very middle was a metal object about the size of two large cars stacked on top of each other. Dull green and boxy, with a sprinkling of minor details, like maintenance hatches and vents.

"And there's our puppy." Alisia said softly. The tightpulse generator was bigger than it looked in its files. Some kind of large, shielded conduit came out of it, immediately bending down into the ground. Near the other end of the generator was an indistinguishable little wad of electronics hooked up to what looked like a wooden child's toy.

The toy had a glass window that let you see inside. There was a small set of little ramps and a four centimeter metal ball inside.

Alisia kept her distance from the edge of the dome and its gore-filled moat while she gave another quick look around. Alisia broke radio silence. After all, Erebus must know where they were by now.

"One bomb, please. Anywhere." She transmitted, then shut her comm down.

A few moments passed, and a sonic boom cracked in the sky.

A few moments later, the tightpulse made a sudden, short, loud, deep hum. At the same time, the little wooden toy flipped over.

An explosion was heard some distance away. Then everything was silent, except for the toy. The steel ball had been flipped to the top, and it clacked its way down the little slides. When the ball reached the end a second or two later, it struck a little button that Alisia had not previously noticed. An identical button sat on the other end of the toy.

"Alright. That explains a little." Alisia said.

Regan tilted her head. "Fuhhh?"

"Well, Erebus has to shut down all his nanites before the pulse, or they get fried. Problem is, he's just a program now too... he has to shut himself down too.. So how does he start up again?"

"Um.. some kind of timer...?"

"Yeah, *fine*, but any kind of electronic timer would get fried too.. remember my watch?"

"So.. he's using the time it takes that ball to fall down....?"

"To hit his restart button. Let's take his toy."

Chapter 64: One Shot

Regan looked at the bloody trench around the dome's perimeter. "We can jump that." Alisia nodded at Regan, and they began running towards the gap. Almost immediately, the moat of gore began to move. "Aw hell!" They stopped a couple meters before the gap, and backed off.

The moat of gore rose up inside the dome frame, filtering the sunlight into a sickly dark red shadow. It seemed at first that it was trying to coat the inside of the dome, but soon structure began to emerge. Pieces came out, riding the bloody ooze; smaller bones forming larger structures... ribs, limbs...

"Are... are those wings?" Alisia asked. They were. From the far end of the moat, as most of a body assembled closer by, two large bony wings assembled. Between these supports spanned translucent sheets of leather, human skin, dripping blood on the floor below. The combined wingspan was around half the diameter of the dome.

"Dammit, let's not just watch, spread out and shred it!" Alisa broke left, Regan right, firing into the forming musculature that was growing around the huge skeletal structure. Firing near-constant streams as they moved, some of the rounds ricocheted off the supports of the dome.

A horned skull the size of a small car assembled from bone pieces still being supplied by the flowing gore. No questioning now, it was a dragon. Bone and muscle but no skin except for the thin, translucent, flowing layer of blood, which still streamed from the moat. Alisia yelled over to Regan. "That idiot! Making a flying monster inside a giant cage."

"Are the bullets doing any good here?" Regan yelled back. The flow of gore which coated it seemed to be very good at quickly repairing damage. Bits that fell off onto the ground just crawled like a worm back to the moat to be fed back to the beast's supply.

"WHO DARES DISTURB MY SLUMBER!?" The dragon's voice was a distorted version of Erebus, being piped out through a speaker in the dragon's skull.

"Idiot!" Regan yelled, redirecting her fire to the skull, smashing off some sections. Regan's rage wasn't terribly productive. The pieces that broke off were already flowing back into place, but Alisia saw this as a good enough distraction. The two of them had traveled far enough apart that the dragon Erebus' focus would be away from her if Regan kept attacking.

Alisia jumped the moat and started running towards the tightpulse and its reset toy. A piece of indistinguishable gore that had fallen from the dragon grabbed onto her ankle, causing her to trip.

Alisia suddenly found herself flat on the ground, in front of one of the partially completed Erikas, staring into its dead eyes. This close, she could see that it was moving it's lips a little, as if talking to itself silently. Choking down a wave of panic, she checked her own leg. The gore blob had moved on. Its senseless programming had already realized that hanging onto Alisia was taking it the opposite direction from its destination moat. Alisia jumped to her feet and got running again.

Regan was fairly close to the dome. Erebus could potentially reach her, but Regan was using the dome's supports as obstacles to the Erebus dragon's grasping claws. "*Fucking moron!*" She yelled while quickly swapping yet another clip of ammo. Erebus was getting a little frustrated. The skull aimed itself at Regan and opened its mouth enough to reveal a metal nozzle with a little blue flame in front of it. "*Oh, BULLshit!*" Regan quickly ducked behind one of the dome's supports in time to shield herself from a flood of 'dragon breath'.

Alisia only saw fire where she knew Regan had been. "*Regan!*" Erebus turned around to look at Alisia. Safe for a moment, Regan peeked out and waved at Alisia. Alisia turned on her comm just long enough to yell into it; "*Bombs! Now! Lots!*"

Erebus cursed himself. He'd been following the wrong target, and to make things worse, his fire breath gimmick didn't turn out to be such a good idea. Sure, it looked great, but he had accidentally cooked five meters worth of the moat, and the nanites in it. Time to go take care of that redhead. He pushed himself off with his back legs and soared across to Alisia, grabbing her easily in his front claw as he landed.

An all-too familiar sonic boom cracked overhead.. and another, and another. Dammit. He squeezed Alisia tightly before having to shut down for the pulse.

Alisia groaned as the large bony fingers seemed to want to crush her, but before Regan could scream her name, the grip relaxed, the hand starting to 'melt'. Below her somewhere, she heard the toy attached to the tightpulse flip over and the low sound of the pulse firing as the ball knocked its way down the slides. That damned toy was so close, yet so far.

The ball hit the bottom and the grip strengthened again as Erebus regained consciousness. Air being squeezed out of her, Alisia called out to Regan as more sonic booms fired overhead. "*Can you get it??*" Fire began to flood towards her face and stopped just short, the grip relaxing again. Wondering if she had any eyebrows left, Alisia heard the tightpulse fire again.

She tried to get free in the few seconds she had, but the lifeless grip was still very stiff.

She got a foot up to try to push a bony finger away as the grip began tightening again. She heard a single shot being fired. The flame thrower in Erebus mouth warmed up once more as sonic booms cried out again.

"Goodbye Jonathan!" Regan's voice came melodic and gleeful.

Before he had to shut down again to protect himself from the tightpulse, Erebus turned his head to look at Regan. She was just standing there, smiling, hands behind her back, holding her P90. Crazy bitch. Erebus' world grew black again.

Alisia felt the grip go loose, and some distance away, Regan's laughter could be heard. Alisia stopped struggling, realizing that the time had come and gone for Erebus to reawaken. The dragon continued to melt, setting a cautious Alisia down on her feet gently. The bony hand came apart around her.

Regan dropped her P90 and ran madly to Alisia. They threw their arms around each other, Regan ecstatic, Alisia confused, until she looked over to the tightpulse. The toy was shattered from Regan's shot, the steel ball missing, having rolled away.

"He's gone! He's dead and he's gone!" Regan said, still giggling with adrenaline. Without the tightpuse being triggered repeatedly by Erebus, missiles were now impacting various parts of the city.

Alisia gently pushed Regan away. "He's asleep." She walked the few steps over to the remains of the toy and the tightpulse control panel. She knelt down and bashed off Erebus' attachment with the butt of her rifle, exposing the manual trigger. Keeping a hand on it, she reached over to the reset button in the broken toy. Hitting the reset, the dragon's body began to twitch to life. Regan ran for her P90. "What the hell are you d-"

Alisia fired the tightpulse, with its short, deep blast. The rising dragon pieces fell again, this time with a faint smoke rising from it, and from the gore trench. With a momentary lapse in the bombing sounds, nanites and servers all over Meston fried.

"Now he's gone. Now he's dead."

Alisia relaxed and sat against the side of the tightpulse, holding an arm out to Regan. Regan flew to her side, and held Alisia as tight as she could. Regan was a fountain of emotions. Thrill of victory, remembrance of her brother, the joy of having Alisia. Her giggles melted into tears. Alisia was profoundly tired, and just squeezed Regan back for a moment. She then turned on her comm and Vtag. "Okay boys, enough with the bombing. It's over. Kris, come get us." Confirmations came back and the bombing ceased. They waited silently in the surrounding quiet, which had gone from eerie to peaceful. They held each other.

"How about we go home?"

Chapter 65: Ashes and Sand

It had rained in the Yute desert since the second fall of Autar.

The ruins had been charred dust for some time, but the rain had caked the ash in most places. Their boots disturbed the surface, occasionally kicking up a little ash that was sucked away by the wind, down the streets to find the horizon.

Alisia followed a few paces behind Regan, who wandered around trying to see the city that had been her home for so long. The streets were easy to make out, although wreckage blocked them in several places. Walking more than a block meant getting your hands dirty, climbing over some barricade of toppled, burnt buildings.

They made it to an intersection and Regan stood on the hood of a burnt out car. She gazed down one direction, then another. Alisia looked up at her and wondered if Regan was remembering the Autar before the first fall, full of people, or was it the fallen Autar, the one she had to herself for so long? Maybe she was just trying to see a memory of her brother.

Alisia sat on the hood of the car and latched onto Regan's calf lazily, sympathetically. Regan looked down and put her hand on Alisia's head, her somber expression gently melting into a smile. "Alright. I'm done here. We can leave this behind."

A little over a month later, the AZU-1 airlimb set down on a familiar sandy shore, this time next to a civilian class aircraft parked not too far from a large, newly built beach house connected to a large new pier.

"Coming?" Parker asked Kris, who was making herself comfortable in the ops room of the airlimb.

Kris casually looked at him with a wry smile, and politely declined. "Nah, I'll wait."

Parker paused, but decided not to fight it. "Kay." He hopped out of the airlimb bay door and started walking towards the house. After four steps, he stopped and decided his boots weren't needed for this mission. He plunked down, and took his boots and socks off, tossing them back into the airlimb before continuing barefoot in the sand. He neared the pier and looked down it. He saw a figure sitting at the end that he barely recognized. She looked so civilian that if it weren't for her unmistakable red hair, he might have thought her to be a stranger. He walked down the pier to greet her.

Alisia didn't stand, but turned around with a smile, her hands sorting out a tackle kit. A fishing rod sat nearby. "Parker! Hey kiddo! They let you out!"

Parker chuckled, "Yeah, I'm going back on duty soon. Not sure where, or doing what though. We managed to work a detour in to say hi." He smirked, and glanced out across the sea. "Retirement seems to be treating you pretty well, Major." He sat next to her on the pier.

"Pretty damn nice, actually. And make it 'Alisia'. No Majors here anymore. Kris here?"

"She stayed in the 'limb. She's... still got issues with Regan I think, I dunno."

Alisia rolled her eyes in the relief that she didn't have to deal with it. "So, uh, you and her....?"

"Yeah. We're gonna give it a try, anyway. It's been a bit more... normal between us since I got zapped."

"Er, sorry again 'bout that... "

"Pfft. No biggie. It was that or watch Erebus use me like a meat puppet to kill you, so, hey! Worked out OK. I guess Regan's broke now, huh? That house over there sure went up fast, and the new plane..."

"Oh lord no. She's friggin loaded. I thought she just took wads of *cash* out of Autar. It was all these stocks and bonds and stuff!"

"Oh I get it now!" Parker joked, "You're all about the bling bling! Some girly comes along with a couple zillion bucks, and suddenly you're all 'oh, yes, I'm a lesbian!'"

Alisia rolled her eyes and slapped Parker's arm. "Gimmie a break."

"Yeah, yeah, the Major has a sugar momma, wait till I tell everyone." Parker smiled, and looked around. "You're so relaxed. Nice to see."

"Nice to feel, too. I highly recommend it. Hey, if you and Kris get serious, maybe you two should buy a tropical island and retire."

"Hmm, yeah, sounds good. I'd have to loot a zombie-ridden city for a few years though."

"Ah, right." Alisia patted Parker on the back, and went back to her bait kit. "Staying for lunch?"

Parker took a sigh, and stood. "No time, really. Next time maybe. Well, I guess this is goodbye, Major." He stared out across the sea.

"Nah." Alisia said, "Just so long."

TO: General Herbert Westmore
FROM: Ret. Major Alisia Terone
RE: future threats

General Westmore,

I realize the need to show confidence to the public now, and the victory over Coll/Erebus helps affirm public confidence, but I wanted to assert to you that this is not the time for relaxing about nanite threats.

The Erebus A.I. was not defeated by our readiness, because we had very little in place for this kind of threat. Erebus was defeated by his own mix of overconfidence and the fact that victory was not his primary objective. He was trying to have fun. I could list a dozen examples where he chose to have fun or show off, when tactically he could have made much better decisions. Coll was not a dumb person, and his A.I. self, as far as we know, was just as smart.

Despite such presumed genius, Ms. Grier and I were permitted to find the Tightpulse Generator. Instead of being simply shot, we faced an elaborate, impressive, but ultimately ineffective opponent. I can see no other reason for this tactical lapse on the part of Erebus, other than his wanting to have fun with us.

As grateful as I am to have survived, it scares me terribly that he could have easily won if he really wanted to, and had prepared appropriately.

Jonathan Coll may have been the first to use nanites in such a horrific way, but it would be shortsighted to assume he will be the last. Nanites have reached a level of effectiveness that can't be un-invented. I don't know how we should prepare for a dedicated nanite threat.

I would hate to see a day of immunizing people with anti-nanite nanites, keeping ahead of hostile technologies with regular updates, but even if such a measure would be effective in preventing future zombies, that is only one way that nanites could be used to catastrophic effect.

I don't know what should be done. Right now we are woefully unprepared. Some great minds played vital roles in defeating Erebus. Please find more such minds. Encourage and support them, while making sure none of them would become another Erebus. General, I am scared.

Major (ret) Alisia Terone